scartissue

THE ORDER OF RAVENS AND WOLVES

T.L HODEL

CONTENTS

AUTHOR WARNING

<u>Author Warning:</u> This book is a dark romance and contains violence, profanity, references to child abuse both physical and sexual, non consensual and dubious consensual sexual scenes, sodomy, and alcohol, tobacco and drug use. If you are a reader sensitive to such material, this might not be the book for you.

The first book in the series is Aftereffect

Playlist

'Can't stop the feeling' by Justin Timberlake
'Scars' by Boy Epic
'Cherry Pie' by Warrant
'Arsonists Lullabye' by Hozier
'Watch Me Burn' by Michele Morrone
'Man In The Mirror' by Michel Jackson
'Filthy' by Justin Timberlake
'Cool' by Jonas Brothers
'Break Stuff' by Limp Bizkit
'Cry Little Sister' by Sisters Of Mercy
'Cowboy Casanova' by Carrie Underwood
'Way Down We Go' by Kaleo
'I Shall Believe' by Sheryl Crow
'I Hope' by Gabby Barret
'The Time Of Our Lives' by The Venice Connection
'Unsteady' by X Ambassadors
'Twice' by Christina Aguilera
'Hands On You' by Ashley Monroe
'Black Horse And The Cherry Tree' by KT Tunstall
'Blank Space' by Taylor Swift

For Ashley, Stella, EJ and all the other TeamJoe members.
TeamJoe forever.
We love you Vivian Murdoch

THE ORDER OF RAVENS AND WOLVES TITLES

KINGS:

Louis Kessler (King of Kings)

- Dean Whitley
- Sebastian Creswell
- Dr. Martin Creswell
- Ryker Hudson

KNIGHTS:

- Micha Kessler (Future king of kings)
- Mason Kessler
- Logan Hudson
- Parker Whitley
- Preston Whitley
- Silas Creswell
- Finn Creswell

NAME PRONUNCIATION

- Micha: Mike - ah
- Ryker: Rye - cur
- Silas: Sye - lass
- Riley: Rye - lee
- Paisley: Pase - lee
- Derek: Dare - ick
- Marnie: Mar - knee
- Trina: Tree - nah
- Logan: Low - gan
- Mason: Mase - on
- Preston: Press - ton
- Parker: Park - er
- Finn: Finn
- Junior: June - your
- Shelby: Shell - bee
- Naomi: Nay - oh - me (bitch)
- Chase: Chase
- Tanner: Tan - er
- Amy: A - me
- Ava: A - va
- Whitley: Witt - lee
- Kessler: Kess - ler
- Creswell: Cress - well
- Mathers: Ma - th - ers
- Grier: Gr - ear
- Harper: Har - per
- Louis: Lou - is
- Lana: La - na
- Sean: Sha - awn

The two most prominent horsemen visited this field today.

Death and war.

They hung in the air with the taint of blood and whimpering cries. I couldn't see them, but I heard their silent call. I'd felt it tugging at the darkest parts of my soul since I was a kid.

They were the monsters in my closet. The things under my bed that demanded to feed, and I answered. Because that's what all it boiled down to, in the end. There was nothing else.

Just death and war.

I rode out the last spikes of my adrenaline surge and sucked in a deep breath. Minutes ago, this place was anarchy, filled with roaring bikes and a hail of bullets.

Now, there was only a soft breeze blowing through the grass. Calm, like the eye of a storm. Except my old man wasn't just any storm. He was a motherfucking hurricane. I could still hear his voice in the back of my head.

'It's time to pay the piper, boy.'

The Order of Ravens and Wolves thought they were infallible. That no one could touch the Kings. They ruled from behind their wall of secrets and golden towers.

They seemed to forget one important fact. My old man was a King. There was no way he'd have started this shit if he wasn't prepared.

While everyone else was patting themselves on the back, I waited for the punchline. The second-rate guns for hire we took out were nothing more than cannon fodder.

There was a bigger picture here. That much I knew. My old man always told me, the best way to catch someone off guard was to let them think they won. Whatever his endgame was, this shit was part of it.

Lou wanted my old man taken alive. Micha's dad was an idiot. The only way we'd have captured mine, was if he wanted us to. Otherwise, he wouldn't have wasted his time taking Mase and Riley.

He would've put a bullet in their heads from a thousand yards away. If Lou wasn't so busy playing King of Kings, he'd see that.

I looked at two bikers lounging on their Harleys and scanned the scythe on the back of their leather jackets. Above were the words *'Lost Souls, Miami, Chapter 11'*. Gotta say, I'd thought Micha lost his damn mind when he asked their president for help.

Chase Mathers was Riley's uncle—though he acted more like her dad—and according to Preston, the guy had a higher body count than Bundy. When Preston is sketchy about someone, that's when you need to worry.

I half expected him to slit our fucking throats when we walked into his tattoo parlor. We were the reason Riley was in danger, after all.

Instead of painting the walls with our blood, Chase came back from the dead and called his boys in. Not sure why he let people think he was offed with his wife and kid, and I didn't really care. We all had the same agenda: rescue my stepsister, Riley, and my brother, Mason.

My endgame was different, though. Eight years ago, I shot my old man and dumped his body in the ocean, thinking that was it. The boogeyman was dead. Saving Mase and Riley was a bonus. I came here for one reason. To finish what I started.

All this shit, the hired guns, taking Mase and Riley, was just my old man's way of saying *surprise motherfuckers'*. Riley was to make Micha suffer—he never did like him—but Mase… that shit was all for me. Another one of his twisted lessons. Like when he made me kill my puppy. I loved that fucking dog.

One shot of epinephrine and Mase woke up. Riley was still unconscious when the ambulance took off. I'd never seen Micha cry before. Not even the first time he had to kill a man, and most of us at least shed a tear for that test. My old man had finally broken the one person I never thought he could.

My eyes locked on the open wing doors and the staircase leading into the dark.

He's down there right now.

"Shit kid," Chase's vice president, Tanner, pointed at the seeping wound in the left side of my abdomen. "You're hit."

I glanced down at one of my old man's men groaning on the ground and popped one in his skull.

"I'm fine," I said, shrugging off the dull ache crawling up my spine with the recoil.

Lou wanted to keep my dad alive, and the King of Kings word was law. Fucking Order hierarchy. Except Lou wasn't my King. Micha was, and he'd want the son of a bitch dead.

Fuck the King of Kings, and fuck the Order.

I cocked my 9mm and marched for the stairs.

"Whoa kid," Tanner pushed on my shoulder, "Where are you going?"

"To talk to my old man." I pressed my gun to his head and growled, "Why? You gonna stop me?"

He held up his hands and took a step back. "Who am I to stand in the middle of a family reunion?"

A smirk tugged at my mouth as I stormed past him and down the stairs.

Stupid Lou. Leaving the bikers to watch me. There was one rule every MC I knew about had. You don't fuck with family. Those assholes wanted blood more than I did. Lucky for them, I was more than happy to play avenging angel.

Torches burned in the sconces on the walls, casting the tunnels in a shadowy illumination. Some might find it eerie. I, however, didn't need light to know where I was going. The only person who knew The Basement better than me, was Preston. Hence why he recognized the room Riley and Mase were being held in.

I was usually too lost in what I was doing to pay attention to the details of my surroundings. When the Order wanted someone to disappear, they called Preston. When they wanted them to suffer, they called me.

"Do yourself a favor, Ryker," Lou's voice echoed down the hall from the branding room, "And tell me. Where is he?"

My brow rose. *He?*

"An eye for an eye, old friend." It'd been eight years since I'd heard my old man's voice, and that cocky drawl still grated on my nerves.

"Tell me where he is," Lou demanded again, "And I'll give you a quick death."

My finger twitched on the trigger

Don't worry, Lou, I got that covered.

My old man laughed. "You might let me slip quietly into the night, old friend, but Dean won't. How is your lovely daughter?"

"Motherfucker," Dean growled.

The resounding sound of flesh hitting flesh rang through the air, followed by a grunt. Dean Whitley wasn't like the other Kings. He was a hard bastard—had to be, to raise a kid like Preston.

Unfortunately, my old man knew exactly which buttons to push. He'd raped Dean's daughter with a pool cue when she was ten. Now, Ava couldn't have kids. I know he did this, because the sick fuck made me watch. I was seven.

"You should learn to control your emotions, Dean." My old man tsked and I could almost see the grin on his face. "Like your son. Then again, Preston doesn't feel much, does he?"

"Keep talking, dickhead," Preston's voice was just as calm as ever. The fucker didn't get angry often, but when he did… "You're only digging yourself a deeper hole."

A hole I planned to drop his body in.

"Perhaps I should've taken Parker instead? Mason was such a disappointment. But your brother…"

He was asking for it now. If Preston had a weakness, it was his baby brother. He stabbed one of their nannies once. Because she spanked Parker.

"Quit stalling, Ryker."

"Smart boy." My old man said.

"Let me guess," I heard Preston sigh, along with the click of a gun cocking, "You've got back up coming?"

"More like… deliverance."

I rounded the corner and saw him. My old man on his knees, with his hands cuffed behind his back. Blood streaked his blond hair and stained his shirt. A lot more blood than what would come from the minor bruises and cuts on his face.

More like claw marks. Though my blood was boiling, I smirked. My stepsister didn't go down without a fight. Bet the fucker didn't see that coming.

Lou stood on one side of my old man, with Dean on the other. The second I walked in, they all stopped and turned my way. Lou and Dean eyed me warily, while a smile spread across my old man's face.

"Ah, and here it is now," he said, nodding at the gun in my hand. "Come to finish the job, boy?"

"What is it you always told me?" I looked him dead in the eyes and raised my hand. Finger ready and on the trigger. "It's time to pay the piper."

"Calm down, Logan." Lou's gaze shifted to my 9mm. "Think about what you're doing."

"Oh, I think I know exactly what I'm doing."

Out of the corner of my eye, I saw Preston push off the wall and stand up straight. Dean muttered under his breath, and Lou took a cautious step closer. They were all ready to pounce. Muscles tense and backs straight, with their alert eyes focused on me. I almost laughed. Did they really think they could stop me?

"Put the gun down, son," Lou coaxed, while taking another step in my direction.

"You need to back the fuck off, Lou. I will shoot you."

He'd survive a leg shot.

Tension rolled off us in heavy waves. They all knew I'd do it. The only question was how far they'd have to go to stop me? They could put a bullet in my head for all I cared. As long as mine struck it's target first.

In true shrink fashion, Lou kept his voice calm and even. "It's forbidden to kill a King, Logan."

I snorted. *Fucking Lou.*

"A King can't kill another King. You were the one who told us that, and I'm not a King yet."

Lou's face dropped.

That's right asshole, I pay attention.

"That's it, boy. Don't let anyone get between you and your prey." My old man's eyes sparkled with amusement.

I hated those green fucking eyes. The same brilliant color girls swooned over was a curse to me. A constant reminder of whose nut sac I spawned from. I couldn't wait to watch the life bleed out of them. "Just don't fuck it up this time."

"Can't fuck up if I hit you between the eyes."

Goodbye, you piece of shit. Hope you enjoy hell.

Someone crashed into me, slamming my back against the wall and making my shot go wild.

Fucking Preston!

"Get the fuck off me!" I snarled in his face.

He grunted and pinned my armed hand to the wall. A smart move, considering I'd have shot the bastard.

"You don't want to do this."

"The fuck I don't!" I struggled against his hold. Preston might be the shortest of us, at six foot even, but the prick was deceptively strong. "He deserves to die."

"He deserves to suffer," Preston argued.

Okay, he might have a point. Why give the bastard a quick death, when he can live in agony for a while? My eyes locked on one of the scars on my arm.

This one was a cigarette burn he gave me when I was six and fell off my bike. Because boys don't cry. There were dozens more blended into the ink covering my upper body. People didn't notice them, but I knew they were there, and I remembered how I got each and every one.

"Still a disappointment, I see." My old man sighed and shook his head.

Fuck letting him live in agony. My old man needed to die!

Rage burned, flowed through my system, giving me the strength to push Preston back.

"Fuck," he grunted, struggling to maintain his hold.

Lou and Dean's mouths were moving. They were yelling something, but I couldn't hear them. All I could see was that smug fucking smile I needed to wipe out of existence.

"Come on, boy," my old man taunted. "Better stop me before I get ahold of your mother."

"You'll never fucking touch her again!" I roared.

I almost had my arm free. One more good tug and this mother-fucker would be done.

"Perhaps the sheriff would like to watch his second wife suffer. Though they're not really married, since I'm still here and she's *my* fucking wife!"

"I'm gonna rip your fucking heart out!"

For years after he was gone, Ma walked around on eggshells. She hid in the house and jumped at her own shadow, afraid he would come back from hell for her. I couldn't stop him when I was a kid.

I wasn't a kid anymore.

"You always did have a soft spot for your mother. Is that why you shot me? To protect her." My old man tsked. "You didn't do a very good job, boy. Here I am, and I *will* get my hands on her."

"Shut him the fuck up!" Preston called out over his shoulder.

I tore my arm out of his grip and lifted the gun. "I'll shut him up."

Preston reared back and punched me in the gut, landing his strike right on my bullet wound. I grunted and flinched long enough for him to slam me into the wall.

"Fuck you!" I growled, glaring in Preston's cold steel eyes.

"You're giving that fucker exactly what he wants."

I looked over at the delight on my old man's face, and sighed.

Fuck! Preston was right.

Still, I couldn't force the tension out of my body. I needed to see his brains on the floor. Needed it so bad, it made my skin crawl.

Preston lifted his hand and slapped me. "Tell me where she is."

Despite the burning need to hit him back, my eyes snapped up to his.

"What's she doing? Are you playing with her?"

And just like that, my mind was on something else.

Shelby fucking Grace.

My walking, talking, wet dream.

"Close your eyes, Logan. Tell me where she is."

My lids slowly shut, allowing me to picture the blonde that'd been taunting me with those long legs and perfect ass.

"She's in my room."

Arms strung up over her head, with red welts marking her creamy complexion. My fucking marks.

"What are you doing to her?" Preston's voice urged me deeper into my fantasy.

I could hear the slap of leather. The resounding echo making my dick swell. I could see the tears dripping off her face, streaking her creamy white skin. Fuck, I wanted to taste her tears. Lick them off her while she pleaded for mercy.

Too bad Shelby was still a little girl. Her room was full of frilly pink and white crap, along with a pile of stuffed animals. Including three unicorns. Fucking unicorns! That girl could never handle what I'd give her.

"Is she crying?"

I licked my lips and nodded. "Yeah."

"No one else will touch her, because she's your little doll to play with, isn't she?"

"My fucking doll," I growled, wanting to punch him for reminding me about something I could never have.

But his trick worked. By the time I opened my eyes, I'd calmed down enough for him to let me go.

Preston cocked his head at me, "You good?"

Yeah, I was good. Still wanted to kill my old man, but I didn't have to anymore.

"Give me a fucking smoke," I barked out.

I should've known my old man wouldn't let it go. Two puffs in and he opened his fucking mouth.

"First thing I'm going to do when I get out is pay the Grace girl a visit."

Preston tackled me before I could pull the trigger.

Chapter 1

Logan

"I'll talk to my dad," Micha said, as he steered the Jeep around Ma's tacky fountain.

Every time I saw that thing I snickered. This house was tainted. It was the last place a cherub would go.

"If anyone has a right to pay that bastard a visit…" He paused to release a long sigh, "I could call a council meeting."

That made me huff out a snort. "What the fuck for?"

If Micha thought any of the Kings would vote in my favor, he was sorely mistaken. We all had our tags. Micha was the hard one, Mase was damaged, Silas angry, Parker the good boy, and Preston cold. I was the unstable one. *His* son, and they were all waiting for me to crack.

Shakespeare said, *'the sins of the father are laid upon the children'*. My old man sins weren't just laid upon me, they tainted my family line like a fucking plague. He was the boogeyman. The beast people whispered about in secret, hoping he wouldn't hear them call his name.

"I could talk to my dad. Make him see–"

"Don't waste your breath," I interrupted, "His mind is made up."

I told Lou I'd go in unarmed and supervised. That wasn't good enough. He said I didn't need a gun to kill someone. While he had a point, I'd grown to like the idea of my old man suffering. It'd be nice if I could fucking partake in it.

But the King of Kings decrees it, so we must follow. I was so tired of the politics crap that came with the Order. Fucking rules, rituals, and all that other shit. Fucking hypocrites, that's all the Kings were.

My brother is my bond, his family is mine. Bullshit. I'd like to see one of those pompous assholes claim my old man as family.

I couldn't wait for Micha to take the throne. Then we'd show those pricks how shit should be run.

I was so fucking frustrated over this shit that I was ready to punch Micha for a little satisfaction. And that was before I saw the pink Camaro parked in front of my house.

Fan-fucking-tastic.

"Looks like my mouse has company," Micha snickered.

"I can fucking see that," I groaned, and slumped back in the passenger seat. "Doesn't she have other friends to visit?"

It was sacrilege for a 69 Camaro to be the same color as bubble gum —poor fucking car. I'd give it a proper paint job if the driver wouldn't take it the wrong way. The last thing I needed was Shelby Grace thinking I was being nice. It was hard enough staying away from her.

The leggy blonde with a body built for fucking was my heroin, and I was an addict before I even had a taste. I had this insatiable need to know what she was doing. Last night, I watched her sleep for three damn hours.

It was fucking annoying.

"You might not want to look over there."

"Why?" I said, turning my gaze to the garage.

Fuck my life.

Shelby's head was under the trunk of Riley's shitty Volkswagen Bug. Why they put an air-cooled engine in the back was beyond me, but it seemed to work. Not in Riley's car.

That thing was so close to death I could smell the reaper. Guess she turned to her friend when I refused to fix it, again. Couldn't really complain right now.

Goddamn.

My eyes traveled over a streak of grease on Shelby's creamy thigh, and up to a pair of tiny black shorts that were hugging the greatest ass ever made.

I'd fuck up shit on my stepsister's car just to watch Cherry Pie fix it. The roads would be safer, and I'd get spank bank material. It was a win-win situation.

"I'd fucking kill Riley if she wore shit like that."

"Huh," I grunted, while staring the hint of pink lace peeking out from the bottom of her shorts.

She couldn't be wearing some plain white cotton panties. No, it had to be lace, which I had a thing for.

The things I could do with that ass.

"Jesus Christ," Micha growled. "What the fuck are you waiting for?"

Someone's in a foul mood.

If he hadn't told Riley to change this morning because she looked like a slut, she wouldn't have slapped him. My stepsister might be a tiny little thing, but she had no problem putting Micha in his place. It was funny as fuck to watch.

"What's wrong, grumpy? Couldn't make her change?" I laughed when he shot me a dirty look.

That was a no.

"Should I stay out here and stare at that?" I cocked my head at Shelby's ass. *Goddamn that looked good.* "Or go inside and check out my sister's cleavage?"

"I know what you're doing."

I cocked a brow at Micha. "Remembering the taste of Riley's nipples?"

He knew I was changing the subject, and I knew I was changing the subject. Didn't mean I'd admit it.

Huffing out an unimpressed sigh, he shook his head. "You're worse than Mase, you know that?"

I wouldn't go that far. Unlike our brother, I freely admitted that I wanted to be balls deep in that shit. Mase was too stubborn. Did he hate Harper, yes. The bitch stabbed him in the back.

Personally, I thought he should hate-fuck the shit out of her. Why not get some payback? I even offered to hold her down. Not that I'd have to, she couldn't weigh more than ninety pounds soaking wet.

"You're constantly pushing Mase."

My eyes rolled Micha's way. "Do you have a point?"

"Follow your own advice." Micha tipped his chin at Shelby. "She's right there."

"It's not that simple."

"It is that simple, Logan. You want her, so take her."

I released a long sigh. "Micha–"

"You threatened to rip Mase's arms off and beat him with the bloody stumps."

"He shouldn't have touched her." I shrugged.

"She hugged *him*." He arched a brow, "In the hospital."

"I fail to see the problem."

I lost count of how many guys my best friend fucked up because they *looked* at Riley. And that was before he decided he wanted her. I knew I wanted Shelby.

Right now I was thinking about all the ways I could fuck her on that car. *Bend her over the hood and plow into her from behind, while I choked her with the fan belt.*

Fuck!

I shifted to adjust myself. Every time this girl was around, I swear my pants shrunk two sizes.

Micha closed his eyes and pinched the bridge of his nose. "Do us all a favor and take what you want, before you kill one of us."

"We've been through this. That girl," I waved my hand at Shelby, "Couldn't handle my shit."

"You don't know that."

Yes, I did.

"She has thirteen stuffed bears, six cats, and three unicorns in her room. Fucking unicorns, Micha!"

"You've been in her room?"

I may have spent a little time in there. Okay, more than a little, but in my defense, if Shelby didn't want anyone in there, she should lock the window.

Micha's brows knit together. "Why didn't you tell me you were watching her?"

I couldn't help but feel a little guilty at the tinge of hurt in his tone. Micha was my best friend. My brother. I used to sneak into his room to escape my old man. He knew more about what happened than anyone else. But this… he wouldn't get this.

"How long have you been watching her?"

Since the day I met her.

"Doesn't matter," I said, turning my attention back to Shelby.

She was swinging a wrench with an annoyed glare. Couldn't blame her. Why the fuck Micha let Riley drive that death trap was beyond me. I loved him, but he was a demanding asshole.

Riley couldn't leave the house without him knowing. She thought he'd given her some freedom. He didn't. Micha was always a paranoid fucker, and that was before my old man took his girl. Riley was lucky he didn't chain her in the basement.

"All you're doing is delaying the inevitable," he said, staring at Shelby with a far off look in his dark eyes. "If you think it was bad when I took my mouse, it's gonna be ten times worse for you. You have some control now. You won't for long."

My cheeks puffed out with an exhale. People around me suffered when I lost control. Shot Preston in the foot once. Fucker didn't even bat an eye. He did toss my keys in Cherry Lake, though. Took me two fucking weeks to find them.

"It was different for you and Riley. She was into the shit you were."

Micha barked out a laugh. "No fucking she wasn't."

I cocked a brow. Who the hell did he think he was talking to. Her room was next to mine. I heard them.

"You're such a fucking idiot." He rolled his eyes and shook his head. "You know what the beautiful thing about virgins is?"

"Tight pussies?" Virgins weren't my thing. I preferred my meat hot.

"They don't have enough experience to know what they like." Both of us watched Shelby straighten up and flip her blonde hair over her shoulder. "One hundred percent trainable."

Huh?

"So, what you're saying is…"

"She might not like pain, but you could train her to respond to it."

I had my playmates, like Amy. That misogynistic bitch moaned when I whipped her. Don't get me wrong, I wanted them to get off on it. Seeing a woman come apart was a beautiful thing.

That was nothing compared to the way they shivered as they pleaded for mercy. That's what I craved. Tears of agony while their body broke in ecstasy. I wanted their pleasure, but I needed their pain.

"Just because she's trainable, doesn't mean she'll respond to it." Some people couldn't handle pain.

"All you need is something small. A hint that she can be pushed the right way. And something tells me a girl that runs track and beats up cars in her spare time, can be pushed that way."

I cocked my head as she tossed the wrench. Micha was one of the best people readers I knew. He picked up on body language and subtle facial expressions like a goddamn lie detector.

"What if you're wrong?"

"I'm not," he stated confidently. "The only question is how much you'll have to push her."

"Well shit," I said, climbing out of the Jeep, "Let's go fucking find out."

Everything else disappeared as I slowly stalked up on the forbidden fruit, trying to decide which part I wanted to play with first. They were all so tempting.

Firm breasts, a narrow waist, and curvy hips. I could wrap those legs around my head and watch her tits bounce. My eyes fell back down to her swaying hips.

That ass, though…

"Stupid car," Shelby growled from under the hood, making my dick harden with her husky tone.

I'd had my fair share of beautiful girls, including Naomi Prescott, Ashworth Academy's queen bee. Shelby Grace was in a whole other league. Long golden blonde hair, with just the right amount of curl. Firm tits that were at least a C-cup, big cinnamon-colored eyes, and pouty pink lips.

Damn, our kids would look good.

I stopped and cocked a brow. Where the hell did that come from?

"You listen to me, car," she grumbled. "You're gonna give me this friggin' spark plug."

My hand twitched. Instinct told me to smack her ass and correct her behavior. My girl would watch her fucking mouth. All those filthy words were for me and me alone.

Technically there was nothing wrong with the word friggin'—other than how incredibly sexy I suddenly found it. Exactly why I didn't want to hear her say it to anyone else. Even a fucking car.

Would she squeal when I spanked her?

She clacked her pliers off the engine and muttered, "Goddamnit."

Let's find out.

My palm landed on her ass with a firm smack.

Fuck, that felt good.

"What the hell!" Shelby shrieked and jumped up, banging her head off the open trunk.

"Careful, Cherry Pie," I snickered, "Wouldn't want you knocking yourself out."

I wanted her fully conscious. *On her knees, with her mouth wrapped around my cock...*

"Ugh, Logan," she groaned and spun around, momentarily stunning me.

The girl looked like she just got fucked. Hair stuck to her sweaty forehead with grease marking her left cheek. What really got me was the way her eyes deepened with desire. I knew that look. Chicks were always checking me out. But when Shelby did it...

"See something you like?"

Pink tinted her cheeks as her pouty lips parted, "What do you want, Logan?"

You bent over the hood, taking it good and hard.

"Depends," I said, licking my lips at the sweat glistening off her ample cleavage, "What are you offering?"

She rolled her eyes—something else I'd have to correct. I couldn't stand bitches rolling their eyes. "I'm kind of busy. So if you could piss off, that would be great."

"Come on, Cherry Pie," I tilted my head and pursed my lips, "Don't you want to talk about the weather, or football again?"

My mouth curled at the hurt glimmering on her face. She'd tried a few times to 'make nice', striking up a conversation about random bullshit. Her latest effort was the Jets and Bills game.

Even if I was a sports guy—which I wasn't—I would've blown her off. My guess was that she wanted to be friendly, to make things easier on Riley.

How fucking sweet of her.

"I'm not in the mood for your crap."

"If I gave a fuck what you were in the mood for, I'd have some stuffed unicorns and bunnies to play with."

"Why do you always have to go there?"

Maybe because you have a hundred fucking stuffed animals in your room.

"I'm not a child."

"No, you're not," I said, pulling my gaze down her tempting body. What did she taste like? Would she stop me if I licked her? *She could try.* "What you are is an inexperienced brat. That's alright," I took a step and leaned in closer, "I can play daddy."

I was too distracted by the way her throat bobbed with a nervous swallow, to stop her from shoving me back.

"I already have a dad, thanks."

The confidence in her tone didn't hide the pain and betrayal shining in her eyes. Was poor little Shelby upset Daddy moved in with her track coach?

"Aw, did Daddy leave you?" I popped my bottom lip out. "I bet he still comes to every one of your meets, though."

Shelby wasn't that much shorter than me—maybe a foot in heels—but she still had to lift her chin to look me in the eyes.

"Is there something wrong with a parent supporting their child?"

"Oh, he's supportive alright. How much you wanna bet that while you're practicing, he's fucking her in the locker room?" I smirked and slowly dropped my eyes down to Shelby's pert ass. "She does have a nice ass," *nowhere near as nice as yours*, "I'd tap that shit."

Okay, so I wasn't very nice to the girl. I had my reasons. Plus, it was hard not to hate her when she made me want her so much. Wearing those tight little outfits while looking at me with sin and sweetness in her eyes. She was asking for it.

Especially on Halloween. All dressed up in that short white dress with angel wings. She was lucky I didn't fuck her right there in that maze.

Did she figure out that was me yet?

"Aw, are you gonna cry now?" I wanted her to cry. My dick hardened just thinking about licking those tears off her face.

"Fuck you, Logan!"

"A solid offer, Cherry Pie." I leaned in and whispered, "You sure you can handle me?" in her ear.

She shot back, "And what makes you think you could handle me?"

That was laughable. The girl probably didn't know how to get herself off properly. "Don't worry about me, Sweetheart. I know what I'm doing."

"I'll just bet you do," Shelby snorted and shouldered past me to dig through the toolbox.

I damn near slapped her. Had to fist my hand to stop myself. Then she had to go and roll her fucking eyes again. Which was when I reached out for her.

"Been with enough girls," she quietly muttered.

I stopped, fingers inches from Shelby's arm and I smirked. Did I detect a hint of jealousy?

Interesting.

"Do you think about what I did to them." I stepped up behind her and braced my palms on the toolbox and leaned in to breathe in her ear, "Sit alone in your room at night with your hand down your panties, imagining all the ways I made them scream."

I'd popped a few cherries in my time, but virginity wasn't something I sought. That timid crap, blushing while nervously shying away, didn't do it for me. Shelby wasn't like that.

She rose to the challenge, spinning around with a sultry smile on her face.

"Have all the random hook-ups you want," she purred, and pressed her soft body up against mine. "When I give myself to someone," her hands slid up my chest and around to the back of my neck, sending a shiver up my spine, "He won't be able to think about anyone else."

A slow smirk spread across my face.

Oh fuck, it's game on now, sunshine.

The toolbox clattered as I pushed in and ran my nose up the column of her neck. She smelled fucking mouth watering—jasmine and diesel. Combine that with her breasts pressing against my chest with her sharp inhale, and I didn't give a fuck anymore if she could handle my shit. The devil himself couldn't drag me away.

"Fuck, you smell good," I growled, fisting her hair and yanking her head to the side so I could have better access. "I want to fucking eat you."

Why the hell did I wait so long for this?

"Logan… w-what are you d-doing."

I heard the stutter in her voice. Felt her nervous tremble. Too fucking bad. Cherry Pie better get used to this shit. The second I touched her, she was fucked.

"Stop it."

I hummed and grazed my mouth across her soft skin, darting my tongue out to sneak a taste. "Don't tell me you're tapping out already, Cherry Pie?"

Her body stiffened for just a second, before she relaxed into me.

That's it, sweetheart, come out and play.

"If anyone's going to tap out," she purred and slid her hands around to grab my ass, "It'll be you."

My hand dropped from her hair down to her hips.

"Big words," I said, pulling her in closer, "For a little girl."

She bowed her back over the toolbox and looked up at me with a cocky smirk on those pouty pink lips. "Don't worry about me. I'm a winner, remember."

She was referring to the race she won this summer, and that was only because she damn near ran me off the track.

I tsked and followed her lead. Leaning in until her hot breath warmed my lips. "Cheating won't win you this one."

"Someone's a sore loser," she breathed out, while trying to wriggle away.

"Careful, Cherry Pie," I growled and tightened my hold, digging my fingers into her hips. "I will fuck you."

Right here, on Riley's shitty fucking car.

My cock couldn't take much more of her little struggles. I could practically taste the heat coming off her pussy. Shelby was about two seconds away from finding herself bent over the hood.

Then she gazed up at me, cinnamon eyes sparkling with challenge, and said, "You can try." I was fucking done.

I dove in.

My mouth crashed down on hers, swallowing her shocked gasp. This girl didn't just look like sex on legs, she fucking tasted like it. And fuck me if she didn't part her lips and swirl her hot tongue over mine.

My cock ached to slide into her wet pussy. Fuck every hole she had until I was consumed with everything that was Shelby Grace. I was done fucking around. It was time to claim what was mine.

Hungry for more, I pressed in, devouring her mouth. Sucking in every ragged breath she released.

It wasn't enough.

I speared my fingers in her hair and yanked hard.

"You're fucked now, Cherry Pie," I growled against her mouth and bit down on her bottom lip, digging my teeth in her flesh.

The sweet coppery tinge of her blood had my dick trying to punch through my jeans.

"Ow!" Shelby cried out, tearing her mouth away.

Most chicks didn't like my brand of fun. I expected the usual anger or fear—neither of which detoured me in the past—but the scowl on Shelby's face was the only thing that suggested anger. Her pupils were blown up in arousal, while her chest heaved with shuddered breaths. Gotta say, I was a bit shocked.

Fuck me, Micha was right!

If this shit was going to work, I'd have to ease her into it. Though it was damn near impossible to reign myself in and take a step back–especially when her tongue darted out and swept up a drop of blood on her lip–I somehow managed to pull myself away.

"You bit me!" she snarled.

I chewed on the gum I'd stolen from her and smirked. "You liked it."

"I don't know who you think you are, Logan Elliot Hudson…"

How cute, she was middle naming me. I'd have to have a chat with my stepsister about that.

"But you are *not* God's gift to women. I, for one, am not interested."

My brow arched. "The way you're looking at me says otherwise."

"I am not looking at you."

"It's okay, look away." I tilted my head and dropped my gaze. "I am."

Her nipples were hard and pressing against the pink fabric of her shirt. I salivated at the thought of having my mouth on those pert little nubs. Hearing her cry out when I bit down.

"Humph!" Shelby grunted and crossed her arms, pressing her tits up. Which was not helping my hard on any. "Not every girl wants to stare at you."

"Is that so?"

"Yes."

I snickered when I lifted my shirt and her eyes locked on my abs.

She tried to not to stare, but failed horribly. A little lower and she'd see exactly how much I wanted her.

"If you ask real nice," I grabbed my cock through my jeans, drawing her gaze where I wanted it. "I might let you touch."

She stood there with her mouth hung open and eyes locked on my package as pink flooded her cheeks.

That's right baby, this shit is all for you.

A second later, she shook her head and snapped out of it. "I'm not one of your groupies, Logan. You can't flash me a few muscles and win me over."

My brow rose. "You want me to up my game, is that it?"

"Go ahead. It won't matter."

Poor little Shelby. She had no idea. I hadn't even begun to play yet.

"You sure about that?"

"Yes." She stated in that all too serious tone people used when they were full of shit.

Shelby Grace was an intermediate challenging a master. She didn't stand a chance. I'd be feeding her my cock by this time next week.

"See you around, Cherry Pie," I said and sauntered away.

This was going to be fun.

oo high an opinion of oneself.

That was the definition of conceit in the dictionary.

In other words, Logan Hudson.

It fit him so well, that there should be a picture of him under the word. Not too small. He wouldn't like that. His face would have to take up at least half the page. That way, when someone opened the book, there he was. Looking up at them with that stupid charming smile.

The sad fact was, the boy was beyond cute. Sexy, gorgeous, breathtaking, those were a few words that came to mind. Basically, Logan Hudson was fucking hot. Bastard knew it too.

Strutting around with his perfectly tousled blond hair, and showing off his lean, well-cut body. As if he couldn't get any more perfect, he had those eyes. The same deep green as the leaves of a mahogany tree. Even when he was being a dick, they sparkled. And he was a dick a lot.

His abs were permanently ingrained in the back of my mind.

Grisly tattoos curving over firm ridges. Like an enticing gothic picture show. I'd put my hands on him, felt the power in those hard muscles.

What would it be like without fabric separating us? Nothing but his firm body warming up my skin. I couldn't stop thinking about it. Tempting as it was to go there—and trust me it was tempting—Logan Hudson was so off limits it wasn't even funny.

The guy had a rather extensive track record. I wouldn't be surprised if the only girls he hadn't slept with were sitting at this table. Riley, my best friend who lived with the guy, warned me to stay away from him.

Well, she warned me to stay away from every guy—Rye wasn't what I'd call a people person—but that was beside the point. Logan was a one-way ticket to a broken heart, and I wasn't about to join his flavor of the month club.

My face scrunched at Marnie's ponytail. It looked like she'd quickly tied her auburn hair up before walking out the door. It went well with the baggy t-shirt and black tights she was wearing.

I called it her librarian look.

This was her preferred fashion choice when she was working on a story. Which I assumed was on Florida state education regulations, based on the book her nose was buried in.

Her twin, Trina, sat beside her, wearing a blouse that matched her aqua eyes and a black skirt. Unlike Marnie, her hair was curled and she had make-up on. Not that she needed it. Neither of them did. Trina just liked looking her best. Something else she liked was boys.

I looked over at the guy sitting at our table. Trigger, or something stupid like that. There wasn't any point in getting to know him. He was her third lunch date this week.

"How's Rye?" Trina asked, popping a cherry tomato in her mouth. "She coming to the Causgrove on Friday?"

She was only asking because she hoped Rye would bring her step-brother. Trina hadn't shut up about Logan since Rye moved in with him. I don't know why she was so interested. It wasn't like he was the monogamous type. Then again, neither was she.

Was anybody?

My hands fisted at the memory of seeing my dad's bare ass and hearing my coach's moans. "Yeah, Rye's coming."

Why would my dad choose some random girl when he could really drive the nail in my heart? I thought I could trust Coach. Boy, was I wrong. He begged me not to tell my mom, and I didn't.

Last night I stared at my bedroom door for an hour, thinking I should tell her, but I kept chickening out. I didn't want to be the one to break her heart more. My pain, I could handle.

Besides, my dad wasn't there anymore. Mom threw him out last month when she got tired of the missing money. He had gambling problems, and I guess she finally had enough.

There was still this voice clawing at the back of my head, pushing me to tell her. Make sure she had all the facts before they got back together. But the little girl in me held out hope for a happy family. At this point, I didn't know which one would win.

A cherry tomato bopped off my forehead, bounced off the table, and dropped on the floor.

My gaze rolled over to Trina. "Seriously?"

"I asked you a question," s he said, cocking a brow back. "When's your date with Noah?"

Trina didn't like being ignored. That didn't warrant having food thrown at me?

"Saturday," I grumbled, "And I'm not doing a double date again."

That was a disaster. Not only did my date spend more time gawking at Trina than he did talking to me, but we got front row seats to the world's worst foreplay.

"Please tell me you're going to do more with Noah than you did with the last two?" Trina openly sighed and waved her hand between her sister and me. "I'm tired of hanging out with the virgin squad."

I rolled my eyes. Unlike my friend, I wasn't going to lose my virginity in the backseat of a car, or at some party. Noah might not be as nice to look at as Logan—I don't think anyone was—but he was sweet and kind.

He brought me a rose this morning. Pink, my favorite color. He paid attention to little details like that, and he wasn't bad looking.

Noah was one of the hottest guys in school. He had the whole tall, dark, and handsome thing going on. Not to mention he was on the football team and had a fairly high GPA.

He was the kind of guy a girl took home to mom. The perfect boyfriend material. Logan was the kind of guy that would do your mom.

So stop thinking about his kiss.

I couldn't help it. The memory was so vivid. I felt his soft lips on mine. All firm and demanding. His heady taste lingered along with the cool, clean scent of his body wash.

Logan wasn't here. We didn't go to the same school, or run in the same social circles. Yet there he was. A whisper of a voice in the back of my mind.

Trina's date tilted his head at me. "Noah Torres?"

"Yeah." I eyed the confusion on his face. "Why?"

"No reason," he said and kissed Trina on the cheek. "I gotta go to practice. See you after school."

That was weird. Ah well, for all I knew the guy collected cat skulls or something.

Trina dropped her chin in her palm and released a dreamy sigh. "I think he's the one."

Marnie and I shared a knowing glance. She said that about every guy she went out with. Might even believe it. Problem was, Trina got bored quickly. Maybe someone like Logan was the solution? I was sure he'd be interested.

Logan was a whore, and I had yet to see a guy turn Trina down. Maybe they were meant for each other? Two players coming together. What better match could there be?

Why did that piss me off?

"You should just pick a guy and stick with him!" I snarled, a little shocked by my attitude.

Trina cocked a brow. "I think that soggy pizza is going to your head."

"It was this, or fish sticks," I muttered.

And the fish in fish sticks was a relative term. Because whatever was in those, it sure as hell wasn't fish. The last thing Ashen Springs High should have issues with was seafood. It wasn't like we lived in a coastal town or anything.

"What do you think Rye's eating right now?"

"I don't know," I said, wondering if Rye sat with Logan at lunch. She was dating his best friend. Maybe she was with him right now? "She was talking about some weird salad the other day."

I swept my tongue over the bite on the inside of my lip. The coppery tinge of my blood still lingered. That crap hurt. Was it wrong that I kind of liked it?

Stop thinking about him!

"Whatever." Trina waved her hand. "It's probably better than this crap."

"You're not even eating cafeteria food!" Marnie piped in. "Mom packed you a lunch."

Trina scoffed at her twin, "I still go to this school, you know. What happens here affects me."

"The only thing that affects you is who's on the top of the pyramid."

"Hey, that happens to be a very important position. You'd know that if you did something other than write stupid articles."

"At least I'm keeping people informed."

"About what? The misuse of school funds? No one cares, Marnie."

I sighed and shook my head. The twins probably came out of the womb arguing. They loved each other, though. Trina destroyed anyone that messed with her sister, and Marnie wrote an article about a guy that tried to take advantage of Trina last year when she passed out at a party. He did not have a good year.

Boys were mean, but girls were cruel.

"Oh my God, I forgot to tell you!" Trina exclaimed, slapping her hand on the table. "Evan's back. He's not looking so good. There's a big scar down the side of his face."

"Good," I muttered.

Everybody knew that Micha put him in the hospital. What they didn't know was why. Riley told me what those jerks did to her and as far as I was concerned, Evan got exactly what he deserved.

Lance should've gotten worse, but his family moved to Washington. People were saying it was because the Knights ran him out of town. Maybe they did, and maybe they didn't. Either way, he was gone, and I, for one, wasn't about to cry over it.

"I wonder what he did. Did Rye say anything?"

"No," I lied.

Riley didn't air her shit. I respected that. That part of my best friend never bothered me. It was the secret she was keeping that picked at the back of my brain. I don't care what anyone said. She was not in a car accident. People didn't get bruises on their neck like that from car accidents.

Chase tried to convince me that Mason was drunk when he crashed the car, and that's why he was sent to rehab. It was a lie. That much I knew.

Riley would *never* get in a car with someone who'd been drinking. She'd kick Mason's ass for just thinking about it. I wasn't angry—we all had our secrets—I was worried. Someone hurt her, and she wouldn't tell me who.

At first I thought maybe it was Micha. He never treated Riley well when we were kids. I changed my mind when I had to pry him away from her bedside long enough to take a shower. He might be an asshole, but I'd never question whether he loved her.

"Are you sure Rye didn't say anything?"

"Nope." If Riley wanted Trina to know, she'd tell her.

"Let it go, Trina," Marnie grumbled. "It's none of your business."

"What's up with you, lately?" Trina said, eyeing her twin. "You should be all over this, Miss Reporter."

Marnie shifted in her seat. "Some things are better left alone."

Even I cocked my brow at that. Nothing stopped Marnie from getting her story. Not being arrested, or making political enemies. Our principal had it out for her since she outed him for having an inappropriate relationship with a student.

Marnie was like a hurricane. This secret society crap was all she talked about for years. Considering some of those rumors involved Micha Kessler and the other Knights, she should be knee deep into this Evan thing. Maybe she finally gave up? Can't prove something that doesn't exist, right?

"You have PMS or something?" Trina said, "Cause you're not due for another two weeks."

Marnie's gaze shifted over to her. "It's seriously disturbing that you know that."

"What? Shell's due in a week."

"Sorry." I shook my head. "Got my shot last week. I'm Aunt Flo free for eleven more weeks."

"God, I wish mom would let us take birth control."

Trina's contraceptives came in pill form from the school nurse. Something her parents didn't know about. Their dad was a pastor at The Church of Holy Trinity. He expected them to be good girls. If only he knew.

"I don't want birth control. It opens up doors I prefer to stay closed."

Was Marnie was having issues with Collin again? He thought because he was the editor of the school paper he deserved 'special treatment', and Marnie was on the top of his list.

"You know," I reached out and placed my hand on Marnie's. "You can talk to us? We won't judge you."

Trina might have the football team pay Collin another visit, and I might make sure his car won't start, but we'd never judge her.

"I'm fine, Shelby," Marnie said, giving me a small smile. "I promise."

"Okay, but if you need me to talk to Collin again, I will."

"Ugh," Trina shivered, "That guy's a creep."

"Collin's the least of my worries," Marnie muttered.

Figuring she was just worried about her next story, I turned my attention to Trina, and we quickly got lost in gossip. Discussing who was wearing what, and the upcoming Christmas dance. I still had to go dress shopping. Wasn't sure if I'd go with Noah or not. That depended on how our date went.

The dance was about the only thing I was excited for this holiday season. Kind of hard to get in the Christmas spirit when my family was in shambles. I loved my baby sister.

Mags asked Santa to bring snow because she thought it would cheer me up. While it was a sweet gesture, this was Florida. It didn't snow here. At least, not where we lived.

I stopped talking when I noticed how eerily quiet it was. Weird, considering sometimes we had to yell over the cafeteria chatter just to hear each other. Also, people were staring at us.

Did I miss something?

"Are you Shelby Grace?"

I shrieked at the new voice. Standing beside me was a man dressed in a white uniform.

Where the hell did he come from?

"Um, yeah?" I said, eyeing the *'Mauve's Bakery'* written on the black box in his hand.

I knew the place. Our family went to the high end bakery on main street every New Years. I absolutely loved their cheesecake, but it was too expensive for more than a yearly treat.

He placed the box on the table, said, "Enjoy," and walked away.

I stared down at the mauve flower emblem. This had to be a joke, right? Mauve's didn't deliver. At least that's what they told dad last year when Mags was too sick to go.

"Who's it from?" Trina chirped excitedly.

I shrugged. "I don't know."

"Maybe it's from Noah?"

I smiled. It probably was. This was the kind of sweet thing he did.

"I'm dying over here. Open it already."

"Alright, alright," I said, carefully untying the ribbon and letting the sides fall away.

My face instantly dropped. It wasn't from Noah.

Sitting on the table in front of me was a big, sugary slice of cherry pie.

Son of a bitch.

Chapter 3
Shelby

When I told Rye about my date with Noah, Logan was less than impressed. He followed me outside and demanded I cancel. I told him where he could shove his demand, and thought that was the end of it. Apparently not.

Friggin cherry pie.

I didn't know if I wanted to scream or laugh. Rye was right. It was kind of hard to hate the guy- I was sure going to try though.

"Come on Shell," Trina whined, "You have to tell me who sent it."

"The magical pie fairy," I said, while shoving my books in my locker. Trina had been pestering me about this all afternoon. Never thought I'd be thankful for math class, but it was one of the few I had without her. "Your whining is starting to get irritating."

"The only thing that irritates you is dogs in dresses."

"Hey," I waved my finger at her. "Animals wearing people clothes is creepy."

Trina rolled her eyes. "Just tell me who sent it. You know I'll find out."

25

The twins were both natural born reporters. Trina preferred to use her talents for gossip, and like her sister, nine times out of ten, she'd get the information she was looking for.

I eyed Trina's black and blue uniform. There wasn't much she took seriously. Cheerleading was one of them. "Don't you have practice?"

"Ugh! Fine," she grumbled and backed down the hall. "But I'm engaging detective mode."

Great.

No one here personally knew Logan, so other than Riley being my best friend, there was no connection between the two of us. At least, I didn't think anyone here knew him.

I glanced down the hall at two girls flirting with a football player. One twirled her hair while the other giggled at something he said.

He seemed to be enjoying the attention, looking down at them with the same glint I saw in Logan's eyes. Had Logan slept with any of the girls here?

Probably.

"Rumor has it, you got a present this afternoon?"

Normally, I'd be happy to hear Noah's voice, but I wasn't looking forward to explaining the new complication in my life.

"It was just a stupid prank," I said, deciding to avoid the question. "Probably Riley."

His brow rose. "Why would Riley send you pie?"

"She has a weird sense of humor," I shrugged, not sure why I'd lied.

I didn't do anything wrong. Well, I did kiss Logan. Technically, he kissed me, but I didn't stop him. How was I supposed to know he'd do that?

He'd been a complete jerk since I met him. The last thing I expected was a kiss. Mags made my head spin less, and she was nine-year-old with ADHD.

"Well, that's good." Noah cocked his head and grinned. "I was starting to think I had competition."

"You have nothing to worry about," I said, feeling guilt crawl up my spine and fill my chest. Here was this great guy, gazing down at me with warm brown eyes, and I was thinking about kissing another man.

I'm no better than my dad.

"You know," as if he could sense my tension, Noah dug his fingers into my shoulders and began kneading my muscles. "We don't have to wait until Saturday. I'll be done practice in an hour."

Noah was the guy I actually wanted to go out with, so I tried to sink into his touch. I closed my eyes and leaned back, resting my head on his shoulder, and for a second it worked. Everything else faded away and it was just him and I, standing in the hallway while I listened to the steady thrum of his heartbeat.

"What do you say, Sweetness?"

The smooth timber of Noah's voice poured through me like a bucket of ice water. Images of my dad flashed through my mind. The sweet way he used to sneak up and hug my mom from behind. The sparkle in her eyes every time he kissed her... and then my coach moaning his name.

Before I could stop myself, I blurted out, "Logan Hudson kissed me."

Noah's fingers stilled and he cocked his head down at me. "Umm, okay? Wasn't expecting that."

"I'm sorry. I should've stopped him." I sighed and pushed off Noah to scoop my backpack off the floor. *He probably can't stand to look at me.* "I was fixing Riley's car and he came up behind me..."

"Shelby..."

"I thought the guy hated me. I wasn't expecting him to do that."

"Shelby..."

"I know it's no excuse." I hung my head and blew out a breath. "If you want to cancel our date, I understand."

"Why would I want to do that?"

It was good while it... Wait... what?

"Um... I kissed another guy," I said, lip curled in confusion.

"It's not like we're exclusive," he pointed out. "Don't you think we should at least go out on one date before we agree to stop seeing other people?"

That made sense. Why commit to someone if you weren't sure things would work out? Still… "But I kissed someone else, and you're okay with that?"

"Sure." He seemed more amused than angry. "I have a date with Chelsea tonight."

Ugh, really? Chelsea?

"Unless you want to go out instead?"

"I can't. My mom's working a double and I have to pick up my sister." I glanced down at my watch and groaned. "Which I'm late doing."

"Well, go get your sister," Noah said backing down the hall towards where his best friends, Dirk and Evan, were standing. "I'll see you tomorrow."

I glared at Evan, who was staring at me with a sneer on his face. *Prick.* "Try not to have too much fun with Chelsea."

"Don't worry sweetness," Noah smiled. "I always use protection."

Eww.

Well Noah just lost some points, but he was right. We weren't exclusive. At least he was honest about it, which is more than I could say for most of the guys in this school.

Except for Dirk, and that was only because I'd never seen him with a girl. Rumor was that he batted for the other team. I didn't think that was true, though.

The football players here were jerks. They ran an openly gay student out of school last year. I highly doubted they'd be okay sharing a locker room with one.

I liked Simon. He was a nice guy, but as much as Rye and I tried to stick up for him, he just couldn't take it anymore. I'd never forget the day she brought big bad Lance down to his knees. One ball crush and-squeeze and he dropped. Was that why Lance and Evan attacked her?

Evan smirked as I walked past. "Looking good, Shelly." 'Shelly' had been the running gag since I was a kid. After *'Shelly's Chicken Shack,'* A place known for salmonella as much as it was for chicken. "How's Riley doing?"

"Eat shit, prick," I growled and sauntered outside to my car.

I had bigger things to worry about then some jackoff trying to get on my nerves. Like Christmas. Since my dad left, Mom was working extra hours so she could afford a good Christmas for Mags. I chipped in what I could. Working at Pop Pop's garage didn't give me much money.

Mags wasn't taking the separation well, and I hated seeing her stress about something she couldn't control. I did what I could to take her mind off it.

Took her out for ice cream, and played whatever stupid game she wanted. Monopoly was her favorite, which took forever, and what she'd probably want to do when we got home. And then there were my dad's gambling debts.

I kept waiting for someone to show up at the house, looking to collect. The first time I saw my dad get his arm broken, I was six. The only thing that saved him the last time was Riley. She was there when two men showed up with a baseball bat.

Not only did she demand the bookie's collectors get out of my house, but she marched right up to them and got in their faces. All five foot three of her. When one of them threatened to hit her, Riley just smiled, and said, *"Go ahead asshole, but I should mention, my dad's the sheriff."*

If I had one ounce of her strength, maybe I wouldn't be worried all the time. Worried about Riley, worried about Christmas and Mom, and whether or not I could save Mags from seeing something she shouldn't.

Hell, I was even concerned about my dad. As angry as I was at him, I still loved him. I didn't want to see him hurt or unhappy.

By the time I pulled up in front of Mags' school, I was wound tighter than a lug nut. Thankfully, I didn't have to wait long for my little sister to come bounding over.

"How come I can't sit in the front?" she whined, climbing in the backseat.

"Because you're too little."

She huffed and crossed her arms. "I'm not little."

We'd had this conversation before. There were regulations for airbags, which Pop Pop made me install.

"Are you thirteen?"

"No."

"Do you weigh a hundred and fifty pounds?"

"I might?"

I raised my brows at her in the rear view mirror. "You don't."

I got my height from our dad. In heels, I was almost six foot. Mags took after our mom. She was a tiny little thing.

Her face scrunched up, displaying her discontent, but she didn't argue any more.

"Okay, let's go," I said, and paused when I spotted a boy with dark hair shuffling down the sidewalk.

Isn't that Junior?

Micha brought him over to Riley's a couple times. The kid had it rough, that much I knew. Didn't know why though. He was guarded and didn't talk much. Right now, he looked downright miserable.

His jeans were scuffed up and it looked like his lip was bleeding. Everybody needed someone, even if they didn't want them. I couldn't leave him like that.

I pulled up beside him and called out my window, "Junior, right?"

He looked my way, dark eyes narrowing. "Yeah?"

"You remember me?"

"I've seen you around." He shrugged indifferently.

God, this kid was so much like Micha it was scary. Junior couldn't be any more then a year or two older then Mags and he already had the, *'don't fuck with me'* face down pat.

"I'm Shelby," I said, and sighed inwardly. "Riley's friend?"

"So?"

I'm gonna start calling this kid mini Micha.

"You want a ride?"

Junior didn't seem too thrilled about the idea. He stood there eyeing my car, like I was going to sell him on the dark web or something. Kids shouldn't be suspicious like that.

Mags talked to anyone, including people she shouldn't. I once caught her having a conversation with a couple guys trying to break into our neighbor's car.

Mags popped her head out of the window, and said, "Come on, my sister's car is really cool. But you have to sit in the back unless you're thirteen," she added, giving me a snotty lip curl.

I stuck my tongue out at her in response.

Brat!

Mags held the door open for him and slid over to the other side. Junior eventually shrugged and headed over.

"So, where to?"

Junior gave me his address and I instantly understood why the kid had it rough. Riley's old neighborhood was the Plaza compared to the crime riddled crap hole where Junior lived.

I knew his apartment, because my dad had clients there. All of which were hardcore addicts. I got that some people couldn't afford much, but the school was at least a forty minute walk. So why didn't his parents pick him up? Weren't they worried about him? I was.

"So, Junior, what do your parents do?" I asked, attempting small talk, and maybe fishing for information.

"Nothing."

"They must have some sort of career. You have to eat, right?"

His answer shocked the hell out of me.

"Is sucking cock a career?"

How was I supposed to respond to that?

"Um… so… your mom…"

"Gotta eat, right?" he said, shooting my words back at me.

Well, okay then.

I wasn't going to fault Junior's mom for doing what she had to do.

Mags hummed and said, "Why would anyone want to suck on a rooster?"

I wasn't sure if I wanted to shake my head, or laugh. One thing I wasn't going to do was explain things to her. That was Mom's department.

"What about your dad?" I asked, interrupting Junior when he opened his mouth. I could just imagine what he'd say.

His gaze met mine in the rear view mirror. "What about him?"

"What does he do?"

"Don't know," Junior shrugged. "Never met him."

Plenty of people's parents weren't together, but I couldn't fathom not knowing one of them. Here I was worried about getting Mags the presents she wanted, and Junior and his mom were all alone.

Did they have anyone to spend Christmas with? Maybe I could help them? I could take donations at Pop Pop's garage and start a toy drive at school. Everyone should have a good Christmas.

I eyed Junior in the mirror, wondering what kind of things he'd want. Did he even like toys, or believe in Santa? It was then that I noticed his lip wasn't bleeding. It was fat, split, and looked fresh.

Like it happened today. He had other marks. One of his eyes was black, and there was a bruise on his arm that I was positive wasn't caused by a kid. It broke my heart. No wonder he was guarded. Someone was hurting him.

Just like Rye.

Every instinct told me to drive him to the police station, but if Riley taught me anything, it was that kids like this didn't ask for help. Or accept it. Anytime I said something to Riley about her mom's drinking, she'd shut me out and I'd have to pry my way back in.

Junior wouldn't say anything to the cops, just like Riley wouldn't tell her dad her mom was drunk when she crashed the car. The only thing someone could do for a kid like this was be there for them. Which Mags, apparently, had covered.

"How come I never see you playing with anyone? Don't you have any friends?"

I shook my head. Gotta love my sister's unfiltered mouth.

"I don't need friends," Junior grumbled.

"Everybody needs friends." Mags reached over and grabbed his hand. "I'll be your friend. I'll play with you every day."

Junior curled his lip as he yanked his hand away. "I didn't ask you to be my friend."

"You don't ask for friends, silly. You just get them."

I listened to Mags ramble off all the ways they were going to have fun and almost felt sorry for the kid. My little sister was tenacious.

She won over Riley – who was the most closed off person I knew – and trust me, Riley tried to run her off. But Mags wouldn't be detoured. Poor Junior didn't have a hope in hell.

He practically threw himself out of the car when I pulled up in front of his apartment.

"Bye, Junior," Mags sang happily. "See you tomorrow."

He glanced back, shooting her a *'what the hell is wrong with you'* look and quickly disappeared into the apartment.

I looked at the rundown building and over to a group of degenerates hanging out on the corner. There was no doubt in my mind that if I left my car parked here, they'd have it stripped in five minutes. And they weren't the worst people I saw. The creepy guy across the street that blew me a kiss took that prize.

How could I leave Junior here without at least saying something to someone? What kind of person would do that? I could call Riley's dad, but I had a feeling the sheriff showing up in this neighborhood would only bring Junior unwanted attention.

I was pretty sure the matching bandanas on those guys' wrists meant they were a gang, and gangs didn't like cops. Or the people that brought them around.

I pulled out my phone and texted the only person I could think of. Riley. She could at least let Micha know. He seemed to care about Junior. Maybe he could help?

> Me: Hey just wanted to let you know, I gave Junior a ride home and he didn't look that great. I think someone beat him up.

I didn't expect Rye to call, but a few seconds later my phone rang. The deep, gruff voice that came across wasn't hers.

"What the fuck do you mean someone beat him up?" Micha demanded.

"I-I don't know," I stuttered. Micha Kessler was scary on a good day. "He has some bruises, and I don't think he got them at school."

"Fucking Julia," Micha growled, before the line went dead.

Well, isn't he pleasant.

I shot Riley a quick text before driving away. Creepy guy was inching closer.

Me: Tell your asshole boyfriend he's welcome.

Rye: Sorry, I'll slap him for you later.

Me: Make sure it hurts.

Rye: Balls it is.

She texted with a smiley face emoji.

Chapter 4
Logan

Shelby's room was annoyingly girly. There was fucking pink everywhere. The blankets, the curtains, even the damn carpet was a faded salmon color.

This place should make my dick die faster than seeing Ma naked – which thank fucking God has never happened – but the only thing I wanted to do was defile this place of innocence. Devour myself a slice of cherry pie, while all of Shelby's stuffed animals watched.

I plucked a brown bunny off a chair by the window. "What do you say, Thumper? Want me to show you how it's really done in the animal kingdom?"

He stared back at me with beaded black eyes and a stitched smile.

"Good to know you're with me, buddy," I said, and tossed him on the bed beside a unicorn.

Thumper I could handle, but the unicorn… I shook my head. What was it with chicks and this shit? Naomi had dolphins, and Amy cats. Even Riley had fucking Minnie Mouse everywhere, and she wasn't girly at all.

Time for something more interesting.

I moved over to the small desk in the corner. Shelby's journal was in the top drawer and I knew she wrote in it everyday. I was curious what she thought about my present?

It wasn't hard to convince Mauve to deliver. She was an old family friend after all. Ma had her over every Sunday for tea.

My lips curled when I flipped open her journal and got to last night's entry. The first words written were, *Logan Hudson is an ass.* Cherry Pie may not have liked my present, but she was thinking about me, and that was the point.

I sat down on her bed and read through her latest dream. There was something about a spanking – nothing like the one I'd give her. There wouldn't be any of this playful slapping crap.

I wanted to see my handprint on her ass. Know that every time she sat down, she felt me. Other than the spanking, the rest was pretty tame. A touch here. A kiss there. Boring, really.

Ah well, what could I expect from a virgin?

She had nothing to go on. At least she better fucking not! Just the thought of another cock tainting my pussy had me ready to kill a motherfucker.

From what I could tell, the most Shelby had done was kiss a couple pricks. Both of whom I paid a visit to. I kind of liked the last one. He was a squirrely fucker. Even took him out for a beer afterwards.

I wrote a couple suggestions in Shelby's journal and dropped it on her desk, just as my phone dinged.

Micha: Where the hell are you?

What the fuck did he care? It wasn't the first time I'd skipped school. One good thing I got from my old man was his intelligence, and the exact reason Lou should've put a bullet in his fucking head.

Me: Had something to do.

Micha: Do you want my dad on your ass?

I don't know why Lou felt the need to act as my father figure. I didn't ask him to, yet there he was, scolding me every time I fucked up. Last week he had a conversation with me about my attendance record.

Apparently, I needed to think about my future. He should worry about his own kid. I already got accepted into MIT, while Micha was thinking about opting out of Stanford to go to the University of Miami so he could be close to his girl.

> Me: I don't swing that way, but I can hook your old man up if that's his thing.

> Micha: Asshole.

I sent him a kiss emoji and pocketed my phone.

Why waste my time in math class when I could be going through Cherry Pie's delicates? She literally had it labeled that. Delicates.

I snickered at the small tab stuck on the corner of her drawer.

Shelby must've done it when she was a kid, because most of the labels were peeling, or half hanging off. I could picture her walking around with pigtails and a label maker, tagging everything she owned. So fucking cute.

While her room looked like it was decorated when she was ten, her 'delicates' were all woman. Lacy little thongs and G-strings in every color imaginable. Fuck that candy *taste the rainbow* crap, I want to eat this shit. What was hiding at the bottom of the drawer was even better.

Well, well, well, what do we have here?

Tucked in the far back corner, was a small silver bullet, along with a book. I scanned the cover, making a mental note of the title and author. *'Daddy P.I.'*, by E.J Frost.

I picked up the toy and flipped the switch, letting it vibrate in my palm as I flipped through the book. Right away it got bonus points for the guy's name being Logan. I didn't know what it was about yet, but I knew he'd own that shit. The sex scenes were particularly interesting.

My Cherry Pie has a naughty side.

I was part way through chapter eight when I heard a familiar hiss.

Shelby's fat gray tabby was standing in the doorway, crouched up in a Halloween cat stance.

Hissss!

"Really?" I sighed, "I thought we were past this shit?"

He growled and let out another hiss, before turning around and prancing away. I shook my head and kicked the door shut.

That cat was one ornery motherfucker. Can't say I blamed him. Poor bastard's name was Fluffy Whiskerson. He had to wear that shit on his collar. Which was, of course, pink.

I tucked Shelby's book back in the drawer and turned around to eye her bed. It wasn't anything special. A double mattress with a light pink blanket and a couple of pillows.

It was the frame I liked. Solid metal, with a headboard and footboard sturdy enough to tie someone to.

The bullet vibrated in my hand as I stood there picturing Shelby on her back with her legs spread. How many times had she come on that bed?

I grabbed my cock through my pants and sucked in a deep breath. I could smell her in here. That sweet jasmine scent that made my dick hard. I wanted to watch her. See how she played with her little toy.

Did she think about me when she was touching herself? Or did she think about someone else?

Like her fucking date!

I went from turned the fuck on, to pissed the fuck off in point two seconds. I was still hard as hell, but now I wanted to hurt someone. Her date would be ideal. Except I still didn't know who it was. I'd find out, though.

What I really wanted to do was slit the motherfucker's throat, but that would be what Lou called an 'overreaction'. As much as I wanted to, I couldn't kill him. If I did everything I wanted, the Order would've put me down a long time ago. Micha wouldn't have had a choice. Even I knew the shit in my head was fucked up.

I slipped the bullet in my pocket. The next time Cherry Pie wanted to play, she'd have to ask permission.

Let's see who she fucking thinks about then!

I glanced down at my watch. Time to go. I hopped out the window and climbed down the lattice to the backyard. Shelby's house was one of those two storey, white picket fence deals.

There was a flagpole in the front yard. A firepit in the back, with matching patio furniture, and a sandbox in the corner. The same all-American family bullshit as half the houses on this block.

It was the inside that separated them. And not the decorations, or happy family pictures. That shit was fake as fuck too. It was the people and the things they did in the dark.

Shelby's neighbors had secret swinger parties, and the guy down the street was a regular at Malum. His wife didn't want to know the sick shit he did there. Everyone had secrets, even sweet little Shelby. What would she do to keep Riley from finding out about the skeleton in her closet?

I rounded the corner and reached for my car door, pausing when I spotted a red BMW parked down the street. Was that Preston's car? Did Lou tell him to follow me? I wouldn't put it past him.

It wasn't like Preston to leave his car in plain sight, though. Especially when he was tailing someone. Of course, it could be someone else's car, but who in this neighborhood could afford a BMW?

Curiosity had me sauntering over to look in the window. Yeah, it was Preston's. I recognized the skull and crossbones Zippo on the dash.

So where the fuck is he?

The thought had barely left my head when I spotted someone hopping over a fence behind one of the cookie-cutter houses lining the block. There was no mistaking that jean jacket. It'd become an identifying mark for Preston. The other Knights talked about it, wondering why he favored the thing.

It was pretty generic. At least, to them, but I was with him when he got it. He took it off one of my old man's friends. The same guy he used to invite over to play with Parker.

Let's just say, what that fucker did to his brother was nothing compared to what Preston did to him.

"Fucking dog," Preston grumbled and turned around, freezing when he saw me.

His hair was dishevelled – nothing new there – and he had blood dripping down his arm. Probably why he was cursing a dog. A brief moment of surprise flashed across his eyes before he casually strolled over.

We were two sides of the same coin, him and I. Both ruthless and cold. Neither one of us had an issue taking someone out. I enjoyed it. Took pleasure in pain and suffering, but Preston... he just didn't care.

There were only two things Preston actually gave a shit about. His siblings, and the Knights. His parents didn't even make the list. There was no doubt in my mind that the fucker could pop a bullet in one of their heads and sleep like a baby.

I tipped my chin at him and said, "Shouldn't you be in school?"

"Shouldn't you?" he shot back.

"I'm not missing midterms." I pulled out a pack of smokes and lit one. "Aren't those kind of important?"

"Don't have any today."

"So, you had the day off and decided to. . . what? Explore the suburbs? Didn't take you for the barbequing and mowing the lawn type."

His cold eyes rolled up. "Curiosity killed the cat, Logan."

It wasn't like Preston to be evasive. He didn't have an issue telling someone what he was doing. If they didn't like it, it was their fucking problem. Especially if he thought they might cause him trouble. Then they became his problem.

"I'm not a cat," I said with a smile.

What could I say? I liked poking the fucker. He came close to shooting me once. I kind of deserved it, though. Never take away someone's revenge kill. They earned that shit.

"No, you're a pain in the ass," he muttered. "What the fuck are you doing here?"

"Checking out Shelby's thong collection."

I didn't have a problem telling people what I was up to either.

He huffed out a sigh. "Micha talked you into going for her, didn't he?"

Preston was the one that told me to stay away from Shelby because she couldn't handle my shit. He was also the one that said if I kept denying my urges, they'd find a way to come out.

That was after I was given my first girl at Malum and Lou gave up on his psychiatric bullshit. I was pretty sure he wrote me off as a lost cause after that.

Preston didn't. He stepped in and gave me the *'put your demons on a leash'* speech. Considering he had to do the same thing, his advice wasn't just helpful, it worked. Now, I had a lot more control.

"She's my doll to play with, remember," I pointed out. "Maybe I just decided to play?"

"That's the problem, Logan. That girl isn't ready for your kind of play." He opened his car door and reached in to grab his Zippo. "You don't know how to tame shit down."

"I can tame shit down."

"Sure. Now you can. But she's gonna do something to piss you off, and then what?"

I took a long drag, pulling a lungful of smoke down my throat. Don't get me wrong, I valued Preston's opinion, but how I handled mine was none of his fucking business.

"Why the fuck do you care?"

"I don't," he said, lighting his own smoke. "Do what you want, but if you're not careful you'll end up with a broken doll."

Why did I get the feeling he wasn't talking about me?

He leaned back against his car and exhaled a stream of smoke. "Broken dolls aren't any fun."

"Are you worried about my doll breaking," I glanced at the fence he'd hopped over and said, "Or yours?"

His jaw clenched and his nostrils flared.

Bingo.

"Don't tell me you've got her locked in a cage somewhere in one of these houses?"

"That's a good fucking idea," his eyes shifted my way, "But no. She's too young to take."

My lip curled, "You're not into some toddler, are you?"

I was only half joking. With Preston, you never really knew.

"She's sixteen, asshole!" Preston snarled, "I'm not a kiddy diddler."

"Well, that's a relief." I let out an exaggerated sigh and slapped my hand over my heart. "I was worried for a minute there."

Preston shook his head and grumbled under his breath.

"Sixteen's not too young." Shelby was sixteen.

"Not to an eighteen-year-old. I'm twenty-one, dickhead," he huffed out a puff of air, "And trust me, sixteen's too young."

"So, you're just going to wait two years?"

He shrugged in response.

Huh? I had to hand it to him. I'd be surprised if I made it to the end of the week. "What if someone else takes her?"

"She knows her place."

"Ah, so you've paid her a visit then?"

"Don't you have somewhere to be?" Preston grumbled, while taking a drag of his smoke.

"Actually, I do." Cherry Pie would be walking out of school in about ten minutes. I flicked my butt and said, "Good luck with your two year long case of blue balls."

"Asshole," he muttered. "Do yourself a favor, Logan. Find a play-mate before you take shit too far and break the girl."

"That's what Malum's for," I sang over my shoulder as I sauntered away.

Chapter 5

Shelby

I slammed my locker shut as Marnie grumbled, "Here comes the skank patrol."

Chelsea Thompson waltzed by with her minions in tow. None of whom bothered to spare us a glance, and why would they?

They were the 'it girls.' The group that ran this school and walked the halls like royalty. We were meant to be nothing more than loyal subjects, which of course, we weren't.

"Bet Rye's happy to be rid of them."

"Probably," I agreed, rolling my gaze over Chelsea's red dress. "From what she said, there's someone worse than the Black Queen at Ashworth, though."

"What? No way."

It was hard to believe that someone could out bitch the Black Queen. Even harder still was that I used to be friends with her. Or at least I'd thought she was my friend. That all changed one afternoon when I was asked to do something and prove my loyalty.

"Some girl named Naomi," I said, remembering a day I wish I could take back.

It took seeing Riley beaten down and humiliated to realize that she was right. The only thing popular girls cared about, was their image. They didn't care about me, not like Riley did.

Her only thought was for my safety. Telling me to run while she was being assaulted. I'd like to say I stepped in right away. That I had her back from the beginning, but she'd have never been there in the first place if it wasn't for me.

"Naomi Prescott?" Marnie cocked her head at me. "The mayor's daughter?"

I shrugged and huffed out a sigh when a group of girls sauntered past, pointing and whispering.

The pie incident had thrust me to the top of the rumor mill. Everybody, and I mean everybody, wanted to know who sent it. Some people even had a bet going. Friggin Logan Hudson.

I left them to their speculations. Sooner or later they'd find something else to talk about. That's how high school worked. One rumor after another. It was worse than one of those gossip magazines.

After saying goodbye to Marnie, I swung my backpack over my shoulder and headed for the parking lot. My first thought when I saw the crowd gathered was that Alice and Leo – Ashen Springs' bipolar couple – were at it again. Last week she smashed out his windows because she was convinced he was cheating on her.

The time before that, it was a rather loud and very public verbal lashing because he thought she was cheating on him. Those two were the definition of a toxic relationship.

Two steps out the door and all the attention wasn't for the couple.

You've got to be kidding me.

Leaning back against his midnight blue Mustang with an amused smirk on his lips, stood Logan.

Was this some kind of cruel joke? Did the universe hate me? Because whatever I did, I was pretty sure I didn't deserve this. And if I did, why couldn't my stalker be some hideously deformed beast of a man, instead of this model of male perfection?

Even the damn sun shone down on him like he was some kind of filthy idol of lust. He stood there with his ankles crossed and black ink crawling up his chest, making Ashworth's crisp uniform look like something from a dirty magazine.

My hand twitched at my side. I couldn't stop thinking about the hard ridges hidden under his white shirt.

Okay, so he might be nice to look at, but that didn't mean I wanted to touch. Right?

A giggle pulled my attention to the girl at his side.

Ugh, Chelsea Thomson.

Of course the Black Queen would be here. Logan was rich, powerful, and hot. Hell, he could be married and Chelsea wouldn't care. If anything, she'd try harder. She got a thrill out of stealing another girl's man. Enjoyed the pain she caused people, hence the title.

I watched her bat her eyelashes and run her hand down Logan's arm, and openly groaned.

I can't believe Noah went out with her last night.

Did I really want her sloppy seconds? Then again, what guy around here hadn't taken the Chelsea ride?

Look at her, staring at Logan like he's some kind of god.

"Pfft, god," I snorted.

Bet he'd love that. Having a flock of subjects following him around, vying for his attention and begging to worship at his feet.

Dick.

"Hey," Dirk tipped his chin at me and wandered over. "Any idea why Logan Hudson is here?"

To push me off the edge into insanity.

"Why ask me?" I eyed Logan's Mustang parked right beside my car. *How convenient.* Guess ignoring him is out of the question.

"Isn't he Riley's stepbrother?"

He had me there. Everyone knew Rye was my best friend, so it stood to reason that I would know her stepbrother.

"Doesn't mean I know him."

In fact, the only time I saw Logan until recently, was when he was bringing home some girl. And even then he'd only pause long enough to poke fun at me.

"Do you often get deliveries from people you don't know?" Dirk argued. "Speaking of which, aren't you going out with my best friend this weekend?"

"Correct me if I'm wrong, but didn't your best friend go out with the school slut last night?"

He grunted and rolled his eyes.

At least I wasn't the only one that didn't want to kiss the queen's ass.

When Chelsea released an obviously fake giggle while pressing her breasts up against Logan, Dirk crossed his arms and snickered. "Looks like Noah isn't the only one interested in a little pre-date action."

I sneered at the playful little flip she did with her dark hair.

Could she be more desperate.

"You sure know how to pick em', Shelly."

"Trust me," I grumbled, "I didn't pick him."

Dirk wasn't my biggest fan. The other day I overheard him trying to talk Noah out of our date. Why, I had no idea. I'd never done anything to him. For some reason, he just didn't like me. Logan showing up at my school probably wasn't helping that situation any.

"What the fuck is he doing here?!"

Yay, another prick.

My skin crawled as I rolled my eyes up at Evan, who was standing behind me. Trina wasn't lying. He did not look good. Micha really worked him over.

Not only did he still have bruises healing, but there was an angular scar on his right cheek. The line so perfectly cut in his skin, that one might think it was put there on purpose. I smirked inwardly.

Not so pretty anymore, are you, prick?

"Back off March, that one's mine."

Both Dirk and Evan cocked a brow at Logan's very loud proclamation.

I groaned and dropped my face in my palm.

Lord, kill me now.

"Don't know him, hey?" Dirk muttered.

I rolled my eyes and grumbled. "Stalking doesn't constitute a relationship."

"Doesn't sound like she's yours, Hudson," Evan called out with a smug smirk and threw his arm around my shoulders.

The stench of his cologne made me want to vomit.

"Get your slimy hand off me!" I growled, shoving him away.

"Now, now Shelly." The asshole actually chuckled and ruffled my hair, which I was now going to wash the second I got home. "There's no need to get feisty. I was only–"

A fist flew past my sight, slamming into Evan's face. I was too stunned to do anything other than stand there as Evan's head twisted to the side and he stumbled back.

Did that just happen?

My gaze locked onto the word fuck tattooed across the assailant's knuckles and up to a pair of green eyes burning with rage.

I opened my mouth to say something, but nothing came out. The person I was staring at looked like Logan, just not the one I knew. This one scared me.

"You hard of hearing, March?" Logan growled. "This one's mine. Don't touch her. Don't even look at her, or that pretty little scar on your face won't be your last."

Evan spat out some blood and wiped his mouth with the back of his hand. "Go ahead, Hudson," he said, glaring at the crowd watching. "There's plenty of witnesses this time."

"You think I give a fuck about these idiots?" A slow smirk spread across Logan's face, and if I didn't know better, I'd say he was enjoying this. "I prefer an audience."

He wanted Evan to give him a reason. Say or do something so he could unleash hell. That much I knew. I could see it in the fiery inferno raging in his glare, and in that moment, I was truly afraid of Logan Hudson.

The really messed up thing was how deeply masculine I suddenly found it.

Here I was, next to an unhinged beast, and all I could think about was having his hand wrapped around my neck while he held me down, and growled in my ear. That's what scared me the most. I even took a step back, which was when Dirk moved in.

"Ease off, Hudson," he said going nose to nose with Logan. "This isn't Ashworth. Your boys aren't here to back you up this time."

"You think I need back up?"

"I think I'm the least of your problems." Dirk tipped his chin at a couple football players making their way through the crowd.

Logan scoffed out a snicker. "You care to test that theory?"

Even I could sense Dirk's apprehension. Which was stupid, considering Logan was outnumbered.

"I'm not looking for a fight, Hudson. But I'm not going to let you kick him around either. Your friend did enough of that."

"You often go to bat for guys that attack little girls?"

Dirk cocked a curious brow and glanced back at Evan, who was grinding his teeth at Logan. "What the hell is he talking about?"

Funny how Evan didn't say anything. Guess he didn't want his friend to know he was a rapist scumbag.

"Maybe you should ask your friend what earned him that pretty scar on his face. You want him around your girl, that's fine, but he better stay the fuck away from mine." Before I knew what was happening, Logan had grabbed my arm–not too nicely either–and was marching me across the parking lot.

His fingers dug in my flesh as he murmured, "Great friends you have there, Cherry Pie."

Alright, that's it!

"First off, I can take care of myself," I snarled and tore my arm out of his grasp. "And I'm not *your* girl."

I don't know what was more infuriating, Logan's lack of response, or the coy smirk on his face.

"Take a hint Logan. I told you I'm not interested."

He cocked a brow at me and sat on the hood of his Mustang. "Was that before, or after you shoved your tongue down my throat?"

"You kissed me!"

"And, *you* kissed me back."

"You kissed her?" Chelsea scoffed with a snide eye roll. "Were you drunk?"

Why is she still here?

"You two are perfect for each other." I turned my glare on the Black Queen. "Clearly neither of you can tell when someone obviously wants nothing to do with you."

Chelsea's eyes narrowed and her lips tightened in the cruel sneer Riley and I had come to know well. "Why would he pick you, when he could have me?"

Logan gave Chelsea a quick scan and said, "You're at best a six," before placing a cigarette between his lips and flipping open a gold lighter. "I don't roll out of bed for anything less than an eight. So unless you got a beer flavored pussy, go find someone else's dick to suck."

I couldn't help but snicker. It was kind of nice seeing queen bitch taken down a peg. Even if it was by Logan.

"What are you laughing at?" Chelsea ground out, "This is my school, and *you* are nothing but a second rate grease monkey."

Grease monkey wasn't that bad. If anything, it was a compliment. I worked hard and was proud of my accomplishments. My car was nothing but a rusty body when Pop Pop found it, and look at her now. Suzie Q was beautiful.

"What exactly do you have to look forward to?" I challenged, "A stellar porn career?"

Chelsea scowled and Logan laughed.

"You must be watching some fucking terrible porn, Cherry Pie."

Did he just insult us both in one sentence?

"Shelly's a good girl," Chelsea sang. "She doesn't watch porn."

My inner-self shook her head. Quick wit was not her strong point.

"No, she prefers to read it. Isn't that right, Baby Doll?"

My stomach flipped. "W-why would you call me that?"

"It's okay," he said, lips curling in a mischievous grin. "Daddy's not mad."

My mouth fell open. A book I was reading had a Daddy/Little

kink. I kept it hidden in my drawer so Mom or Mags wouldn't find it. But he couldn't possibly know about that.

Was I that easy to read? Did I walk around openly broadcasting my secrets? Suddenly, I felt extremely exposed, standing there with Logan and Chelsea staring at me.

Say something!

"I… well you…" I stuttered, desperately searching for something to throw back at him. *Damn him for being so friggin perfect.* "That tattoo's crooked," I cried out, and immediately felt like face palming.

Quick wit apparently wasn't my strong point either.

Logan smirked and leaned back, exhaling a cloud of smoke. "I can give you a more intimate look if you want?"

"Screw you, Logan."

"Anytime, sweetheart. Just name the place."

"You're kidding, right?" Chelsea piped in. "You aren't seriously picking her over me?"

He didn't even look her way, which Chelsea was not happy with. She stomped her foot and marched away, grumbling under her breath.

I'll pay for that tomorrow.

While I was happy to be rid of Chelsea, there was still another asshole to contend with. One that was staring at me like he could see what was under my clothes.

"Well, this was fun," I said, pulling my sweater tighter around my chest. "Have fun with your fan club."

I nodded at the group of girls giggling in the grass, and sauntered around my car. Why I thought it would be that easy to dismiss Logan, I had no idea.

Because like the gazelle that turned its back on the lion, I quickly found myself trapped. Logan was on me, pressing me up against my car door before I had a chance to open it.

"Did I say you could leave?" he purred in my ear. Hot breath wafting over my skin, causing me to shiver.

"I didn't ask," I pointed out, and twisted my neck to look back at him.

That was a mistake. Not only was I sucked into those deep pools of green, but I could taste the faint hint of tobacco with each breath he took.

"A valid point," he said, stepping in closer and sliding his hand around my waist.

My heart picked up pace when he began toying with my shirt, slowly tugging it free of my skirt.

"Logan," I whispered, licking my lips and trying desperately to ignore the hard ridges of his chest pressing against my back. "People are watching."

Most had left, I assumed right after the showdown between Dirk and Logan. They'd gotten their amusement. A few remained, not really paying attention, except for the girls in the grass. None of whom looked very happy with me right now.

"Are they?" he breathed. "You better be quiet then."

Whatever I was going to say was lost in the gasp I sucked in as his fingers dipped under my shirt and skimmed over my stomach. I wriggled, trying to get enough room to open my door and slip inside the safety of my car. Logan wasn't having any of it. He pressed in, sandwiching me between the metal door and his hard body, and shoved his hand down my skirt.

"Admit it, Cherry Pie, you want me."

When his fingers dipped lower, tracing the outline of my panties, I squeezed my thighs shut. Both out of absolute mortification that there were people around, and because I didn't want him to feel the dampness on the lace fabric.

"Are you forgetting I have a date Saturday?"

It just came out. An anxious burst of word vomit. Because his hand was no longer just snaking down my abdomen. He'd forced his way between my tightly clenched thighs and was cupping a place no one else had touched.

"Ah, that's right," Logan said, pressing his finger down on my clit.

No matter how many times I'd touched myself, or the countless books I'd read, nothing could've prepared me for the electric jolt that shot through me.

"And who's the lucky guy?"

I clamped my mouth shut to stop the moan threatening to bubble up my throat.

"I know it isn't March," he did it again, this time rolling his finger slowly, "And I'm assuming it wasn't the prick you were talking to. He doesn't seem to like you."

"Maybe I like Dirk?" I sang, hoping to shock Logan enough that he'd stop what he was doing.

It wasn't unreasonable to think I'd be interested in Dirk. Like most football players, he was tall, buff, and not bad looking. But he wasn't my type. Which was apparently arrogant blond assholes.

"He is kind of cute."

To my relief, Logan pulled his hand away and dropped it on the roof of my car. "Guess I'll have to kill him then."

It wasn't his threat that stunned me, it was the seriousness in his eyes. Wow, money and power really went to some people's heads.

"Good looking, and homicidal tendencies," I grumbled, "What more could a girl ask for?"

The bastard actually puffed his chest out proudly.

"I have many talents." He took a step back and winked. "You'll see."

Happy to have a chance for escape, I just rolled my eyes and opened the door, tossing my bag in the backseat.

"A word of advice, Cherry Pie. You shouldn't waste your time giving a fuck what other people think."

"This coming from the guy that keeps telling me what to do."

Logan flashed me his perfect white teeth. "I'm the exception."

Of course he was. Logan Hudson was the exception to every rule as far as Logan Hudson was concerned. He expected me to cancel my date because he was him, and the world should fall at his feet. I was going on that date. If for no other reason, than to prove that he wasn't as great as he thought he was.

"And yet, it'll be someone else kissing me good night Saturday."

"Watch yourself," he warned, a dark twinkle in his eyes. "I'm not as nice as you think I am."

"Trust me, plenty of words come to mind when I think of you. Nice isn't one of them."

"And trust me when I say, I've been nice so far. That can quickly change."

Whatever.

"This isn't Ashworth," I said with a sigh. "You're not king here."

"Oh, baby, I'm king everywhere."

Before he could say anything else, I climbed in my car and closed the door.

"Bastard," I muttered, while pinching the bridge of my nose.

This might be a game to him, but this was my life! Deciding I wouldn't let him get to me, I turned my keys and started the ignition.

The song blaring through my eardrums was not Taylor Swift. I tried to turn it off. Fumbling with the radio and clicking buttons. Nothing worked. I couldn't even turn the volume down

'She's my cherry pie.'

I didn't realize how much I hated this song until now. When I glared back at Logan, he grinned smugly and shot me a wink. That's it. If he thought he was the only one that could play dirty, I was more than happy to prove him wrong.

Game on, Logan.

Chapter 6

Logan

Riley pounded on the bathroom door.

"Logan, hurry the hell up!" For a little thing, she was surprisingly strong. The door vibrated with each hit. "Other people have to use the bathroom too."

I pulled a lungful of smoke down my throat and propped my hip against the counter. If my stepsister and her boyfriend hadn't kept me up until two am, I might've left fifteen minutes ago, when I was done. I considered this payback.

"Micha, a little help?" she huffed from the other side.

"I told you to be quiet last night."

That he did. Several times.

"But we're not going to have time to shower together."

I shook my head and chuckled. Riley was a ball of fire and rage, but goddamn, the girl could turn on the sweet tap when she wanted to.

I completely forgot I gave Micha a key until the door swung open. He had it so Riley couldn't hide, not so he could fuck my shit up.

"You're done," Micha growled, "Get the fuck out."

If looks could kill.

"Someone's grumpy. Didn't your dick get enough attention last night?"

"Yeah, and it's gonna get some more this morning. Now fuck off."

I'd be pissed if someone was fucking with my pussy too. I've killed motherfuckers for less. Unfortunately, the person cockblocking me from my pussy, was my pussy. Couldn't fuck the shit out of Shelby if she was fucking dead.

Well, I could, but necrophilia wasn't my thing. I've never had to try this hard for some ass. It was fucking frustrating, and I was loving every second.

Riley popped up next to Micha and snarled, "Are you seriously standing in here smoking!"

"Next time gag her," I said, flicking my butt down the drain, "Or I will."

Micha cocked his brow. "You're just pissed you're not getting any."

"Why haven't you been getting any?" Riley asked, eyes narrowed suspiciously.

"Aw sis, your concern brings a tear to my eye," I sang, laying my hand on my chest. "It's truly heartwarming."

It wasn't like my dick wasn't getting any attention. Amy sucked me off the other day in the library. I was just craving a particular flavor, and so was my dick.

"Well, I'd hate for your dick to fall off from inactivity. Besides, I'm starting to miss your usual parade of skanks. They have stellar conversational skills."

My lips curled. "I don't bring them here for their conversational skills."

She grumbled and rolled her eyes.

"You still haven't taken your girl?" Micha asked.

"Logan has a girl? Did hell freeze over?" Riley said, looking up at him, "Who is she?"

In true Micha fashion, he completely ignored her. "You need to nail that shit down."

"I'm working on it." I could take a page from his book and tell Shelby how shit was, but I was having too much fun playing with her. "It'll be done by Saturday."

"And if it's not?"

Then I kill the motherfucker she's going out with.

"I'd be more worried about what your girl is going to say."

"What the hell is that supposed to mean?" Riley said, glaring at Micha like she was about to kick him in the balls.

Shelby was Riley's best friend. She basically sold herself to Micha to protect her. Something told me she wouldn't be too happy about this shit.

I smirked at my friend and left. "Have fun with that."

I was probably getting punched later.

Halfway down the stairs, I heard Ma's voice. I couldn't remember the last time I heard her sing. When I walked into the kitchen and saw her floating around with a smile on her face, I was a bit shocked. Ma was good at putting up a happy front.

She did it for years. Pretending everything was great in public while life at home was a fucking nightmare. It was nice to see an actual smile on her face. It was in large part thanks to Derek, my stepdad.

I may not like the fucker, but he loved Ma, and I loved seeing her happy. So I wouldn't kill him. For now.

Ma's smile widened when she saw me. "How's my sweet boy this morning?"

"Hey Ma. Whatcha doing?"

"I made your favorite," she explained, holding up a plate of blueberry muffins.

Fuck yeah!

Flashing her a smile, I snatched one and took a big bite. My eyes rolled to the back of my head as blueberries exploded in my mouth, coating my tongue with sweetness. There was only one thing better than Ma's cooking. Shelby's fucking delicious mouth.

"You've been in a good mood lately," Ma said, dropping her elbows on the counter. "Is there a reason for that smile on your face?"

I chuckled at the spark of hope in her eyes. She'd be happy if I started popping out kids right out of high school.

"Maybe it's your muffins?" I teased, and grabbed another one. "Why'd you wait so long to make them?"

"After what–" The smile dropped off her face, "You know."

Yeah, I knew. All too fucking well, and I hated that he still had an effect on her.

"He's dead, Ma. He can't hurt you anymore," I lied.

My old man was locked up in some dark corner of The Order and still breathing. Derek wanted to tell her. I told him not to. Ma was in a good place. I didn't want to see her shaking in fear every time she took a step.

Knowing my old man was out there would only break her. Riley'd known him for less than twenty-four hours, and she agreed with me.

Ma squeezed my arm and said, "We survived, and that's all that matters."

Did we?

I sighed and stared down at the brown sugar and cinnamon heart decorating the top of the muffin. One of the few joys I had growing up was Ma's baking, but she hadn't made these muffins in years. Not since…

PAIN SIZZLED across my burnt palm, lighting up my nerves. I lay on the floor, hearing tears plop down on the tiles, but not feeling them.

My body had gone numb, cutting everything off except the ache in my hand. Like it had done many times before. This felt different, though. I was still here, experiencing it with a clear head. I just didn't care.

"What the fuck is wrong with you, Paisley?"

My dad was looming over my terrified mom with a rolling pin in his hand. I watched him step on a muffin, squishing the heart on top into something twisted and deformed.

"Are you trying to turn my son into a pussy?"

"Please Ryker, we were just making muffins," Mom pleaded. "Logan likes them."

My mom was scared. Down on her knees, shaking like a leaf. We'd both been here before. Hearts hammering in our chests, while we waited for the inevitable pain.

At least that's what should be happening, except I couldn't hear my pulse whooshing in my ears. Didn't feel a thumping against my ribs, or an impending sense of dread. No sickly smell, or spikes of fear. Just a calm wave of nothing.

Why wasn't I scared?

I looked over at a knife laying on the floor. Light glistened off the sharp edge of the blade. It was beautiful. Gliding across the steel in smooth, fluid movements. Would blood look the same?

I could almost see it dripping off the tip, splashing in fat drops on the floor. I could almost feel the hard handle in my palm.

That's because it was in my hand.

I stared down at my burnt flesh wrapped around the handle of the knife and flexed my fingers, pressing the hard edge into my palm. It didn't even hurt. It felt kind of nice. Like for once, I had the power.

"Boys don't bake, Paisley."

My eyes rolled up to my dad as a voice in my head called out, 'Kill him.'

He raised the rolling pin, but stopped and cocked his head down at my mom. Her wide eyes weren't looking at him.

"Sweetheart," she cautiously said with her hand held up. "Put that down."

Was she talking to me?

My dad twisted his neck, looking over his shoulder. "What are you going to do with that, boy?"

My hand shot out, digging the blade into his leg. It was so easy. A simple flick of my wrist and he cried out. It felt satisfying and freeing. I liked it so much that I did it again.

"You little shit!" my dad growled and lunged.

I didn't care what he was going to do to me, because I was too busy smiling at the deep red color seeping into his jeans. Blood. If the boogieman could bleed, then he could die...

Screams pierced the air.

Someone was yelling. It sounded like Ma?

"Logan! Calm the fuck down before I knock you the fuck out!"

I blinked a few times and looked around. It was still the kitchen, but the tiles were different. Not the dark mocha color I watched my old man's blood drip on.

Micha was standing beside me with his hands out, as if he was afraid I was going to fucking kill him. My brows pulled together as I tipped my chin. It looked like he was saying something.

What?

I felt a twitch to my right and turned my head. My stepsister's eyes were wide and wild. I could smell the fear coming off her. The corner of my mouth tipped up as my gaze fell to the hand wrapped around her neck. Someone was having fun.

He had a good grip. Tight enough to make her face turn red, but not enough to choke the life out of her. I watch a drop of sweat roll off her face and land on one of the fingers around her throat. I liked the guy's style. He had fuck tattooed across his knuckles...

Oh shit, that's my hand!

Everything came flooding back at once. The smell of muffins, and Ma's whimpering cries, along with Micha's cautious pleading for me to let his girl go. I looked over at Ma hugging her knees under the table while Riley's pulse fluttered against my fingers.

Why the table? She used to do this shit when my old man was on a rampage. Didn't help her then, either. The fact that she was under there at all was a little insulting. I'd stab myself before ever laying a hand on Ma. Riley, on the other hand...

We had fun that night, Micha, Riley and I. Hadn't really given much thought to fucking her again. She'd become my sister in every sense of the word. I loved her, I'd kill for her, and I liked fucking with her. Right now, though, she looked real good. Pale-faced and quaking. Fear was intoxicating. It made my blood sing and my dick hard.

Micha was probably two seconds away from shooting me in the head. Honestly, I was a bit shocked he hadn't fucked me up yet. Then again, I'd have probably snapped her fucking neck before he could pry me off. It wasn't the first time this happened, though I usually knew exactly what I was doing. I just couldn't stop myself. Nor did I want to. I sighed inwardly.

Ah well, I guess playtime's over.

I smirked at Riley and leaned in to say, "I think your boyfriend knows about us."

"Motherfucker," Micha grumbled, dropping his face in his palm.

I released his girl and took a step back. Riley didn't move. Didn't even blink. She just flattened her back against the wall and watched me. As if I'd pounce if she so much as twitched.

Aw, poor timid little mouse.

Micha slapped his hand down on my shoulder. "I thought I was gonna have to fucking kill you."

"Well," I said, strutting out of the room. "The day's not over yet."

I was definitely getting punched later.

"What the fuck just happened?" I heard Riley mutter behind me.

Two steps outside, I paused, eyeing my car. I swear Betty was parked closer to the fountain.

Huh?

I shrugged and headed over, tossing my bag in the backseat. The second I turned the key and 'Ugly Kid Joe' poured out of my speakers, I knew what'd happened.

Touché, Cherry Pie.

The corner of my mouth lifted as I peeled down the driveway, loudly singing, "I hate everything about you."

PARKER and I were leaning against the lockers in Ashworth when Micha came charging down the hall with murder in his eyes.

"You!" He bellowed, throwing an angry finger in my direction. "You're dead, motherfucker!"

"Oh shit." I grabbed Parker's shoulders and pulled him in front of me. The fucker was big and he'd make a good shield.

"What's going on?" Parker whispered.

"Oh, nothing." I shifted him so he was between Micha and I. "I might've choked his girlfriend a little."

"What?!"

"It was just a little." I rolled my eyes. "She's fine."

Everyone needed to calm down. Riley might have a bruise, but there was no permanent damage.

"You damn near killed her!" Micha argued.

I ducked behind Parker, avoiding his swinging fist. "That's a little dramatic, don't you think?"

Micha huffed out an unimpressed sigh.

"Ugh, fine!" I grumbled, stepping out from my human shield. "You get one–"

His fist landed in my gut before I could finish speaking. I groaned and hunched over. Shit, he could hit.

"You're fucking lucky that's all I'm giving you."

I coughed and looked up at him. "Noted."

"What the fuck happened, anyway?" he asked, eyeing me. "I've never seen you black out."

Parker's brow rose. "He blacked out?"

I could sense the apprehension in both of them. The question practically displayed on their lips. *Did he finally snap?* I wasn't an idiot. They may not be afraid of me, but they sure as hell were terrified of what I could do.

"Who says I blacked out?"

"Don't give me that shit," Micha growled and crossed his arms. "You weren't responding to anything I said."

"Maybe I was enjoying the view." It wasn't a lie. I did enjoy the view. "You know, remembering fun times at the tattoo parlor."

That earned me another punch.

"Guess that means there won't be an encore performance?" I grunted.

"Do you want me to kick your ass?"

Maybe?

I could use a distraction. My old man kept fucking yapping in the back of my head. *'What are you going to do with that, boy?'* If Lou would just let me see him, I could beat this shit into silence. Why the fuck should everyone else have fun? I deserved revenge more than any of them.

"Are you gonna let Parker take her for a ride too?" I said, taunting Micha to hit me again. "He could do you both."

Now Parker was glaring at me. He was a big motherfucker. His punches hurt like a bitch. Not like Mase's, but Mase wasn't here.

Speaking of Mase...

"Come on Parker, you had a taste of Mase. Aren't you curious if big bro is just as spicy?"

Micha's face dropped. "What the fuck is he talking about?"

"Nothing," Parker said, shooting me a *'shut the fuck up'* glare.

He didn't know I knew about that. Mase told me. They didn't fuck, but they did some shit.

"Hey, I'm not judging," I'd had more dick than either of them by the time I was Junior's age. "Have you considered giving Silas a go? That motherfucker is hung like a horse, and I'm kind of curious how chicks manage to swallow that shit."

I smiled when Parker rolled his neck. He was almost there. Fists clenching with that vein in his forehead throbbing.

"Are you sure it's football you really like, cause I'm thinking it might be the group showers."

"Fucker," Parker growled, and shoved me back into the lockers.

That's it. Hit me, you prick.

I was about to ask if he got hard in the locker room when my phone went off. Ringing Warrant's *'Cherry Pie'* from my pocket.

Right on time.

"Hold that thought," I said, answering my phone. "Hey, Cherry Pie."

Shelby's angry voice rang through my ear, "Logan, you son of a bitch!"

"Such hostility," I snickered. "And here I thought you were calling to say good morning."

Shelby was probably having an issue getting into her locker. She'd need the code for that. I had the door replaced last night.

Her shit was locked up tight with a stainless steel door and electronic lock. And because I wasn't a complete asshole, I made sure there was a plaque with my number. In case of emergencies.

"Give me the goddamn code now!"

"I don't know?" I tsked, "I don't just give my codes to anyone. That shit is personal."

"You son of–" The line went quiet for a minute, and I heard her take a few deep breaths before sweetly singing, "Please?"

Oh, I liked that.

"Say please again."

"Logan, come on," she huffed out impatiently. "I'm gonna be late."

I hummed in contemplation. "Okay, but this is a give and take situation, sweetheart. You have to do something for me."

I could practically hear her teeth grinding as she hissed out, "What do you want?"

What did I want? That was a question I'd been asking myself since the day she stormed into my life. Whatever this shit was, it was beyond what my dick wanted, and oh my dick wanted.

I needed to know this girl was thinking about me. Needed to be stuck in that pretty little head, like she was stuck in mine.

"I'm guessing naked pics are out of the question?" Her incoherent grumble was the only answer I got. "Alright, I'd rather see it in person anyway. So I guess I'll settle for you canceling your fucking date."

Now my teeth were grinding.

"You can't be serious?"

"Deadly."

While I was enjoying playing with her, this wasn't part of the game. If Shelby went out with that prick, I'd kill him and string her ass up. Already had the whip picked out.

Parker grumbled out a groan. "We're going to have to clean up a body, aren't we?"

"Depends on his girl." Micha leaned back on the wall and smirked.

Micha didn't just know what I'd do, he understood it. He handed out so many beatdowns, everyone in this town with a dick was too afraid to look at Riley. He was probably hoping Shelby would go out with this prick. Since Riley'd stopped fighting him, he didn't have as many assholes to fuck up. He was itching to let off some steam.

"What's it gonna be, sweetheart?"

"Eat a dick, Logan!"

I chuckled. The girl had sass.

Micha tipped his chin at me. "What'd you do?"

I sauntered over and said, "Upgraded her locker," While holding out my phone so he could listen to Shelby stomp around.

"Nice," he nodded.

Though Parker was obviously leaning in to listen, he still muttered, "You guys are fucked up."

Micha's dark eyes rolled his way. "We'll see if you're saying that when it's your turn."

"I don't know," I said, giving Parker a scan. Other than his sexual preferences, he was a pretty normal guy. "He might try that wine and dine bullshit."

"Better than this crap."

I chuckled when he leaned in closer. "You seem to be enjoying it."

He rolled his eyes and we all went back to listening.

Shelby huffed and a door opened, followed by the sound of wind blowing. She was outside now. When I heard the distinct sound of a car trunk opening and closing, I knew exactly what she was doing.

So predictable.

"Whatcha doing, Cherry Pie?"

"Getting my crowbar."

That was a bad idea.

"I wouldn't do that if I were you," I warned her.

"Fuck you, Logan!"

I tsked. "Watch your mouth, Cherry Pie, there's a time and place for language like that."

"Eat shit, Logan. You don't control my mouth."

"You wanna bet?"

We heard Shelby walk back into the school halls as she growled, "The day you control what I say or do, is the day I kiss your feet."

The corner of my mouth curled. Challenge accepted. Except it won't be my feet she'd be kissing.

Micha sighed and shook his head. "Quit while you're ahead, Shelby."

"Fuck you, Micha," Shelby barked out. "I'm telling Riley."

That was a mistake. Micha might've been a bit on her side. Now she was fucked. He didn't take well to threats. Especially ones that involved his girl.

"You better get her under control," he growled at me.

"I will."

"Fuck you guys." Shelby jammed her crowbar in what I assumed was her locker.

A second later, shrieking alarms erupted from the other end. Micha, Parker and I all jumped back from the speaker, cringing at the sound. Fuck, that was louder than I'd thought. I could barely hear Shelby cursing.

"Well, I'll let you go and deal with that!" I yelled into my phone and hung up.

"Fuck," Micha grumbled, wriggling his finger in his ear. "A little fucking warning would've been nice."

"No shit," Parker agreed, shaking his head.

A couple of people in the hall were staring at us, but I just cocked a brow and they turned away.

"You figured out who she's going out with yet?"

"No." I rolled my eyes Micha's way and smiled. "But I think our good friend Evan might have an idea."

That brightened him up. Evan and his friend attacked Riley, and even though Micha taught him a lesson–a couple times if you include the hospital visits–he wouldn't argue teaching him another one.

Evan was lucky he was still alive. I'd have slit his fucking throat. Almost did. Riley may be a pain in the ass, but she was still my sister.

"Well," Micha looked at me, "Maybe we should pay him a visit?"

"My thoughts exactly," I said, slapping my hand on his shoulder.

My feet pounded off the red turf sending beads of sweat trickling down my chest. I loved it. The fire burning through my calves and the rush of adrenaline as I approached the finish line.

I listened to the football coach yell at his team while sucking in the sweet scent of fresh cut grass. There was only one goal out here, finish first. It was simple, honest, and incredibly freeing.

"That's it, Shell," my dad cheered from beside my coach. His hand was on her shoulder. "Keep those feet moving! You're my star!"

It used to be freeing.

Practice was bad enough when my dad came, and now he was touching *her*. Like what they did didn't matter. Mom told me to be nice. That she was happy he found someone. Would she still be happy if she knew *when* he found her?

Instead of dwelling on it, I used my anger to force my legs to move faster. If I could burn my anger away, I might be able to look my dad in the eyes again. Except when I crossed the finish line, there was no sense of relief.

Just the nausea knotting my gut and threatening to send the contents of my stomach up my throat, when I heard *her* commend my time.

I hunched over to catch my breath and dumped a cup of water over my head. Even the cool drops sluicing down my back couldn't stem the rage boiling through me. He was going to come over here. He always did. I was Daddy's star. The child that'd get him out of this small town and make him somebody. Except he was somebody.

He was my somebody.

I didn't know what to say to him anymore. How could I pretend that everything was okay when all I wanted to do was throw up every time he smiled at my coach? His eyes lit up the same way they used to for Mom.

How could she not know something was wrong? Why didn't I? All the extra training and attention. It wasn't because Coach thought I had talent. She was after something else. Vicky, that's what she told me to call her. As if she didn't tear my family apart.

"You're the top runner this year," Marnie tapped her pen off a pad of paper. "Tell me, what's your secret?"

I sighed. "I love you Marnie, but do you ever turn it off?"

"Well, I could ask you about this morning... I'm sure that'd be a much bigger story."

I muttered under my breath. Friggin Logan! It took two hours for the school to get someone down here to turn off that stupid alarm. And I was the one that got in trouble for it.

"I'm surprised Collin didn't sick you on me." Logan caused enough of a spectacle yesterday, I sure as hell didn't want this crap in the school paper. Enough people were talking about me.

"He tried." Marnie shrugged. "I turned it down."

And that's why I loved her. Marnie was loyal. She'd never turn her back on a friend. Neither would Rye. Though her approach would've been a little more violent. If she was here right now, no one would be bugging me. Trina, on the other hand… The queen of gossip already had her feelers out.

"Which is why I ended up on sports. So, if you don't mind, I'd like to get my story."

I stood up and rolled my neck. "Since when does anyone care about track?"

"The people want what they want."

That caused my brows to rise. This was a football town. The only other sport that got attention was swimming, and that was only because Micha Kessler was captain of Ashworth's swim team.

"The people want hot, hunky football players, and half naked cheerleaders. Not sweaty track runners."

"True." Marnie nodded and tipped her head towards a flock of girls gathered on the bleachers. "Their sudden interest might have something to do with that."

I groaned, already knowing who I was going to see.

Except this time Logan wasn't alone. Sitting on the bench beside him with his arms crossed was Micha, and beside him, Parker. Naturally they were surrounded by a bunch of girls vying for their attention.

Rather desperately, if you asked me. Which seemed to annoy Micha. I heard him tell one of them to fuck off. He wasn't quiet about it either. Not that I expected Micha to ever be quiet about anything. Something Riley and he had in common. God help the person that got in their way.

Parker was too focused on the football team practicing to care about their fans. I knew he was a good running back–our football coach made strategies just for him–but seeing the way his crystal eyes followed their movements made me think he didn't just play. He really enjoyed the game.

Three of the girls were chatting up Logan, who was playing right into their hands. Giving them that stupid charming smile. They didn't even seem to care that he wasn't looking at them. His green eyes glittered as he smirked and leaned back to rest his elbows on the bench behind him.

My gaze narrowed.

He's up to something.

"Maybe you should give him what he wants?" Marnie said. "They're not normal, Shell."

"Last I checked, asshole was a pretty normal personality trait."

Her eyes slid my way. "You can't tell me you don't have questions."

I cocked my head and thought back to Riley lying in that hospital bed. Yeah, I had questions. Questions I tried taking to Chase. All he said was, *'Leave it alone, little girl'*.

That was the really bothersome part. Chase Mathers was the least evasive person I knew. Especially when it came to Riley. I once saw him threaten an eight-year-old kid because he made her cry.

Now that I thought about it, not once had Chase stepped in when Micha was tormenting Riley. And he tormented her a lot. *Why would he threaten a kid that pushed her on the playground, but not the one that made her life a living hell?*

I was about to ask Marnie what she thought, when someone cut me off.

"Miss Grace." A tall man with dark hair walked over and held his hand out. "A thousand meters in under three minutes, that's quite the time."

"Thanks," I muttered, while eyeing his navy shirt.

He looked familiar. Was he one of the football parents? Wouldn't be the first time one of them came up to me. Though usually they were looking for the bathroom or something. Not commenting on my running skills.

"Um, who are you?"

"Where are my manners. I'm Gregory Bantam." He explained. "I coach the track and swim teams at Ashworth Academy."

That's why I knew him. I'd seen him on the field when we had meets with Ashworth. What the hell was he doing here?

My dad and coach sauntered up.

"Oh good," my dad said, slapping his hand on Gregory's shoulder, "I see you've met my little peanut."

Little peanut? He hadn't called me that since I was Mags' age.

"She's our star runner," my coach added in.

I glared at my dad's arm draped over her. The night I caught them, he said he only married mom because she was pregnant. Like it was my fault he wasn't happy. That's how I ended up at the Bluffs, prepared to race. Logan might've been slightly right about that night.

I took a few risks I shouldn't have. The Bluffs weren't a safe place to act recklessly. One wrong move and your car would go careening over the cliff. Honestly, I was surprised I didn't end up in the hospital. Or worse.

"She's quite the star, isn't she?" my dad stated proudly.

I don't like that smile on his face.

"I think she could be." Gregory said looking at me. "With the right coach."

Oh no.

"I'll get right to the point, Shelby."

Don't say it.

"I'd like to offer you a spot on the team at Ashworth. With a full scholarship, of course."

Damnit!

"Isn't that great, Peanut?" My dad sounded so happy, and why wouldn't he be? This was exactly what he wanted. One of his daughters to help him make a name for himself. If nothing else, Ashworth would give him the opportunity to rub shoulders with the elite and wealthy.

God forbid he find out the great Logan Hudson was interested in me. He'd have me fitted for a wedding dress before graduation.

"Yeah Dad, that's great," I grumbled, turning my glare to Logan. *He had something to do with this.*

Did he really think this crap would work? That having me at Ashworth would change anything? The corner of my mouth curled as I cocked my hip. We'll just see about that. I could always reject the offer. *What would you think about that, Logan?*

The glint in his eyes lit up at my silent challenge, and I sighed. Even if I wanted to, I couldn't turn it down. My dad would never let me.

Logan may have thought he won, but I'd never give in to him. Despite how good he looked. And holy crap, did he look good. The boy had style, I'd give him that.

I tilted my head and took in his dark jeans and white shirt. Which, of course, had a couple buttons undone. His lips twisted in a wicked smirk as he kicked his feet up, crossing them at the ankles. I could practically hear him tempting me to take a closer look.

Pfft, dick.

"I have some paperwork for you to fill out…"

I continued to glare my hatred at Logan as my dad and my *new* coach walked off to discuss my future–because why should I be involved in that conversation?

Logan popped his bottom lip out and returned my glare with a mocking frown. I suddenly understood my best friend's violent streak. All I wanted to do was slap that smug expression off his face.

"Wow Shell, drool much?"

My mouth dropped at Marnie's comment.

"I am not… I just…" I threw my hands up in the air and muttered, "This is all his fault."

Marnie's brow rose. "Getting recruited to one of the best schools in the state is his fault?"

"Yes!" I shrieked, watching a blond lock of hair flop over his forehead. Was I the only one who hated this guy?

He smirked and my stomach flipped.

Okay, maybe I didn't *hate* him. I was sure as hell gonna try, though.

Stupid sexy smoulder. I mean, who did he think he was? The friggin king of England? People can just smile, you know? They don't always have to be so damn charming.

And then, just like that, it was all gone. Logan's suave playfulness washed away, replaced with a glare so cold the temperature around me dropped, making me shiver.

"Looks like you have a fan club," Noah chuckled in my ear, causing me to jump a little.

I was so focused on Logan, I hadn't heard him come up behind me.

"Hi," I said, looking back at him with a smile.

He returned my smile and nodded at the bleachers. "I don't think your friend likes me."

Huh?

It was then that I noticed Logan's murderous glare wasn't aimed at me.

Seems the ball's in my court now, buddy.

A slow smile spread across my face as I turned to Noah. "I wouldn't worry about him."

"Yeah?" he said, wrapping his arm around my waist. "The other girls seem to like him."

"Not my type."

"What's your type? Sweaty football players, I hope."

Though Noah did look good in his uniform, with his brown hair stuck to his head, I didn't feel anything. No flutter of nerves, or tingling when his hand brushed down my back.

All I could think about was what he did with Chelsea on their date.

Even Logan turned her down.

I decided to avoid the subject altogether. "Shouldn't you be practicing?"

"Probably," he nodded while gazing warmly down at me. "But I saw you over here and had to come say hi."

Aw!

My heart melted a bit.

"Torres!" The football coach yelled, "Stop fraternizing and get your ass back here!"

"Gotta go." He kissed my cheek and ran back to practice, saying, "See you Saturday, Sweetness."

I'd contemplated canceling our date. Did I really want Chelsea's leftovers? But as I watched Noah leave, I thought maybe it wasn't so bad he'd gone out with her. He was honest about it, and was very understanding about this whole Logan situation. Shouldn't I do the same for him?

There was still some part of me that didn't want to upset Logan. As stupid as that was. Hell, I was looking forward to seeing the scowl on his face right now. He deserved it, and it'd be nice to finally get one up on him.

Except when I turned around, my heart stopped dead in my chest. The expression on Logan's face was far past a scowl. He looked downright feral. I stood there paralyzed, chest heaving, while Micha and Parker fought to physically hold him back.

The strain on their faces was evident as they yelled at him to calm down. I don't know what was scarier, the fact that Micha–who was usually calm and collected–was anything but, or that both of them combined were barely containing him?

Than Logan's eyes locked with mine.

His anger radiated through me from across the field, wrapping around me in icy tendrils. That's when I knew I was screwed. Because the face I was staring at wasn't the charming guy girls swooned over. This man wanted to hurt me.

Chapter 8
Logan

Noah Torres.

That was the asshole I was going to kill. Not quick, either. Shit like that was reserved for fuckers you needed to get rid of, or the pricks too dangerous to continue breathing. Like my old man—worst mistake Lou ever made.

But Noah… That motherfucker was going out nice and slow. So his screams could lull me to sleep at night.

Not only did he kiss Shelby, but the prick looked me right in the eyes when he did it. Pressed his lips to my Cherry Pie's cheek and smiled up at me. A silent fuck you. If Micha and Parker weren't there, I'd have gutted him and painted the fucking field with his blood. He wants to fuck with me…

Alright, you piece of shit. Let's play.

Even Parker said the prick was asking for it. Probably would've helped me kill him too, if it wasn't for Micha. He didn't want to clean up the mess. I was quite capable of cleaning up my own messes.

Some Micha didn't even know about. Like Lance. Everyone

thought he moved out of town. His family did. Preston relocated them right after we buried Lance. His final resting place was beside the car Ava torched in my backyard.

He shouldn't have touched my sister, and as Preston put it, there were some things the King of Kings didn't need to know about. That's why guys like us existed. Plausible deniability. Worked for me.

Now, every time I saw Riley sitting out back drawing, I smiled. Evan March would've been in the spot next to him, but that was Micha's kill. I'd never take that shit from him.

I leaned back on the wall and lit a smoke, snorting at the pink flower stuck on Shelby's bedroom door. Pink. Why wasn't I surprised? It wasn't that bad compared to some of the girly shit in this room. The flower looked half dead. Faded with age, with curled in petals. A lot like the wilted black rose on my right hand.

My thumb traced over the stab wound cutting through the center of my palm. The scar was nothing more than a thin line blended into black ink. But I knew it was there. I could feel the blade cutting through my flesh, pinning my hand to the table.

Unlike my other scars, this one wasn't a constant reminder of the nightmare I was born into. Because this one was the last scar my old man would ever give me. Sometimes, when I closed my eyes late at night, I could feel my finger pulling that trigger. The shot echoing through my ears, marking the moment in my memory. The boogeyman was dead…

"You stay there, boy."

My old man slammed the knife down through my hand and into the table beneath. My flesh screamed as it was torn apart. It took everything I had to hold back my own cry of pain. I'd never give him that satisfaction again. Didn't stop my knees from giving out.

He twisted his neck and glared at Micha, who was on the ground clutching a bullet wound in his side. "Watch what happens when someone fucks with me."

I couldn't do anything but watch as he strutted over to my best friend. I tried to stop him, but that only tugged on the blade skewered through my hand, causing me to drop back down.

I told Micha this would happen. That we couldn't stop him. How were two ten-year-old's and a twelve-year-old supposed to fight the boogeyman? He ate kids for breakfast.

"Look at you. The King of Kings precious heir." My old man lifted his foot, delivering a hard kick to Micha's side. "Not so fucking great now, are you?"

Micha grunted and cried out when my old man's foot struck him again. He wasn't used to this. He didn't live in my house, and his old man made sure mine was never left alone with him. Micha was protected, pampered, and weak.

He couldn't handle what was coming. Maybe that's why I spoke up? To keep the one untouchable pillar in my life strong.

"I'm gonna tear your fucking guts out!"

"I thought you'd have learned by now, boy," my old man smirked at me. "You can't kill the boogeyman."

"You're not the boogeyman," Micha groaned, and I couldn't help but sigh in relief. He hadn't been broken. Yet. "Just a sick, twisted fuck, and he's not afraid of you anymore."

He wasn't wrong. I wasn't afraid, but I wasn't stupid either. There was a big difference between numb and used to it.

"You're right, he's not." My old man tilted his head down at Micha, eyes roaming over the blood seeping from his wound. "But his mother is."

I sucked in a gasp and searched his face. Was he going to hurt Ma? She wasn't here, so I couldn't tell if I needed to protect her from his glare.

"You see that," my old man said, tipping his head back at me. "Love is weakness, Micha. Hate's a much stronger motivator."

"Don't listen to him, Logan." Micha locked his dark eyes on mine. "He's just trying to mess with your head."

It was working.

I looked over at the sheriff's wife, curled up on the ground beside her husband, quietly sobbing. Her husband couldn't do anything to help her.

Even if he wasn't tied to a chair, he was beaten so badly one of his eyes was swollen shut. My old man really worked Maria Adams over. Honestly, I *was surprised she was still breathing, and if her state was any indication of what might happen to Ma...*

"It's no use. The boy's a lost cause when it comes to his mother."

"A bastard like you doesn't deserve a kid," the sheriff piped in. "I feel sorry for him."

My lips curled in a sneer. It wasn't my wife laying naked on the floor. He couldn't even protect his own family. What kind of man was he?

"Quiet down, I'm not done with you yet." My old man's gaze rolled his way, "Or your pretty wife."

Maria whimpered and hugged the leg of the chair her husband was tied to.

"You bastard! I signed your stupid contract!" the sheriff bellowed.

"I never said I'd stop. It's been a long time since I had someone so feisty. It's a pity your daughter isn't here to join in the fun."

That caused Micha to growl loudly. "Stay the fuck away from her!"

He may not like Riley, but she was his and he protected what was his.

My old man smirked. Riley was the whole reason we were here. To save her from him, and she wasn't even home. I couldn't help but snort at the irony.

"Perhaps I'll let my boy have a turn? How about it, boy?" He glanced over his shoulder, green eyes twinkling in delight. "You ready to become a man?"

I had no interest in Riley. He'd make me do it, though. For one simple reason. It would fracture our friendship.

Micha pushed his hand into the floor and propped himself up, causing a sickly wet sound to emanate through the room, and glared up at my old man, hate emanating from his dark gaze. "He'll kill you one day. You know that, right?"

My old man belted out a chuckle. "You think too highly of my boy."

"He's stronger than you think." Micha's eyes shifted slightly to the left, making me notice the gun laying on the table next to my pinned hand.

Do it.

I cocked my head, brows furrowed at the weapon. I couldn't kill the boogeyman.

Yes you can. If you can make him bleed, you can kill him. Take it!

I looked back at my best friend—why did he think I could kill him—and said, "What did you do with Preston?"

Preston was much more capable than I was, but the last time we saw him, he was being dragged upstairs.

Micha's brow rose, as if he could read my thoughts, and he once again shifted his gaze at the gun. This time more insistently.

"I wouldn't worry about Preston." My old man crouched down and roughly grabbed Micha's chin, digging his fingers into his cheeks. "Sweet little Mason, however..."

My jaw clenched as ice flowed through my veins. Mase was my brother too, and so far had remained out of my father's grasp. My gaze fell on the barrel of the gun. Black and shiny, like the knife I used to slice my old man's leg.

If the boogeyman can bleed, he can die.

Micha smirked up at my old man and sang, "I win, fucker."

The amusement fell off my old man's face when he looked back in time to see me lift the gun.

"It's time to pay the piper," I said, and squeezed the trigger...

I SHOOK the long faded gunshot from my memory. My haunted thoughts could wait. There were more pressing matters to deal with. Mainly, the tempting blonde that thought she could toy with me.

Shelby gave me a smug grin before she let that prick touch her. If she thought my head was a safe place to dance around, she was sorely mistaken.

I ripped the flower off her door and crumpled it in my hand.

Sorry, sweetheart, my mind was fucked long before you showed up.

Soft footsteps echoed up the stairs, making my lips curl. Since Shelby's mom was working the night shift and her sister was staying at her dad's place, that meant Cherry Pie was home. It was time to play. I dropped my cigarette in a glass of water on the nightstand and watched the door.

Come on in, sweetheart.

"Yeah, yeah," she sighed from out in the hall, making my dick jump in anticipation. She was right there. I could smell her through the door. "I'll feed you in a minute. Let me change first."

Meow.

Fat fucking cat. I fed that bastard when I got here. It was the only way I could get his grumpy ass to stop hissing at me.

The door opened and Shelby sauntered in. She looked good, always did. In a low cut pink shirt and black skirt. But it was her ass that drew my attention. Eyes focused on the fabric bouncing off those firm globes. I wanted to do things to that ass. Like see my handprint on it.

The cat trotted in behind her and meowed.

"Go on," she said, shooing him. "I'll be down in a minute."

No you won't.

I couldn't help but shake my head. Shelby was completely oblivious. Walking around like she was alone, but Fluffy saw me.

His eyes landed right on me, before he meowed and pranced away. How fucking sad was that? She didn't see the six foot four man in her room. The damn cat did.

Shelby sighed and pulled her shirt over her head. Maybe it wasn't so bad that she didn't notice me. I cocked my head and rolled my gaze over the smooth creamy mounds wrapped in red lace.

What the fuck was I here for?

Whatever it was, it could wait. I had pert little nipples to stare at. Red was my new favorite color. Bold against her fair skin. A lot like blood, and I'd been dying to mark that perfect complexion.

Do her panties match?

Shelby turned around and froze. Standing there with wide eyes and her mouth hung open, begging me to face fuck her. That look on her face—somewhere between confusion and fear—wasn't doing her any favors. All I could think about was forcing her down on her knees and watching her choke on my cock.

I could. Push her down and wrap those perfect pink lips around...

"Logan?"

That's right, baby, say my name.

"What are you... I mean..." Her face flushed in frustration, "How did..."

I might've found her stuttering cute, if I wasn't too busy growling internally at her cheek. The same fucking cheek that prick kissed. Before I left this room, my come would be the only thing marking her tainted flesh.

Let's see if that fucking prick wants to kiss her then!

"What are you doing in my house?"

What the fuck did she mean, what was I doing here? She should fucking know.

"Hello," she sang, while waving her hand through the air, "Are you going to answer me, or just stand there?"

My brow arched. Cherry Pie better watch her fucking tone, or I'd have something other than her mouth wrapped around my cock tonight.

"Answer me, damn it!"

Making demands now, was she?

My old man's voice piped up in the back of my head.

'Are you going to let her talk to you like that? Get over there and do something about it, boy.'

I was tempted to do just that. March over there and teach Shelby a lesson she'd never forget. Preston's words were the only thing that stopped me. *'Broken dolls aren't any fun.'*

Still...

I cocked a brow at her ass, hand twitching at my side.

"This is breaking and entering, you know," she insisted with a far too cocky head shake. "I could call the cops."

She could. Wouldn't do her any good, but she could call. I doubted they'd even make me leave. And if they did, I'd be back. Then she'd really be sorry.

"Please say something."

No. I don't think I will.

She wasn't liking the silent treatment. It made her uncomfortable. Feet shifting on the carpet while her hands toyed with her skirt. She still hadn't covered up, though, and my eyes kept falling back down to her full breasts, bouncing with every move she made.

'So easily distracted,' my old man scoffed. *'You're weak, boy.'*

"If this is some trick to get me to kiss you like I did Silas, it isn't going to work."

What!? She fucking kissed Silas! That motherfucker.

"Logan, you're kind of freaking me out."

Good.

My nostrils flared as my gaze rolled up to hers.

Fucking Silas. Really?

"Look, if this is about this afternoon…" Shelby cleared her throat and licked her lips. "Noah didn't–"

"Don't say his fucking name," I hissed through gritted teeth.

Silas, I could forgive–might hit him a couple times–but that motherfucker Noah… He'd be six feet under before he went anywhere near her again.

'So much for the silent treatment,' my old man snickered.

Shut the fuck up!

That fucker wouldn't leave me alone. Even in death he was there, yapping in the back of my mind.

'But I wasn't dead, was I? You couldn't even do that right.'

"Logan, Noah–"

"I said don't fucking say his name!"

She yipped and jumped back.

That's right sweetheart, now you're getting it.

I kept reminding myself to heed Preston's warning, but I didn't know how long I could hold back. Especially when Shelby demurely glanced down at her wringing hands.

Didn't she know that shit was my aphrodisiac? The nervousness thick in the air and subtle glances got my dick hard. Lucky for her, the beast hadn't consumed me, yet.

And then she opened her fucking mouth.

"Did you hurt him?"

I glared at the concern in her eyes. "Not yet."

Why the fuck did she care if I hurt that prick? I should fuck him up for that question alone.

My Cherry Pie was obviously scared. She still tried to put up a strong front, though. Staying right where she was, with her feet firmly planted on the ground. But she couldn't hide that shit from me. I spent my childhood watching my old man torture fuckers.

In the end, everybody gave themselves away. And sweet little Shelby, with her quiet shivers and shifting glances, may as well have had *'I'm terrified'* tattooed across her forehead.

"What do you want?" she asked, bright eyes searching mine for the answer to the question on the tip of her tongue. The one she was afraid to ask.

A fine film of sweat glistened on her heaving chest, making me lick my lips. There was nothing quite like the taste of fear. The heady feel of tears rolling down my throat was addictive.

Finally her pouty pink lips parted and spilled out, "Are you going to hurt me?"

There it is.

Was I going to hurt her... fuck yeah I was going to hurt her. But she'd like it.

"Yes," I said, eyes locking on her nipples, pert and pressing against the lace fabric of her bra.

Maybe that's what she's afraid of?

"Why?"

I'd never been harder in my life. I pushed my hand in my jeans and readjusted myself. No need to be discrete. She'd be getting real personal with my cock in a minute.

"Why not?"

The look on her face made me chuckle. Big eyes wide and locked on my package.

"Logan," she held her hand up, as if that was going to stop me. *Too cute.* "You need to leave."

"Oh, Cherry Pie," I pushed off the wall and kicked the door shut. "I'm not going anywhere."

Chapter 9

Shelby

When scared, people usually run away or hide, and right now, staring into those green eyes glimmering with dark intent, I was terrified. It was moments like this that I wished I was more like my best friend. Rye stood up to pricks like Micha her entire life and not once did I see her back down. Even when she should've. If I had one tenth of her strength, then maybe my pulse wouldn't be whooshing loudly in my ears. But bravery wasn't my strong point.

Apparently I wasn't smart, either. Did my panicked heart give me a sudden surge of courage, letting me fight back? No. It didn't even send me fleeing from danger. It sent me barreling right for it.

The door clicked closed and like that girl in horror movies who ran up the stairs, I charged for the only exit. Which was right behind the person I was trying to escape.

The coolness of the metal doorknob on the tips of my fingers caused hope to swell in my heart. That tiny spark was all I got.

Logan grabbed the back of my neck, digging his fingers painfully into my flesh as he slammed me face first against the door.

All I could think as I watched the white wood come closer, was how ironic fate's cruelty was. How many times had I cursed that horror movie girl's stupidity? Only to have it turn out that I *was* that girl.

"I thought you were supposed to be fast, Cherry Pie." Logan's tongue clicked in my ear, further mocking my stupidity. "Coach would not be happy."

Okay, I made the wrong choice and epically failed, but making fun of my time. Nah ah. Not happening.

"I'd run circles around you on the field."

"Sure you would," he snickered.

I'd been running for years, and still I couldn't help but think maybe he was right. I had yet to see the guy fail at anything. Just last week he told Riley he could draw a better flower than her. Guess what - he did. It was annoying how perfect the arrogant ass was.

"You know what, Logan, you're not as great as you think you are."

"Oh yeah?" he purred and ran his finger down my spine, chuckling when I openly shivered. "You seem to like me."

I silently cursed myself and spat back, "In your dreams."

Which only made him bark out a laugh.

"You're not fooling anyone sweetheart." He leaned in to whisper, "I can smell your pussy."

The fact that he was right only fueled my anger. Every time his deep voice wafted in my ear, wetness seeped into my panties.

"If you squeeze your legs together any tighter, I'm going to need a crowbar to get them open."

"You'll never get them open," I snarled.

I felt him smile and my heart sunk. Logan liked to toy with me. Of course he would rise to the challenge. I may as well have been dangling bait in front of a hungry lion. The man I was facing off against wasn't only a conceited asshat, he was the guy girls dreamed about.

The charming smile on their fantasy stranger. The dirty things whispered in their ears and the tingle deep inside that made them squeeze their thighs in shame. Logan Hudson was lust personified, and as much as I hated to admit it, he already had me in his web.

He knew it, too.

Stepping in to press the solid planes of his chest against my back as his breath warmed my ear, "Admit it, Cherry Pie. Your pussy's begging for me."

I wasn't mad at him, per say. I was mad at the need pulsing in my core and how I couldn't get enough of his scent. None of which should be happening in this situation. Yet my senses soaked it up like a glutenous whore.

"Fuck you, Logan."

I yipped when his heavy hand landed on my ass, sending a loud smack ringing through the air.

The pain still had me on my tiptoes when he delivered another strike and growled, "How many times have I told you to watch your fucking mouth!?"

A weird thing happened when he did it again. The burn radiating across my backside turned into something else. A tingly zing that caused my clit to throb.

It was amazing and uncomfortable at the same time, and I wanted it to stop. But it didn't. Logan continued unleashing smack after smack, until I wasn't sure which burned hotter, my tender flesh, or my unwanted desire.

Stupid books tainting my sexuality.

"Fuck," Logan grunted in a deep husky tone that sent a shiver down my spine, "Your cries are music to my ears."

I didn't even realize I had tears trickling down my face until he said that.

"Fuck you!" I snarled over my shoulder at him.

"That's strike two, Cherry Pie." His fingers speared in my hair and roughly yanked my head back. "Trust me, you don't want to get to three."

Under normal circumstances I'd have some witty comeback–Riley taught me the fine art of sarcasm—but my capacity to formulate complex thoughts was gone. My brain had left the building.

The only thing I could think to do was swing my hand back, raking my nails down his arm. And that was my mistake. I could feel his skin under my nails, so I knew I got him good. Except Logan didn't so much as twitch or cry out.

Dread washed over me when he pressed in and darkly chuckled in my ear, "Strike three, baby."

He was going to hurt me again. I could hear it in his voice. The truly terrifying part was the undertone of desire.

I couldn't disguise my fear anymore. My body openly quaked as I held my breath, waiting for the next strike to come. But Logan wasn't just after my body. He wanted to toy with my mind as well. I knew I was in trouble the second I felt his hand drop from my hair and smooth down my side.

"You liked it when I spanked you. It got you wet, didn't it?" he purred in my ear and then released a throaty groan that made my knees weak. "God, I hoped you'd be like this."

Be like what? Pathetic? Weak?

"Leave me alone," I whispered, dropping my forehead on the door and pressing my body away from his heat.

I just had to get away from him. Then I'd be able to think straight. It wasn't the burn in my butt causing a deep seated ache in my core.

Or Logan and his charming, pretty boy ways. It was all those stupid books I'd read. Making me think that stuff like this was hot. Trapped in the arms of some sexy muscular guy. Except it wasn't hot. I didn't like this.

Yes you do.

Logan snickered in my ear and followed my lead. Stepping in until there was nowhere left for me to go. No gap or space I could escape into. Just him, and his hard body, surrounding me.

The coolness of the door only heightened the heat rising inside me, and every breath I took left Logan's taste lingering on the tip of my tongue.

My entire system lit up. Begging to feel his lips again, and hear the dirty things he whispered to me that day in the garage. That's when I knew, he'd won. My body had already given in, and my mind wasn't far behind.

"Please go away."

"Oh sweetheart," I could feel his eyes on me, as vividly as if he were caressing me. "I'm not going anywhere."

My heart fluttered while my stomach flipped. I was so on edge that when he nuzzled in and ran his nose up the side of my neck, I jumped and squeaked out a protest. Nothing I'd experienced before—no kiss or touch from a boy—ignited my skin like he did.

This was bad. Logan Hudson was a whole lot of sin wrapped up in heartbreak, and as much as my body wanted to, I couldn't go down that road.

I twisted my head away from his hot breath and stared at the flowered picture frame on my dresser, pulling my eyes over each individual petal.

Logan snickered, causing a puff of air to toy with the small hairs on the back of my neck. "Are you trying to ignore me, Cherry Pie?"

"No."

A purple petal, next to blue.

"Uh huh." He hummed and swept his tongue over the sensitive spot behind my ear.

Oh God that feels good. No, focus on the petals. Pink and another purple...

The flowers were no longer enough to distract me when he sucked my earlobe through his teeth. My gaze fell down to the peeling label on my top drawer that read *'delicates'* and cocked my head.

Things had gone missing in here. From that drawer, specifically. I'd thought it was Mags messing around, but what if it wasn't...

"Have you been here before?"

"Does it matter?"

Yes.

No.

Maybe?

I couldn't think right now.

Silence hung in the air and I swear I could feel every breath he took vibrate through my soul. Like some doomsday clock ticking away the seconds to the apocalypse.

Inhale.

Tick.

Exhale.

Tick.

I prayed for him to do something. Touch me, hit me, talk, anything that might break the tension coursing through my bones. The anticipation was killing me. Was he going to hurt me? Touch me? Maybe just tease me? Whatever it was, I wanted him to get it over with.

And then he grazed his lips over the shell of my ear and asked, "Are you gonna fight me?"

What the hell kind of question was that?

My heart was now beating so fast, I expected to see the door thump with each echoing thud. I slowly twisted my neck to glance over my shoulder. Another mistake. My breath hitched the second I met those deep green eyes. The desire in them was so thick it was palpable.

I licked my lips, wetting my dry mouth. "Do I need to?"

Did I want to?

"Depends." His shoulders lifted in a casual shrug. "Either way, I'll get what I want."

A lock of blond hair flopped over his forehead. Dangling there as if pointing at the intensity of his glare. He said he was going to hurt me, but that was just a mind fuck, right? Who would get that turned on hurting someone?

"Go on, ask," he said, searching my eyes for something. "I know you want to."

"Are you really going to hurt me?" The words spilled out before I could stop them.

The corner of his mouth lifted in a malicious smirk that matched the dark glint in his eyes. "Scared?"

Yes.

"No."

His brow arched. "Don't lie to me."

"I'm not."

I totally am.

"Besides, you're the one that broke the law. You should be the scared one. Not me."

With one phone call, I could send him to jail. Problem was, my phone was on the dresser. If I could just get to it…

"Is that so?" He chuckled and tightly wrapped his fingers around my hips. "Are you gonna send me to jail, Cherry Pie?"

"Yes. You broke into *my* house," I explained, hoping to knock some sense back into not only him, but myself as well.

"Did I? There's no broken windows and all the doors are locked." His tongue darted out, leaving a hot wet trail on my skin. "Gotta say, Cherry Pie, it kinda looks like you let me in."

My mouth fell open but nothing came out. Was he right? I mean, I didn't know how he got in, so maybe the cops would think I let him in?

What! No, that's the stupidest thing ever!

Without another thought, I reached for my sweater pocket, where I usually kept my phone. Except it wasn't there. Neither was my sweater, or my shirt! I slowly tipped my chin down, glancing at my bra clad breasts.

Shit.

The first thing I did when I got home from school was change into comfy clothes. I'd been standing here the whole time in just my bra and skirt.

Way to send the wrong signal, Shelby.

"Logan, I'm not going to sleep with you," I said, needing to clarify the situation.

He snickered, "Sleep is the last thing I have planned for you."

Yup, this is bad!

"That's not happening."

"I'm way past asking permission, sweetheart," he said, sliding his palm around my hip.

This couldn't be happening. Logan was arrogant and conceited, but even he wasn't that bold.

"You're mine now, Cherry Pie," he growled, and shoved his hand down the waistband of my skirt. "And after tonight, you won't fucking forget it."

I sucked in a deep breath and mustered the last bit of strength I had left. "Stop it."

"No."

All I could do when his finger slid over my panties and pressed down on my clit, was gasp a shocked response. I'd touched myself there before. Even bought a toy to play with, but neither sent tingles shooting up my core like one touch from him did.

"Fucking lace," Logan groaned, and pressed in.

What was wrong with lace?

"I want to fucking eat it off you."

Shit, did I say that out loud?

His finger swirled and suddenly that bundle of nerves became the center of my being. Everything else shut down. I tried to fight it.

Squeezing my eyes shut and gritting my teeth against the spikes of pleasure. But it was no use. Logan not only knew what he was doing, he was a master.

"Stop," I panted, while digging my fingernails into the grainy wooden door.

"Not a fucking chance," he said, skimming his other hand up my stomach and pinching my nipple so hard I cried out.

The small spike of pain allowed me to regain some of my senses. I slapped his hand away from my breast. All that got me was another smack on the ass and my hands pinned above my head. The whole time Logan continued to work my clit.

"You let another man put his hands on you, Cherry Pie."

So? Fuck you.

"Did you think I would let that go?" he growled while picking up speed, applying just enough pressure to make me want more. "That you wouldn't get punished?"

"How many girls have you touched this week?"

"One," he hissed in my ear. "And she's right fucking here."

Like I believed that. Would've told him as much too, if I could've made my mouth work. Instead of speaking, I moaned and let my head fall back on his shoulder.

"Look at you. One finger and you're all ready to be my dirty little slut."

"I'm sorry," I whispered as pleasure overtook me.

"You're sorry, are you?"

His curt words should've been my first clue that something was wrong. But I didn't care. I'd give Logan whatever he wanted, as long as he kept doing what he was doing.

In a matter of seconds my skirt was torn away and my panties obliterated, leaving me bare except for my bra.

Logan shoved a finger inside me and growled, "You haven't even begun to be sorry."

Oh.

My.

God.

My entire body seized as my walls clenched tightly around him. Whatever I was chasing was right there. I could feel it. Yet it seemed so far away.

"Please," I moaned out, shifting my hips back into him.

"That's it, sweetheart, give in to me."

My brows furrowed.

What the hell was I doing? I couldn't let this happen. But it was too late. Logan shoved another finger inside me and I went off. Screaming out his name as waves of ecstasy rocked through my body.

Stuck in a cloud of bliss, I couldn't react when he grabbed the back of my neck and held me against the door. Didn't care when he palmed my ass, or when I heard the rustle of a belt. I was happy to remain in my satisfied state. Until I felt it.

The smooth, hot, head of his very erect penis. Satisfaction fled and I instantly tensed. "W-what are–"

"Shut up," he snarled, tightening his hold on the back of my neck to a painful grip. "Did you think I'd play with your hot little pussy and that would be the end of it? Sorry, sweetheart, that's not how this shit works."

The scent of coconut assailed my nostrils as something cool slid down the crack of my ass. It smelled a lot like the oil I had on my bedside table. I held my breath as he smoothed it over my skin, but when his finger dipped down, toying with my back hole, panic set in.

"I don't know what you're thinking but–"

My sentence was cut off with a loud squeal. I threw myself forward, completely forgetting the door was in my way. Because there was a finger in my ass! Forcing it's way past that tight ring of muscles to slowly pump in and out of my ass. My ass!

It was the most invasive, strangest feeling I'd ever had. It was wrong, dirty and painful. So, why could I feel a bead of wetness trickle down my thigh? Oh, fuck it. Who cared? I had bigger things to worry about. Like the finger in my ass.

My ass!

I did what any normal person would do. I struggled and threw my arms behind me. Even managed to hit him a few times. That taught me two things. First, Logan Hudson was deceptively strong, and second, he hit back. Only a lot harder.

"Are you gonna let that prick kiss you again?" he growled, while forcing another finger inside me.

Let me just say, one finger, much better than two.

Defeated, I sucked back my sob and shook my head. "I'm not going out with Noah."

I was cut off when Logan viciously shoved his fingers as far as they would go.

"I told you not to say his fucking name!"

"I'm sorry," I blubbered, tears reigniting the sing in my cheek from his slap, "I canceled the date. I swear. I'm not going out with him."

"Did you?"

I could hear the disbelief in his voice, but I really did cancel. Noah was a nice guy. It wasn't fair to lead him on just to prove a point. Not to mention, if he got hurt because of it, I'd never forgive myself.

"I did. I promise."

"Ah huh." Though he still sounded mad, I was relieved that his fingers had slowed to more of a soft caress. It wasn't so much painful anymore, as just uncomfortable. "And why would you do that?"

"I didn't really like him," I explained, hoping I wouldn't upset him again. "Not like I should."

"So, douchebag didn't get you wet?"

"No."

Was it wrong that some sick part of me was enjoying this? Having him touch such a forbidden part? It was even starting to feel kind of good.

"And who does?"

I knew what he wanted, but I couldn't say it. Because that would mean I'd have to admit it to myself. And that I couldn't do. I shook my head and clamped my mouth shut, refusing to give him an answer.

"God damnit!" Logan roared and lifted me off the ground with one arm around my waist. "You want to fuck with me! Alright sweetheart, let's fucking play."

There wasn't time to respond, because the next thing I knew, I was flying through the air. My body bounced on the mattress before I had time to process what happened. After that, I stayed still, listening to my heart pounding painfully in my chest.

I wasn't that tiny little girl men could manhandle. In heels, I was close to six foot, and Logan lifted me like I weighed nothing. It was both terrifying, and exhilarating. The terror was what won when I heard the distinct sound of clothes falling on the floor.

I felt the mattress dip as the springs squeaked, and would like to say I jumped up and fled. But I didn't. I laid there like a coward, too afraid to move, as Logan's heavy body crawled over me.

It was his bare ass straddling my thighs that finally knocked the sense back into me. I squirmed and failed, fighting to get away. It was useless. One resounding slap, and my will to fight was sucked away with the air in my lungs.

"I'd stop fighting if I were you." Something a lot bigger than a finger lined up with my back hole, making me instantly freeze. "You're only making this harder on yourself."

I opened my mouth to tell him off at the same time he pushed forward.

Sharp slices of fire raced across my skin as Logan forced his cock past that tight ring of muscles. God it hurt. I felt like I was being split open. I fought to push him out while cramming the blanket in my mouth to muffle my scream. But he didn't care.

Tears dripped off my face and onto the blanket I was biting down on as I whimpered and reached back to push him away.

He answered by pinning my arms against my back and giving me another smack. My torment seemed to go on forever. So achingly slow and wracked with pain that I was pathetically relieved when his pelvis met my backside.

"Jesus fuck." He released a satisfied grunt and squeezed my sore ass cheek. "You feel fucking amazing."

I could care less how he thought I felt. At least that's what I told myself. The flutter in my chest suggested otherwise.

"I hate you," I grumbled through the stuffing crammed in my mouth.

Next thing I knew, the blanket, my one comfort, was ripped away. "Get that shit out of your mouth. I want to fucking hear you scream."

Terrified and thoroughly confused, I decided to try another approach.

"Logan, I'm scared." There was no point in hiding it anymore. His uncompromising hardness was lodged inside me. If he couldn't see me shaking, he could feel it. "I won't fight you anymore. Please don't hurt me."

"You'll be a good girl now, will you?" he said, pulling his hips back and snapping them forward. Giving me a taste of what he had in store.

I pressed my face into the mattress and slowly nodded. If this was the consequence of fighting him, then it wasn't worth it.

"Spread your legs."

I did.

"Get up on all fours."

I did that too, because if I listened, maybe he would make it nice for me.

"Still scared, sweetheart?" He gave me a small thrust and snickered when I trembled.

I whimpered out a cry. "It hurts."

He grabbed a fistful of my hair and pulled me up against him. "Good. I want to hurt you. The louder you scream, the harder I come."

Then he fucked me.

There was nothing tender or soft about the way Logan took me. His thrusts were hard, fast and brutal. Raw animal lust. As much as I wanted to hate it, a bigger part of me didn't. It loved the way he used me.

The smell of sweat in the air, and deep grunts. It hurt, yes. So much. But there was this dark pleasure behind it. Like some twisted part of my soul was surfacing. Pain mixed with euphoria sending me off that orgasmic cliff. Again, and again, and again.

By the time the fourth orgasm was cresting, I couldn't take it anymore. My energy was sapped. That blissful cloud I was so eager to chase before was now painfully intense, spikes rolling up my spine.

"Please," I begged with tears trickling down my face. "I can't... no more."

"You're done when I say you're fucking done." Logan wrapped his hand around my neck, pulled me up to him, and licked the tears off my cheek "Your ass feels way too fucking good. I could fuck you all night."

I whimpered. I wouldn't survive much more of this.

"You want me to come, sunshine?"

I actually allowed myself to believe he'd taken pity on me. Relief washed over me as I nodded. I should've known better.

"No other boys. No going on dates." He tipped my chin, forcing me to look into his hooded eyes. "You're mine until I say otherwise. Say it."

I'd promised myself I wouldn't go down this road, but I said it anyway. "I'm yours until you say otherwise."

The hard look on his face softened.

"Good girl," he whispered, sliding his fingers through my folds and strumming my clit.

I squeezed my eyes shut and shook my head, and still he didn't stop. He thrust his fingers inside me, hitting a spot I was way too sensitive to enjoy.

"You can give me one more."

Was it possible to die from an orgasm? Because I was pretty sure I was about to find out.

"No more," I whined, but I didn't have much of a choice.

Logan sped up, pumping his cock furiously in my ass as he thrust his fingers harder. Brushing that damned spot over and over, forcing me off an orgasmic cliff that had me seeing spots.

It felt like my heart stopped. Seized right there in my chest, as my vision blackened. I heard him growl, felt his teeth clamp down on my shoulder, and that was it.

My last thought as darkness leaked in, sweeping me to the blissful void of nothing, was that Logan Hudson was the devil. And I just sold him my soul.

"Mother fuck."

I'd never come so hard in my life. All I wanted to do was go again. Fuck. I squeezed her ass, spreading her cheeks so I could watch myself pump into her a few more times.

Seeing my shaft sink inside her was one of the most erotic things I'd ever seen, and I watched a lot of porn. Made a few personal videos myself. No fantasy compared to this shit. I could stay here, feeling her clench around me, forever.

My Cherry Pie, on the other hand…

Her hair was a tangled mess, stuck to her sweaty forehead, while her eyes fluttered behind closed lids. I couldn't help but snicker. She was dead. I'd fucked the girl into a coma.

"We're going to have to work on your stamina, baby."

My dick wept when I slid out of the greatest ass ever made and laid down over my sleeping beauty. Shelby whimpered and shifted back, which wasn't helping any. My dick was still hard and ready for round two.

There was no way in hell I was going to be able to fuck this girl out of my system. Don't know why I ever thought I could. She was too fucking perfect.

I damn near blew my load watching her change head gaskets, and she was so sweet it made my teeth hurt. Never thought I'd be the one to go for the nice girl, but here I was. Swooning over little miss sunshine.

I propped myself up so I could see the red handprints on her ass. Seeing her creamy complexion with my marks caused a weird feeling in my chest. This heavy swelling.

It threw me so much that I smacked my ribs to make it stop. And then there was the bite on her shoulder. That one had me seriously thinking about taking Cherry Pie for another ride. She was passed out, so it wouldn't hurt as much.

Broken dolls aren't any fun.

I sighed and got up, headed for the bathroom to flush the condom.

Fucking Preston ruining my good time. I'd punch him for it, but like it or not, he was right. Fuck sakes, I rode her for less than an hour and she passed out on me. Another round might break her. Which really fucking sucked.

My dick was used to pounding holes for hours. Then again, that's all those girls were. Holes. Shelby Grace was different. How? I hadn't figured that out yet. All I knew was I wanted to keep her, and that meant easing her into things.

Try telling my dick that though. I was tempted to pump one out when I rolled the condom off and flushed it. Rule number one, never leave your baby juice around for some crazy bitch to find.

This time it didn't feel that way, though. It felt wrong. Like it belonged inside her. Was Cherry Pie on birth control? I'd never bare-backed before, and she was mine...

Her old man signed the contract yesterday. It was amazing what a gambler would do to get rid of his debts. Still pissed me off, knowing he'd so quickly sell his daughter. Exactly why I bought his debts instead. Fucker owed me now.

I was halfway down the hall, when I stopped with my brows knit and stared at Shelby's bedroom door. Why the fuck was I still here? I didn't stick around after. Girls tended to get clingy if you did that cuddle shit. Not to mention the questions that came when they noticed one of my scars.

That shit was none of their fucking business. So why the fuck didn't I want to leave now?

My fingers brushed over one of the scars on my chest.

Shelby hadn't seen them yet. What would she do when she did? When she found out that my family line was spawned from the stuff of nightmares, would she give me that pitiful pathetic look?

What about when she found out other things? The shit Micha didn't even know. Twisted, sick things no father should do to his son. Would she still want me if she knew about that?

'Who fucking cares what she thinks, boy. Now get in there and fuck her again.'

My dick instantly jumped to attention, ready to give in to my old man's demands, but I didn't move. Not because I didn't want to fuck her again, that's what every inch of my body was screaming to do.

It was that voice that stopped me from giving her a good hard dicking.

My old man.

Ma was his wife and some of the bitches he fucked were treated better. Not my girl. My girl would be treated better than the sluts I used. Only problem was, I had no idea how to do that.

I thought back to how fucking annoying it was when Naomi spent so much time in the bathroom. I told her to do that shit at home, but of course she didn't listen. Naomi was always primping herself. Come to think of it, so were Ava and Amy.

Maybe girls had a thing about being clean? Well, shit. I could do that.

Nodding to myself, I walked back into the bathroom to get a cloth. Plus, I was fucking starving and rummaging around in the Grace girls' unorganized cupboards gave me a chance to place an order.

With a warm, damp cloth in hand, I went back to Shelby's room. I was Logan fucking Hudson, I could take care of my girl. Fuck, I'd probably own that shit.

I'm a goddamn Rockstar.

I couldn't help but chuckle when Cherry Pie squeaked and snapped her eyes shut. It was cute how hard she was trying to pretend to be asleep. Laying there with her body stiffly still and mouth clamped shut.

Her fear though, I could taste that shit, and it was fucking delicious. Her horrible acting career came to a crashing halt when I crawled up on the bed and swiped the cloth over her sore flesh.

"No, don't," she whimpered and shuffled up the bed. Which was a bit aggravating, considering I was doing this crap for her.

"Stop fucking squirming," I growled, and smacked her ass. That seemed to work.

"No more. I can't."

I sighed. "Whining like that is only making me hard." My dick was good to go before I walked in here. This shit wasn't helping. "Unless you want me to use this tight little ass again, I suggest you shut the fuck up."

Shelby lifted her head, rolling her curious eyes back at me. "You're not going to do… that again?"

Fucking adorable.

"I hadn't planned on it." Didn't mean I wouldn't. "I could always change my mind if you're up for another round."

She shook her head and remained silent while watching me. Real careful, as if she was afraid I'd pounce. It was fucking amusing, and I may have taken a little more time to clean her up than needed.

I was oddly intent on making sure she wasn't torn or bleeding. Which was also annoying. I shouldn't give a crap, but for some reason, I did.

Once I was done, I tossed the cloth in the hamper and did something else fucked up. I laid down beside her and pulled her into my arms.

Shelby stiffened. "What are you doing?"

"Holding you."

"Why?"

Even she thought this was strange behaviour, and still, I didn't let her go.

"Because I want to."

Son of a bitch, I really did. Huh?

It went quiet for a bit. The only thing I could hear was her uneasy breathing. I sucked in a deep breath, taking in her scent, and nuzzled in.

This was comfortable, having her soft warm body pressed up against mine. I liked it. For once I didn't feel the need to fuck with someone, or hit them. The voices that taunted me in the back of my mind had gone quiet. Empty and peaceful.

Eventually Shelby relaxed. The first time I saw her, I knew I had her body. Lust was an old friend and the glimmer in her cinnamon eyes was unmistakable. But that was the easy part. Any jackass with half decent skills could make a girl desire him.

Making her want him, now that was another story. And judging by the way her heart was pattering away, her mind wasn't quite there yet. Maybe she was confused? That was cool. I had no fucking clue what the hell was happening either. We'd just have to figure this shit out together.

"Logan..." Guess Cherry Pie couldn't take the silence anymore. "Can I get dressed?"

A smirk tugged at my lips as I propped myself up on my elbow and cocked a brow down at her. "Are you asking my permission?"

Little sassy minx grumbled under her breath and huffed out a sigh. "I'm cold."

"I'll keep you warm."

"I don't want you to keep me warm."

After everything I'd done, she still had her attitude. My doll was stronger than I thought.

"I didn't ask what you want."

"Oh for the love of...." She squirmed out of my arms and sat up. "I'm getting dressed."

I pulled her back down and chuckled in her ear. "You're not going anywhere, Cherry Pie."

"Logan, I'm naked!"

I snickered and rolled my gaze over her pert little rose bud nipples and down to the curve of her hip. "I didn't take you for the shy type."

"I'm not," she said with a growl, which was incredibly sexy. A confident woman always was.

"That doesn't mean I'm going to lay here naked with you."

"I beg to differ."

She snarled, smacked my arm, and started to pull away. My Cherry Pie thought she could fight me? Hilarious. She pushed, and I pulled. Tightening my hold with every little squirm she made.

I had to hand it to her though, the girl had some power in those thighs. When she threw her leg back and kicked me in the shin, I actually winced. Impressive, but not good enough.

It took me two seconds to wrap my legs around hers. Before she could take her next breath, I had sweet Shelby's arms pinned behind her back, with my other hand on her throat.

"You're getting me all worked up, sunshine." I dragged my tongue up the side of her face, savoring the taste of defeat. "I'm starting to think you want me to take you for another ride."

I felt her throat bob under my fingers with a heavy swallow. "Compromise?"

Interesting. Okay I'll play along.

"What were you thinking?"

"You let me put some clothes on, and I'll cuddle with you as long as you want."

If I had considered it, her full breasts pressed out with her arched back changed my mind.

"No deal," I said, sliding my hand off her neck to pinch her nipple.

I liked having free access. She liked it too.

"You can pick what I wear," she cried out.

Now we were getting somewhere. There was all kinds of shit in her delicates drawer. Lacy little thongs I could eat off her.

"Anything?"

"Yes, anything."

My eyes landed on a pile of black fabric on the floor.

"So let me get this straight, you'll wear whatever I want, and you'll lay here with me. No fighting. If I want to sleep with my hand on your ass, you'll leave it there."

"Who said anything about sleep?"

I answered her with a smile.

She grumbled out a sigh and rolled her eyes. Instantly, my hand landed on her ass. God, I loved that sound. Skin hitting skin. It was almost as good as the stinging strike of a leather whip.

"Don't roll your fucking eyes. It's disrespectful."

"You're one to talk about disrespect."

My brow rose. "What was that?"

"Nothing," she muttered.

Uh huh, that's what I thought.

"Can I get dressed now?"

"I don't know," I said, watching goosebumps prick her skin as I swirled my finger around her pert nipple. "You didn't answer my question."

"Yes, fine, I'll cuddle with you, okay?"

"Okay," I nodded and released her.

Shelby sat up and eyed me. "Just like that?"

"Just like that."

My response didn't set her at ease. Her eyes narrowed suspiciously.

"What's the catch? What kind of crap are you going to make me wear?"

"My shirt."

Her face dropped in an expression of disbelief. "Your shirt?"

"Yup."

"That's the catch? You just want me to wear your shirt?"

"That's right."

She stared at me for a second with her lip curled, before getting off the bed to snatch my shirt off the floor.

"Seriously," she sang, eyeing me again, "That's it? You just want me to wear your shirt?"

"That's it."

"Why?"

My lips tipped up in a slow smile. Simple. I wanted her to smell like me. If I could spray her with my come before she left the house everyday, I would. Don't think she'd go for that, though.

"Explanations weren't part of the deal, Cherry Pie."

"Whatever," she grumbled and slipped the shirt over her head.

Gotta say, I never thought I'd find something like that sexy, but watching the black fabric float over her skin and caress her ass was erotic as fuck.

"Could *you* put something on?"

"I don't know." Placing my hands behind my head, I stretched out, letting her see every hard inch. "What's in it for me?"

"Why does there always have to be something in it for you?" Her mouth may be arguing, but her eyes were stuck on something else.

"That's how this works, sweetheart. You want something from me, then I want something from you."

"And what do you want?"

Her tongue darted out, moistening those pouty pink lips, and I smirked.

"A blow job."

I couldn't help but snicker when her mouth fell open.

"You've got the right idea, but my dick's over here."

The moment was over.

"Forget it," she snarled, lip curling. "Stay naked for all I care."

I shrugged. "Okay, but the longer I stay naked, the more likely it is you'll get fucked again."

We argued for a bit and eventually came to the agreement that she would suck my dick in the morning. My guess was she'd try and get out of it.

What my little Cherry Pie didn't know was that I had no problem holding her down and face fucking her. One way or another, she'd be gagging on my cock come morning.

When the doorbell rang and I slipped into my jeans she shot me a dirty look. "Who the hell is that?"

"Relax, Cherry Pie, I ordered pizza." I was assuming by the look on her face that she thought I'd invited some random girl over to fuck with her.

Normally I wouldn't be opposed to the idea, but I didn't want to share Shelby. Even with a girl.

"So you would've gotten dressed anyway?"

"Yup."

"That's not fair!" she cried out with a snide little stomp. "You tricked me."

I looked back at her with a smirk, said, "Who said anything about fair?" and sauntered down the stairs.

I was fucking starving and could smell the pizza before I opened the door. Gotta love ordering apps. There was no need to tip the driver or make awkward small talk.

Everything was already paid for. They gave you your food and that was it. Not this guy. I had half a slice in my mouth before I noticed him gawking over my shoulder.

I eyed the prick peeking into *my* girl's house and took another bite. "Is there a fucking problem?"

"Sorry," he said, jumping back and pausing long enough to give me a quick scan, "I was expecting someone else."

I just bet you were.

His hungry eyes turned back to the stairs as he said, "This blonde usually answers the door."

This mother–

"Oh yeah, I know who you're talking about." I leaned against the doorframe and eyed the prick up. He was kind of skinny. One pop to the face should do it. "She's cute, right?"

"That girl is smoking."

It was bad enough that the prick was practically drooling, but he had the gall to talk to me like I gave a shit what his opinion was. Little pencil-neck dickweed.

"I'd give my left nut for a piece of that."

That can be arranged.

"Sometimes she answers the door in these tight little outfits…"

Why was he still talking? Didn't he notice I was standing here with my jeans half open and no shirt on. What? Did he think I was banging her mom?

"That ass, bro. Fuck me."

I was just balls deep in that ass, motherfucker.

And yet he kept going. "Between you and me, I think she's sweet on me."

This fucker has a death wish.

"Is that so?"

"Yeah, man. She keeps giving me these cute smiles."

Does she now? I'd be having a talk with Cherry Pie about that. "Uh huh."

"She plays shy, but I bet that girl likes it rough."

"And let me guess, you're the guy to give it to her?"

He was too busy yapping to see my fist.

I hit him square in the jaw, scraping my knuckles on his teeth, because he was still fucking talking. His eyes rolled back and he crumpled to the ground.

"Piece of shit," I muttered, and slammed the door.

I woke up the next morning wrapped in Logan's arms. I probably should've jumped up and scampered away, but I didn't. I stayed where I was, staring at the wall, like some drugged out zombie.

If I looked at him, I'd have to face what happened last night and admit that a part of me enjoyed it. The way he held me down, and the things he said. All of it played over and over again in my mind.

Waking up in his arms wasn't helping any. Hearing his steady breaths whisp across my ear while he held me close. It felt oddly natural and comfortable, and was one hundred percent disturbing. Logan Hudson didn't cuddle or take girls on dates.

He played them. Taking what he wanted and then moving on to the next. Sometimes in the same night.

Well, I wasn't going to be one of those girls. The ones that thought for some reason they'd be different. That he would want more than one night of fun from them.

I spent enough time with Trina to know how this game was

played, and I wasn't going to become that pathetic person pining for something that would never come.

Not gonna happen!

I carefully lifted Logan's arm and inched my way across the bed, which was no easy task. Each shuffle or grunt made me hold my breath and silently pray he wouldn't wake up.

I don't how he did it, but ever time I saw those twinkling green eyes or stupid charming smirk, I wound up trapped in his web. Maybe he was secretly an incubus or something. It wouldn't surprise me if he had some supernatural allure.

Bastard.

After what felt like forever, my feet finally slipped off the edge of the mattress. I'd escaped the lustful demon. Or, at least I thought I had. I was just sliding my butt off the mattress when Logan's hands wrapped under my armpits and he pulled me back up.

"Are you trying to sneak away from me, Cherry Pie?"

"No," I grumbled, hating how sexy his sleepy tone sounded.

"That's good." He wrapped his leg around me and nuzzled in, grazing his lips off my ear, "Cause I'd hate to think you were trying to renege on our deal."

Before Logan came along, I was confident in who I was. I had the body I was born with and there was nothing I could do about that. But lately I was questioning everything. Does this shirt match these pants? Did I do that right? Was I good enough? Would my dad be proud of me?

The last one I'd asked myself a lot lately. I couldn't stop this nagging feeling that if I'd tried harder to make him happy, he wouldn't have cheated. Stupid, I know. Still, I couldn't stop thinking about what he said.

'I never would have married your mother if she wasn't pregnant.'

"Why can't men be faithful?"

Though I couldn't see him–I was staring at the wall–I could feel Logan's brow rise.

"I hadn't realized I was unfaithful."

"Oh, please," I rolled my eyes back at him, which was a mistake.

The second I met that piercing green gaze, I froze. Trapped by the way they sparkled as he rolled his eyes over me.

Focus, Shelby.

"Why don't you just leave Logan. We both know you want to."

"Do I strike you as the kind of guy that does anything I don't want to?"

Definitely not. But I didn't want him here.

"Just go," I growled, angry that I couldn't shake the image of my dad sucking face with my coach. "I'm sure your next flavor is waiting outside for you."

"Ah, that's what this is about," he said, propping himself up on an elbow. "So quick to condemn, Cherry Pie. But you're not mad at me, are you?" His lips twisted in a mocking frown. "You're mad at daddy."

It wasn't what he said that had my hand flying through the air. Logan teasing me had become my new normal. It was because he was right.

"Fuck you," I snarled, slapping him across the face.

The second my strike rang through the air, I suddenly understood what Rye meant by her mouth was always getting her in trouble.

Except in my case, it was my hand. Logan's eyes darkened and before I had a chance to contemplate my stupid decision, he had my arms pinned and was glowering down at me.

"Watch yourself, Cherry Pie, I'm looking for a reason to hurt you." His voice dropped an octave, causing my heart to fall with it, pumping nervous pulses through my churning gut. "Don't piss me off."

If last night proved anything, it was how far Logan was willing to go. But did I heed his warning? No. I was too mad to go limp and play sweet little submissive. My body bucked and my legs kicked, while I screamed every curse word I knew in his face.

It didn't do much good. He was bigger and stronger. Still, I didn't stop. The ticking time bomb I'd been suppressing for months had blown. Exploding in a burning rage that not even the cold spikes of fear rocketing up my spine could cool.

I squirmed. I screamed. I would've clawed his eyes out if I could move my hands. I wanted to hurt him. Make someone, anyone, feel my pain. Take the ripping hole in my heart and shove it down their throat, until they were choking on the same pile of disgust and hatred I was.

And then Logan slapped me. Turning that horrible burning rage into a moment of shock.

"That's it," he growled, flipping me over before my brain had time to register the sting spreading across my face. "You want to act like a child and throw a tantrum." He ripped the blanket away, pressed his knee into my back, and swung his hand, landing a firm strike on my still sore ass. "Then I'll treat you like one."

He hit me again, once again fueling that burning ugliness to consume me.

"Let me go!" I snarled, kicking him with my heels. "I hate you!"

He said nothing as he continued his assault. I reached back and clawed his arm, flailed my body and spewed insults at him.

Each time he answered me with a resounding smack. It went on for so long that my body was covered in a fine coat of sweat and it felt like I was sitting in a bucket of lava.

"So Daddy is fucking your coach."

Smack.

"Suck it up and move on. No one gives a shit what Daddy does."

Smack.

"Screw you." I'd met his mom. Paisley was possibly the sweetest person on earth. And Riley's dad might be strict, but he was loving. He had no idea the pain a dysfunctional family could cause. How much a parent could break your heart. "You have the perfect life. What could you know about any of this?"

He full on belly laughed, as if what I'd said was the funniest thing in the world.

"You think you're the only one with daddy issues? You should meet my old man."

"Oh boo hoo," I sang, "Daddy didn't get me the jet I wanted for Christmas."

There was a big difference between disappointment, and being blamed for ruining his life.

The next thing I knew, Logan had a handful of my hair and was twisting my head.

"You see that," he growled, while throwing his arm in my face, "That nice little cigarette burn in the skull's eye?"

I sucked in a breath, because I did see it. Right there in the eye socket, a small circular burn healed with time. And that wasn't all I saw.

The black ink on his tanned skin hid a road map of pain and torture. Cuts, abrasions and rough patches of skin. Scars everywhere.

"What happened to you?"

"These are the gifts *my* daddy gave me."

Until this moment, I'd never given much thought to where his father was. In this day and age it wasn't that big of an assumption to think his parents split.

Even couples people think are truly happy break up. My parents were a prime example of that. Everyone thought they were the perfect couple. At home it was a different story.

I heard the fights. Saw the dried tears on my mom's face. Behind closed doors, away from the prying eyes of others, that was when reality reared its' ugly head.

My heart ached as my gaze rolled over Logan's scars. His reality wasn't just ugly. It was a nightmare.

"Is he in jail?" It would explain his absence.

Logan snorted out a laugh. "Men like my old man don't go to jail, Cherry Pie."

What the hell did that mean? No one was beyond the scales of justice. The law didn't care where you came from, or who you were. Unless they were the president, of course.

"If you break the law, you go to jail." Riley got arrested for graffiti, and her dad was sheriff. "That's how it works, Logan."

"It's fucking annoying how naive you are." Logan sighed and rolled off me. "You need to let go of your Care Bear ideals. The world isn't fluffy bunnies and rainbows."

Why did he always treat me like I was a child? I knew there were ugly things in the world. He was here, wasn't he?

"There's nothing wrong with choosing to see the good in life," I snarled, flinching when I sat up and my ass pressed down on the mattress.

"You need a fucking reality check, sweetheart." He pushed me on my back before I could get another word out. "And I'm going to give it to you."

I was so done with his arrogance. Thinking he was all that just because he was handsome. Okay, he was gorgeous, and had that wicked smirk down pat.

That didn't make him any better than the rest of us. Well, except kissing. His lips were so soft, and the things he did with his tongue. Logan definitely knew what he was doing in that department. And with his fingers, and other parts.

Should my orgasm be that intense? My body kept shivering as if I was still recovering. Logan's mouth twisted in that sinful way that caused goosebumps to erupt across my skin.

He did things to me that I didn't think were possible. Made me feel things I didn't know I could. And a huge part of me wondered what else he could do with those lips.

Focus Shelby!

"You know what?" His lips crashed down on mine before I could tell him what.

My mind struggled, telling me to slap him. Especially since, like everything else he did, Logan Hudson was a master at kissing. I lay there with his heavy weight pressing down on me, giving him nothing more a weak moan in protest.

His taste exploded across my tongue as his mouth worked mine, and I felt another piece of my soul slip away.

I tried to move, regain control of my limbs and push him away. My body wasn't listening, though. I couldn't get my arms to move. Well, that wasn't entirely true. They worked enough to spear my fingers in his hair. I was in so much trouble.

Logan pulled away long enough to softly purr, "I want to fuck you so bad," and dove back in. More demanding this time.

I was helpless. Logan Hudson was like that first bite of Thanksgiving dinner. I'd tell myself, just one plate, and later that night, I'd be lying on the couch wondering how I got so full I couldn't move. Fighting him was a useless endeavour.

I was in so much trouble.

And then his lips were gone. I opened my eyes to see him staring down at me with a cocky grin.

This can't be good.

"Time to pay up, Cherry Pie."

My eyes narrowed. "What are you talking about?"

"We had a deal."

Yup, definitely not good.

"You can't be serious."

"I put clothes on."

"For like two seconds," I argued. "I am not giving you a blow job for that."

His eyes darkened, as if he was happy I was refusing. Which almost made me give in. After what happened last night, I wasn't in a hurry to push him again. Luckily for me, my baby sister decided to kill the mood.

"What's a blow job?"

We both stopped and turned to see Mags standing in my doorway, her little hip cocked to the side. She'd spent the night at Dad's house. I shouldn't have seen her until I picked her up from school.

"Shouldn't Dad be taking you to school?"

"He wanted to surprise you with breakfast."

I rolled my eyes. Of course he did. I started Ashworth on Monday, so naturally he was playing the proud parent. It's funny how quickly he forgot about blaming me for ruining his life.

"What's a blow job?" Mags repeated.

I was about to tell her to get out of my room, but Logan beat me to the punch.

"It's when a girl sucks on a guy's–"

"Oh my God!" I squealed, smacking him with a pillow. "She's nine!"

He shrugged and rolled off me. "She's gotta learn sometime."

"Not when she's nine!"

"I'm not a baby," Mags sang, crossing her arms.

Logan cocked a brow at me, silently saying 'see', and I'd never wanted to smack anyone more in my life. Which I didn't get a chance to do, because another voice wafted up the stairs.

"Are you up, Peanut?"

Oh, shit!

My wide eyes locked on my little sister. "Dad's here?"

"She's up here, Daddy," Mags yelled with a smile.

I don't know why I thought the brat would do anything else. Getting me in trouble was one of her favorite past times.

If my dad found a boy in my room, not only would I be grounded for the rest of my life, but I'd get a lecture from my mom for months. And if there was one thing southern women were good at, it was guilt trips.

"Go distract him!" I shrieked. Mags' lips twisted and I groaned. Don't know why I thought she would help me now. "How much is this going to cost me?"

"Forty."

"What!? What the heck do you need that much for?" My sister's main expenditure was candy at the corner store.

"I want to get Mom a Christmas present."

Aww. Okay, that made my heart melt a bit. Mags may be a pain in the ass, but she had a sweet side. The instant I agreed, she took off, screaming that Dad needed to come and see her new bear. There was a reason I sent Mags out there. The nine year old was an amazing manipulator.

When our dad argued, she started crying and squealed, "You don't love me as much as Shelby."

Logan laid back on the bed and smirked. "I like her."

"Of course you do," I groaned, "You're both extortionists."

Let's just hope my sister could keep Dad occupied long enough to get the boy out of my room.

I wasn't sure how I felt about Shelby pretty much pushing me out her bedroom window. Forcing someone to do the walk of shame was my job, and the one time I didn't want to do it, I was the one being shooed away.

Still not sure why I gave in and ended up climbing out the window without a shirt on. Not that I cared about walking around without a shirt.

I looked good. But I didn't do what girls said, they did what I told them to. Yet, for some reason the panicked look on Shelby's face made me cave.

When did I become such a pussy?

All through school it pissed me off. Now I was parked outside her house. Why? No fucking clue. All I knew was when the day ended, I got in my car and wound up here.

Funny thing was, Shelby wasn't even home. She had an appointment at Ashworth, which I knew about. I might've said fuck it and gone home, if it wasn't for the sleek black Aston Martin in the driveway.

Lou's sleek black Aston Martin.

What the fuck is he doing here?

Even more intriguing was the fact that I didn't see Marco's Escalade anywhere. Meaning Lou came by himself. The King of Kings didn't go anywhere without security. Unless he didn't want anyone to know what he was doing.

"What are you up to, Lou?"

Was he here about Cherry Pie's contract? He knew I requested one, but didn't know who for. Maybe Micha said something? No. He wouldn't do that. While Micha was loyal to the Order, his true loyalties lied with his brothers. The Knights.

He would betray the Order before betraying any one of us. Fuck sakes he covered up my old man's death, back when we thought I killed the bastard. So if it wasn't for the contract, what the fuck was Lou doing here?

Let's find out.

I'd been watching Shelby for months. Spending every waking minute stalking her was fucking annoying and time consuming, and then I thought, why jerk off to fantasies when I could have the real thing? So I had cameras installed in her house last week.

I scoffed out a snicker and pulled out my phone, clicking on the app connecting me to the live feed of the Grace house. He was constantly telling me to be careful because you never knew who was watching, and he walked into a house full of cameras.

"You should pay better attention to your surroundings, Lou." I tsked and zoomed in on Lou and Shelby's mom standing in the kitchen.

"What are we going to do?" Shelby's mom threw her hands up in the air.

Gotta say, for an older woman, Cheyenne Grace was pretty fucking hot. Blonde hair, striking blue eyes with a great figure. Even had the same firm ass as her daughter. I'd fuck her, if I didn't already have the younger model.

"Cheyenne," Lou sighed, "Calm down."

"Don't tell me to calm down! I am calm."

I was kind of digging the accent. If I pissed Cherry Pie off enough, would she get the same southern drawl as her mom?

Lou scrubbed a hand down his face and muttered, "Lower your voice."

"Why?" I was guessing by the glare in her eyes, Shelby's mom liked being told what to do as much as her daughter did. "There's no one here to hear us."

I smirked. *I am.*

What happened next caught me completely off guard. Lou, the all mighty King of Kings, who didn't bow down to anyone, reached out and pulled her into his embrace.

"I'm sorry. I know you're worried."

Well fuck me! Did hell freeze over? Because Louis Kessler didn't apologize to anyone for anything. And he didn't just apologize, he was comforting her. Stroking her hair while she muttered, *'Tell me to calm down'* into his chest. What the hell…

"Don't worry," he shooshed her and continued petting her head. "We'll find him."

Seriously, what the fuck was going on here?

Shelby's mom softened in his arms and cried out. "Oh Louie, I'm sorry."

Louie? That was fucking great. Definitely storing that one for later.

"It's all my fault."

"Don't be ridiculous. It's me Ryker's after. Not you."

I sat up, face hardening at the screen. Why the fuck was he talking about my old man with Shelby's mom? They didn't know each other.

"The first thing I'm going to do when I get out is pay the Grace girl a visit."

My fingers curled tightly around my phone as I stole a glance at the house. What the fuck wasn't Lou telling me?

Shelby's mother raised her head and brushed the tears off her face before gazing up into Lou's eyes. "I should've tried harder to find you."

"How were you going to do that? It was one drunken night in college. You didn't even know my name."

No fucking way! This was Lou's mystery blonde? Cheyenne fucking Grace. She was here all these years and he didn't know. Now that was fucking priceless.

"How could you have told me you were pregnant?"

I cocked my head at the screen. What?

"But I didn't have to give him up."

Nope not hallucinating.

"And what were you supposed to do..."

My brain fought to process the information I'd just overheard. Not only was Cheyenne motherfucking Grace, Lou's mystery blonde, but she had a kid!

Micha had an older brother that I was pretty sure he didn't know about. He would have definitely told me about that shit. How had Lou known? That's when it all clicked into place.

"Tell me where he is, and I'll give you a quick death."

Lou didn't keep my old man alive to find out what he might've told someone else. He wasn't protecting The Order. He was looking for his fucking kid. I just hit the motherfucking jackpot!

I tucked my phone in my pocket and stepped out on the street to lean against my car. Let's see how the King of Kings likes having the tables turned.

The ball's in my court now, motherfucker.

Bet he'd let me see my old man now. God, I couldn't wait. By the time I left, he'd have three scars for every one of mine. That was just my payback. Ma's was an entirely different story.

That was the shit I was looking forward to. The last thing that prick ever saw would be Ma's bright smile. Had the picture in my wallet. My old man would leave this world knowing he didn't win. That's when I'd know I'd gotten our revenge.

My eyes rolled up when Lou strutted out of the house. "Fancy meeting you here."

He stopped dead in his tracks.

"Logan?" he said, taking a second to glance around, "What are you doing here?"

I pulled out a cigarette and flipped open my lighter, enjoying the rush of smoke flowing down my throat before answering him.

"I could ask you the same thing."

"Are you following me?"

Instead of responding, I took another long pull of my smoke.

"If you think I'll lead you to your father," he smoothed down his suit jacket, "You underestimate me, son."

It was the condescending look on his face that made me smile. Lou's shrink mind had me pegged from the time I was twelve. I was the impulsive one that couldn't keep his mouth shut.

Something I was happy to let him believe. People tended not to give a shit what they said when they thought you weren't paying attention.

"I'm much more interested in the illegitimate child you spawned with the lovely Cheyenne Grace."

And there it was. That shocked look I'd been waiting to see my entire life. But if Lou was anything, it was collected. He straightened up and whipped the Kessler's trademark blank expression back onto his face.

"Honestly son, I worry about you." He exhaled and shook his head. "Some of the stuff you come up with makes we wonder whether you're a danger."

Oh, I was definitely a danger, but he already knew that. "Are you going to have me committed, Lou? Think some time in the nut house will fix my brain? Or do you just think it'll shut me up?"

"There's definitely something wrong with your mind, son."

He had me there.

"We tried that once, remember. It didn't go over so well."

When I was twelve, Lou sent Preston and I upstate for 'therapy'. They sent us back.

Lou huffed out a breath and continued down the walkway. "I don't have time for this."

"That's fine," I nodded and flicked my butt. "I'm sure Micha would be interested to see the video. Does he know he has an older brother?"

Lou stopped dead in his tracks. "You're bluffing."

I cocked a brow at him. "Am I?"

Cautious fucker stood there studying me. I could see the wheels turning in his head. Was I telling the truth? Or did I just make a good guess?

"I have to hand it to you son, you've upped your game. I almost believed you for a minute."

You have no idea how much I've upped my game.

"You remember the contract I asked for?"

"Yes, yes," he said, waving his hand dismissively through the air. "Tell me who it's for and I'll get everything signed."

"Shelby Grace." He didn't say a word. Just stared at me. "And I already got daddy's signature."

He muttered under his breath and pushed his fingers through his hair.

Now that made me smile.

"What do you want?"

"You know what I want."

"I can't let you see him, Logan." Lou's eyes rolled up, "I need him alive."

"He'll live."

"But will he be able to talk?"

That I couldn't guarantee.

"I'm sure you'll figure it out," I said, opening my car door and stopping to look back at him, "Oh, and Micha."

"What about him?"

"He's called a council meeting."

Lou nodded. "I'm aware."

Micha was adopting Junior. Why, I had no idea. I personally hated the little shit, but he wanted him, and also wanted him in the Order, as a Knight. That's what the meeting was for.

"You're going to make sure it happens."

"You know I can't," Lou's brows furrowed. "The King of Kings only votes in the event of a tie."

Fucking Order hierarchy. I was so sick of this shit. I knew for a fact that the Creswell's would never vote in Micha's favor.

Their insistence on proper reputation was the main source of Silas's constant scowl. They'd never be okay with trash like Junior joining their ranks, and since the only other vote was Preston's dad, Micha was fucked.

"There is one way." Lou cocked his head, pondering something. "You have your handbook, I assume."

I nodded. The handbook was the Order's list of rules and regulations. I hadn't read it, could care less about the rules, but I still had it.

"Chapter twelve, paragraph three, section four."

I WAS SITTING in the kitchen, eating my third sandwich while rereading my handbook. Most of it was useless. Council meeting rules, lists of family names, and other mundane crap.

There were a few interesting things.

If a King was unable to attend a meeting, his eldest son could cast a vote in his stead. Meaning, since my old man was locked up in a dark hole, I was the one that got to vote. The really intriguing part came with the list of wolves' family names:

Dorian,

Fenton,

and Mathers.

At first I thought it was a coincidence. There had to be a ton of Mathers out there, right? What were the chances Riley's uncle had anything to do with this? Pretty good, it turned out. Mathers Tattooing was on land owned by great granddaddy Mathers, who was born in this town.

Needless to say, Chase was quite interested to learn about his heritage. Okay, that was bullshit. The asshole didn't give a fuck. His exact words were, "Why the fuck should I care if some kid gets in your club?"

He had a point. Personally, I didn't give a fuck about the little shit either. Micha was the only reason I was doing this. Chase had similar motivations, because the second I mentioned how disappointed Riley would be, he changed his mind. He'd be here Monday.

I should be pissed. All this time I could've had a say. Instead, I was shaking my head. The Kings liked to keep Preston and I in the dark. Apparently it was for our own good. Complete bullshit.

Neither one of us would have a problem knocking one of them off. Including Preston's old man. They weren't protecting us. They were fucking scared. And now Lou had dragged Chase into this shit.

Dumb fuck.

There was one thing Mathers cared about. Riley. And Lou's son didn't just claim her. He took her. Why he didn't just slit our fucking throats was beyond me. Maybe he still would.

"You can't do this!"

I turned my head to see Junior storm into the kitchen, followed by Micha, who crossed his arms and growled, "It's done."

Both were scowling so deep, lines of anger were etched onto their faces. Sometimes if was fucking eerie how similar they were.

"This is bullshit." Junior threw his finger up, pointing angrily at Micha. "You said you wouldn't kill her."

Micha rolled his eyes. "I didn't kill her. She left."

"I'll find her. You can't keep me here."

"Actually I can. You're legally mine now."

Junior threw open the patio door and stormed outside. "We'll see about that."

I chuckled when Micha pinched the bridge of his nose and sighed.

"How's parenthood treating you?"

"Go fuck yourself," he grumbled, slumping down on the stool beside me.

"You're the one that wanted the little shit."

The only answer I got was an unimpressed glare. I couldn't help it, I burst out laughing. He brought this shit on himself. And why? Because they couldn't leave Junior with his mother? Little bastard was doing just fine before Micha came along. He was still alive, wasn't he? I tried to tell Riley that.

Speaking of Riley...

"Where's your girl?" She was the one that talked him into this shit. "Shouldn't she be here to hold your hand?"

"She's busy celebrating," his dark eyes rolled my way, "With your girl."

I slipped off the stool and dropped my plate in the sink. "What the fuck are the celebrating?"

"Fucked if I know. Mouse said it was girls' night or some shit." Micha shrugged. "No boys allowed."

Fuck that shit.

"And you just let her go?"

"Why the fuck not?"

"Do you not remember Naomi's last girls' night?"

That was a cluster fuck. When girls drank they turned stupid, and stupid is easy to manipulate. I should know. Had fun with stupid many times.

"Are they drinking?"

Micha's brow lifted. "Mouse doesn't drink."

"Cherry Pie does," I pointed out. "And she did get Riley in that dress on Halloween."

I smirked when Micha's eyes met mine. He didn't like the way Shelby dressed. Said it was too revealing and a bad influence on his girl. I thought it was the other way around. Shelby had too much attitude, which I blamed on my stepsister. And Micha, a bit. He let her get away with too much.

"I know what you're doing. It's not going to work."

"Whatever you say," I shrugged. My best friend knew me well. Unfortunately, I knew him too. "I guess you could always talk to Shelby another day."

His eyes narrowed on me. "Why the fuck would I need to talk to her?"

I smirked.

"Ran into your old man today."

Chapter 13
Shelby

Riley picked up a can of pink paint and sprayed the wall. "The prick hasn't messaged me back."

I sucked in a deep breath, enjoying the chemical scent of aerosol. Rye and I had been coming to the Causegrove for so long that the smell of wildflowers and paint had a calming effect on me now. It let me know I was safe. For a few hours I could forget all the crap going on and just have fun with my friends.

"Maybe he's busy dealing with Junior?"

Junior was officially adopted by Micha today, which was good news to me. Since I dropped him off that one day, I'd been trying to put together a plan to collect donations for his mother and him for Christmas. Every kid should have a good Christmas. That was one thing I knew Micha could give him.

I highly doubted Junior was as happy about the adoption as I was. Mags constantly talked about him. Let me just say, my little sister probably didn't improve his mood any. I swear Megan Ruth Grace was put on this earth to annoy people.

Rye's blue eyes rolled my way. "Micha's not the coddling type."

"And Junior's not the coddle me type," I pointed out.

Tico snorted from his spot on the rundown couch. "Still don't know why you're dating that guy."

It was weird seeing him hating on someone. Tico was a pretty easy going guy, he seemed to get along with everyone. Amazing, considering his home life. He really hated Micha Kessler though. Can't say I blamed him. It wasn't like Micha was nice to Riley growing up.

"I know it's hard to believe, but I think he really does love her." Not sure why I was defending Micha.

He was a complete and utter jerk. But the way he sat by Riley's bedside, begging her to wake up, made me like him just a little. Still didn't forgive all the shit he did to her. It was a start, though.

"You should give him a chance."

"If you say so." Shadows ghosted across Tico's face, deepening the scowl etched in his forehead as he stared into the glowing light of the crackling fire.

Riley mumbled, "There won't be anything left of him to give a chance if the bastard doesn't get back to me."

When she pulled out her phone and sent another text, I knew she was worried. Rye wasn't that girl glued to her phone. Sometimes it was like pulling teeth just to get her to answer a call.

"Like I said, he's probably dealing with Junior."

"I'm sure Junior's fine."

I gave my best friend a sideways glance. On a normal day, that kid was anything but fine.

Headlights lit up our spot under the stone bridge, interrupting our conversation. Rye groaned as a blue Ford Taurus rolled up.

"Holy shit," Trina exclaimed, getting out of the car. "She showed! And surprise, surprise, she's painting."

Riley rolled her eyes and grumbled under her breath.

"Leave her alone," Marnie said, climbing out of the passenger side. "Rye's an artist, she can't help it when the mood strikes."

"Exactly," Riley nodded.

"Whatever." Trina cracked open a box and tossed Tico a beer. "Who's the muse this time, Picasso?"

"Can't you tell?" Riley turned her grin Trina's way, "It's you. After your ten year porn career."

It was Trina's turn to grumble.

I eyed the detailed portrait of a desiccated woman. She was laying on the ground with her head lulled to the side and eyes half open.

My attention was drawn to the open chest cavity and hypodermic needles piercing the woman's exposed heart. From everything I'd been told, I'd have to say the woman represented Junior's mother.

"I don't know," Marnie sang, teasing her sister, "She might have a couple cheesy tattoos by then."

"Good point," Riley agreed.

"If I got any tattoos, they would be classy." Trina waved her hand through the air. "You know, like a flower or dolphin or something."

We all gave her the same look. Somewhere in Miami, Chase was shaking his head.

"Don't ever say that shit to Chase," Riley shook her head and returned to her painting. "He'd slap the shit out of you."

Trina rolled her eyes. "Please, Chase loves me."

"No, he tolerates you."

I couldn't help but chuckle. I missed this. Being here with my friends, listening to the wind blowing through tall grass and the crackling fire. The Causegrove was the place my friends came to get away from the world. To me, it was home. One of the few places I could relax and seek solitude from the mess in my mind.

"Anyway, I'm much more interested in what your stepbrother's intentions are with our darling Shelby."

At least it used to be.

Stupid Trina and her big mouth.

"What?" Riley spun around, slamming her hands down on her hips. "What the hell is she talking about, Shell?"

"Nothing." I huffed out a sigh and glared at the sparkle in Trina's aqua eyes. She did this on purpose. I wouldn't answer her, so she outed me to Riley.

Touché Trina.

"I wouldn't call showing up at our school and punching Evan March 'nothing.'"

Sometimes I really hated Trina.

"That had nothing to do with me." It was a lie, but hopefully one Riley would buy.

"Uh huh?" The corner of Trina's mouth lifted, "Well, according to Chelsea, he practically told the whole school you were his, and hit Evan for touching you."

"Chelsea's full of bull." My hand swept through the air, trying to pass it off as nothing more than gossip. ""Everyone knows that."

"Hold up," Tico sat forward, resting his elbows on his knees. "Are we talking about Logan Hudson? Gorgeous god of a man?"

Trina nodded.

Tico's brow arched. "So, the player of Ashen Springs called our little Shelby his?"

"He sent her a piece of pie too. From *Mauves*."

How did she even find that out?

"And he showed up with your boyfriend at one of her practices."

Shut the hell up Trina!

"Micha knew about this!?" Riley growled and crossed her arms. "Okay Shell, what the hell is going on?"

"Nothing's going on."

That was a definite lie. Something was going on. Like the things he did to me last night. My mind kept replaying over and over, reminding me how he felt inside me.

His hot breath warming my skin while he grunted in my ear...

"Logan's just a pain in the ass."

A deep aching pain that throbbed every time I thought of him.

"Girl," Tico sang, clicking his tongue, "You're in trouble."

"Please." Just because he had pretty green eyes, a charming smile and smelled really good, didn't make him the epitome of masculine perfection. "He's not that great."

Who are you trying to kid?

Tico sighed and flopped back on the couch. "I'd eat the shit outta some pussy if it meant I got to just look at his dick."

"Right?" Trina agreed. "I'd pay to lick him."

Riley made a gagging noise. I was right there with her. Just thinking about Trina touching Logan made my blood boil. Which only pissed me off more, because why the hell should I care?

"Sorry girl," Tico sighed, "But that man is hot enough to turn me straight for a night."

"I told you, sis." Both Riley and I groaned at the big smile on Logan's face. We'd been so caught up in our conversation that we didn't hear him drive up. "I'm irresistible."

Logan looked over at Tico and gave him a playful wink as Parker walked by carrying a keg. I might've thrown up at the pink tint in Tico's cheeks if Micha and Silas didn't march in to join us.

"What are you doing here?" Riley growled at Micha, "This is girls' night."

Micha shot Tico a dirty look, "Doesn't look like girl's night."

Tico was the last person he needed to worry about. Even if he didn't bat for the other team, he wasn't the kind of guy my best friend would go for.

Not because he wasn't cute–Tico was adorable–but adorable wasn't exactly what women went for. Besides, his short stature was not going to help Riley's huge Napoleon complex.

"We brought a girl," Logan said, flashing his perfect white teeth.

That's when I noticed the blonde tip-toeing closer. My eyes rolled over her black silk dress and Jimmy Choo shoes. Hardly the kind of outfit for the Causegrove. Though I had to admit she was rocking it. Didn't so much as stumble on the rocky ground, and those had to be at least two inch heels.

"Bitchy Barbie." Riley's brow rose. "Seriously?"

"What the hell is this, Logan?" the girl huffed and crossed her arms.

I could see why she'd been dubbed Bitchy Barbie. This girl had the best resting bitch face I'd ever seen.

"It's a party," Logan sang, throwing his arms open wide.

"This is not a party." Bitchy Barbie carefully plucked something off the couch, curled her lip at it, and flicked it away. "It's reject day at the homeless shelter."

"Sorry babe," Tico snickered, "If you're looking for cocktails at the Plaza, you came to the wrong place."

The curl in her lip deepened. "Clearly."

"Stop complaining," Parker scoffed. "Think of it like camping."

"I don't camp."

"There's a shocker," he muttered.

"Everything's covered in dirt." She exhaled a puff of air and turned her unimpressed eyes Logan's way. "Where, exactly, am I supposed to sit?"

I don't know why, but it pissed me off that she expected Logan to cater to her. Maybe it was just because I didn't like snooty people. And this girl, whoever she was, was as pompous as they came.

"If you put a little more clothing on, it wouldn't be a problem."

I could feel the judgement in her cool glare as her gaze slowly swept over my black jeans and green shirt. "Oh honey, I don't dress down for anyone."

Admittedly, the shirt wasn't something I would normally wear, but for some reason the color called to me. I stole a quick glance at Logan's sparkling eyes.

Yeah, for some reason.

"Naomi doesn't dress up, either," Riley snarled.

Ah, this girl was Naomi. That made sense. Rye told me a lot about her, and so far, she'd lived up to every one of my meager expectations.

Naomi sneered at my best friend. "It's called class, honey. Something you clearly have none of."

"Hooker isn't a class," Rye scoffed, "I hope you're wearing underwear. I'd hate for the couch to catch something."

Normally I enjoyed my best friend's sarcasm, but Micha was staring at me. Arms crossed with a glare so cold it sent a shiver up my spine. I might've even moved in closer to Logan when he threw his arm over my shoulders.

"Micha and I need to talk to you."

I looked up at Logan and over to Micha, who I was pretty sure was currently contemplating my potential murder. Micha wasn't the only one who had death in his eyes. Riley was eyeing the arm Logan had draped around me.

"We have nothing to talk about." Whatever this situation was, I wanted no part of it.

Micha's booming voice disagreed. "Yes, we fucking do."

"Yeah," Rye loudly agreed. "Like why the hell is Logan touching you?"

"I did a lot more than touch her last night."

I'd never wished the ground would open up and swallow me more than when Riley and Trina's jaws dropped.

"It's not what you think."

"It's exactly *what* you think," Logan smirked. "Just not *how* you think."

Sweet God above, please give me the strength to not murder this man.

"Shelby?" Trina sang in an accusatory tone. "And here I was thinking you might die a virgin."

I rolled my eyes. "I am a virgin."

Right? I mean I still had my hymen, so technically...

"Depends on your definition of virgin," Logan pointed out.

Right now would be a great time for those secret teleportation powers to kick in.

"This is so not... I mean..." Riley's burning blue glare landed on me. "How could you let this happen?"

How could I let this happen? It wasn't like I'd asked for Logan's interest. If anything, I'd prayed it would go away.

"You should've told me. We said no secrets."

"No secrets. Really?"

At that moment, all I could think about was seeing my best friend laying in that hospital bed, and the lame excuse she gave me for it. "Okay then, what really happened to you and Mason?"

"I already told you, it was a car accident."

Right, cause you get bruises on your neck from car accidents.

"You can talk about this later, Mouse." Not once had Micha taken his eyes off me.

"Don't tell me what to do," Riley snarled at him. "She's my friend, not yours."

"This is more important."

"How could it be more important?" Her gaze shifted over to Logan. "If you helped him with some stupid fucking contract…"

Logan chuckled and tightened his hold on me. "I didn't need help for that."

"What?!" shrieked Riley.

Not sure why she was getting so worked up over a contract. My dad was a lawyer. Contracts were a good thing. They protected both parties.

"Micha…"

"It's done, Mouse. Deal with it. You and I need to have a talk," Micha added, pointing at me.

"No." Riley slapped his hand. "You are not pulling the same shit–"

"Jesus Christ, Mouse, this has nothing to do with the fucking contract," he roared down at her. "It's about our goddamn brother."

My eyes snapped up to his.

What?

I DIDN'T BELIEVE it at first. I mean, my mom with Louis Kessler? How laughable was that?

My mom was a country girl. Not the small town wearing cowboy boots type, but the competing in horse shows and sipping tea type. I swear dirt literally avoided the woman. Louis Kessler was… well Louis Kessler.

So, I called my mom, and guess what? Not only was it true, but she had a baby she gave up. I had an older brother! My mom. The Sally Mae, baking on weekends, proper southern girl, got pregnant at seventeen. Seven–friggin-teen!

She claimed she was too busy to talk and we'd discuss it later. Bull crap! This would get brushed under the rug and become another taboo subject in the Grace household. Just like my dad's gambling problem. After all, everything would be fine if you just smiled.

I threw my phone and dropped down onto the grass, letting tears burn angry streaks down my cheeks. Was I so fragile that people were afraid to tell me things? Didn't they think I could handle it?

Even my best friend, the one person I thought would never keep me in the dark, was hiding something from me.

That's what hurt the most. It was like Rye didn't trust me. After all the crap we'd been through, and she couldn't tell me what really happened to her. She didn't tell me about Micha, either.

Not until long after they started dating. Would she have let Micha tell me about our brother? Or would it just be something else to keep from me? A secret they all didn't think I could handle.

Riley always said we were all the same. No one was better than the next. But that wasn't true, because she treated me differently. They all did.

"Shell?" Riley stepped through the trees, invading my dark solitude. "Are you okay?"

Fan–freaking–tastic. Not that you care.

"I'm fine."

"Look at you," she flopped down beside me and brushed some of the wetness off my cheek. "You're not fine."

I didn't want her touching me. Didn't want her arm around me in some pitying version of comfort. Instead of pushing her away, I just hugged my knees and whispered, "Go away, Riley."

I really am pathetic.

"Come on, Shell," I could hear the tinge of pain in her words. I just didn't care. "Talk to me."

I snorted. *Talk to her? Yeah, right. Because she's been so forthcoming with me.*

"You shouldn't keep this stuff in," she said, giving me a gentle nudge. "Friends don't keep things from each other, remember?"

Because I was the one hiding crap.

"Don't make me get Trina."

She was really pulling out the big guns now. If she wanted to talk, fine. We'd talk!

"Alright Rye, why don't we start with what really happened to you."

"Shell…"

"Don't give me some crap about a car accident either," I cut her off before she could lie to me again. "People don't get bruises like that from car accidents."

"Yes they do. Bruises are easy to get."

"From car accidents?" I cocked a brow at her. "On their neck?"

"The seatbelt."

Funny how she couldn't look at me when she said that.

"Sure," I sighed and pushed off the ground. "Whatever you say."

"Shelby…"

"What, Riley?" I barked back at her, "Are you going to feed me another lie, because I'm not really in the mood. I'd rather spend my time drinking than listening to your bullshit."

Should've known she wouldn't just let me drown my sorrows.

"Don't," she said, grabbing my arm. "You shouldn't drink when you're upset."

"Relax, Riley, I'm not your mother," I snarled, tearing my arm out of her grasp and continuing on my way to the keg. "I'm not going to drive myself into a powerline."

Okay, that was a low blow.

Guilt or anger, I'm not sure which, allowed me to turn away from my best friend and head for the keg. Alcohol would help. Didn't need to think when I was drunk. I could almost taste the bitter beer on my tongue when Logan stepped out of the shadows.

"Do you mind?" I growled, pissed that he was in my way. "You're interrupting my date with a drink."

Or a dozen.

"Shelby…"

"Riley…" I sang back at her.

I tried to move around Logan, but he stepped in my way.

Prick.

"Where do you think you're going, sweetheart?"

"It's a party, right?" Screw him and his sweetheart. "I'm just joining in the festivities."

"That's not gonna happen."

Who the hell was he, thinking he could tell me what to do. Oh, that's right. Logan Hudson. The friggin king of everything.

"What's wrong, Logan? Worried someone will take advantage of me?" My eyes locked on Parker. He had the same playful glimmer in his gaze as he did the first time I met him. "Or that I'll let them?"

The version of Logan I'd met last night came back. I stood there watching his eyes darken and felt a deep sense of satisfaction fill my chest. Probably should've been scared.

He wasn't nice to me last night, but I didn't want nice. I needed to take my frustration out on someone. I wanted to fight with him. Craved the sting of his slap. Pain let me forget.

"You're treading a thin line, Cherry Pie."

Good. Let's cross that line, asshole.

"Whatever you say, Logan," I said, and shouldered past him. Fuck him and his stupid brow of disapproval.

The next thing I knew, my feet were lifted off the ground and I was thrown over his shoulder.

"Logan, put her down!" Riley shrieked.

"Go find your boyfriend, sis. I got this." The bastard's palm smacked down on my ass, making me cry out. I was still sore from last night, and that shit hurt.

"Fuck you, Logan," I hissed through clenched teeth while pounding my fists on his back.

"You don't want to keep pushing me, sweetheart."

If Logan felt my strikes, he didn't respond. Simply kept walking us deeper in the trees as I added more strength into each hit, hoping that one would cause him to release me.

It didn't.

The only response I got was a softly growled, "Just so you know, I'm keeping a mental tally of every time you hit me."

That made me stop. Something told me Logan held back last night. A theory I wasn't in a hurry to test. No matter how mad I was.

I sighed and tried to get comfortable, which was impossible when being carried caveman style. Shoulders were hard, especially when digging into your gut. Had a great view of his ass though, so it wasn't all bad.

I cocked my head at the design on his pocket, wondering if all jeans looked this good, or just his.

"Out of curiosity, would smacking your butt count against my tally?"

Logan's shoulders shook with his laugh.

"Baby, you can touch me any time you want." His grip on my backside tightened, fingers digging into my sore flesh. "Anywhere you want."

Anywhere? Because I was a little curious about one part. I mean, I'd felt it, but hadn't really seen it. Was it just as pretty as the rest of him? Could a dick be pretty?

I'd seen a few pornos and I didn't know if I'd call those dicks pretty. Intimidating, scary and big, maybe, but not pretty. Pretty just wasn't the right word for a dick.

I shook my head. That was the last thing I should be thinking about. Unfortunately, my body didn't agree.

The longer he carted me through the foliage, the deeper the growing need in my core got. I blamed it on his scent. All masculine and yummy.

Stupid Logan Hudson.

Was he taking me to his secret love den? I could picture it all silky and full of pillows. Like something out of one of those Egyptian movies. I snorted. It was probably more like the back of a dirty van. Still...

"Are you going to have sex with me?"

Shut up Shelby, don't give him ideas!

"It's not *if* I'm going to fuck you, sweetheart, it's when."

My brain was already far too focused on the hard muscles bulging under me to think of some witty retort. At least, that's what I told myself.

"If that's where you're taking me, you can turn around. I'm not doing *that* with you."

Even I didn't believe my own words.

"Keep telling yourself that, Cherry Pie," he snickered. "You and I both know I'll be balls deep in your pussy soon enough."

I grumbled a string of curses under my breath, because I was starting to think he was right.

He finally put me down when we broke through the treeline. My nose immediately scrunched at the heavy odor of sulphur in the air. I expected to see the sign for Ashen Springs hot springs, but we were nowhere near the top of the bluffs. Couldn't even see the top.

I could hear the geyser roaring from somewhere above us, but the giant rocky wall blocked my view of anything else. That's all there was. Rock in the front, with trees behind, and a small path in between.

If there was a serial killer in Ashen Springs, this is the kind of place I'd imagine him hiding the bodies. It was so far out of the way, no one would ever find it.

Heck, I grew up playing in this forest and I had no idea this place was here. I couldn't even see the small cave in the rock \side until Logan ushered me in it.

It was kind of sweet how gently he placed his hand on my head and helped me duck down. After the night I'd had, it was nice feeling cared for. But willingly going into a dark, confined space with Logan was probably not my best idea. Oh well, today was apparently the day for bad decisions. So I may as well go with it.

"Come on, Cherry Pie, it's just up here."

"Logan I'm not in the–" My breath hitched when I rounded the corner and entered a large cavern.

Everything was cast in a blue glow from phosphorescent plants growing across the top. I walked over to a patch of Chocolate Daisies and brushed my fingers over their soft petals.

Water cascading down the wall beside them bubbled into a small pool that had steam rising off it. It was all so beautiful, as if I'd stepped out of reality and right into a fairy tale. Every new place I looked there was something else to see, but it was the glint in the far left corner that caught my eye.

What I found was the last thing I expected to see. A 1955 Ford Thunderbird, complete with white wash tires. This was truly a thing of beauty, and sad at the same time.

She was sitting here, covered in dust and vines. Lost and forgotten. Not good enough to be cared for. The patches of rust alone were sacrilegious. I felt her pain. Almost cried when I ran my palm over the smooth roof.

Then I saw it.

The remains of a red and blue lighting bolt along the side.

Oh.

My.

God.

"Is this?"

"I think so." Logan came up behind me, wrapped his arms around my waist and rested his chin on my shoulder. "Isn't she beautiful?"

I scoffed out a snort. "Beautiful? She's a friggin legend."

As was her driver. Jumping Jim Kahuna. He was the whole reason we even had a street racing community. Jim didn't solve fights with harsh words or fists. He beat them on the track, and won every time.

Until that last race.

One fatal mistake. A wrong turn down the bluffs sent Jumping Jim careening over the edge. At least, that's what people said, but no trace of him or his car were ever found.

"How did this end up here?" I voiced out loud. It didn't make sense. She was in pretty much perfect condition. Almost like someone drove her here.

"I think someone was trying to hide her."

"Why?"

"Legends have a way of following you, sweetheart. Even the bad ones."

His words tugged at my heart. I glanced down at his arm, thinking about the scars I'd seen there. Scars that his own father had inflicted. My dad was a lying, cheating, gambler, but he'd never hurt me. Not like that. I was his star, after all.

I couldn't take him places if I couldn't run. Was that all I was to everybody? Someone who could do things for them? A way to make themselves feel better, without ever actually telling me anything?

I let out a deep sigh and ran my finger along the edge of the lighting bolt. "Do you ever think about running away?"

"You can't run from who you are, sweetheart."

I lifted my chin and looked over at him. "What if you don't know who you are?"

"Then you stop hiding," Logan breathed in my ear.

On the outside, I was a normal teenage girl. Always smiling and happy. But on the inside, I was slowly dying. Why was he the only person who saw that? It should be someone else, like Riley, or my mom. Not Logan friggin Hudson.

"I'm not hiding." I wriggled out of his arms and spun around. "You are."

He threw his head back and barked out a laugh, which only made me more angry.

"I know what you're doing with all those tattoos. Trying to pretend you're cool, when it's really just a mask for a sad little boy." I sang the last part with a snide head swing.

"Oo, vicious. I like it." Logan stepped in, forcing me to back up into the car. "Don't think you can hurt me with your snotty little comments, sweetheart. I. Own. This. Shit."

He was right. I don't know what he'd gone through, but I'm sure it was worse than anything I'd experienced. Had the scars to prove it. And what was so wrong in my life? People hid stuff from me? So what.

Who didn't have secrets, right? So why did it bother me so much? Why couldn't I shake the hollow throb in my chest? I tipped my chin up, meeting Logan's piercing gaze.

I couldn't make this feeling go away, but he could.

"You know," I purred, while sliding my hands up his chest. "There are many things we could be doing right now."

Logan cocked a brow. "What are you doing?"

I watched my finger glide over his black shirt, mesmerized by the way the soft fabric felt against the hard chiselled ridges underneath.

"What do you think I'm doing?"

He cupped my ass and pulled me, causing a shocked gasp to escape my parted lips.

"Watch yourself, Cherry Pie." I shivered as he ran his nose up my face and around the shell of my ear. "I will fuck you."

I clung to him, letting his warmth melt away the cold spikes pumping through my veins. The sting from his fingers digging in my flesh, his hot breath on my skin, and the hard muscles tensing beneath my palms. It all felt… right. Right now, in this moment, I was free.

"Maybe that's what I want."

"That's the fucking problem, Cherry Pie." In the blink of an eye, he flipped me over, folding my body across the hood. "You have no fucking idea what you want."

"And I suppose you do," I snarled over my shoulder. "Are you going to give me what I want?"

In a matter of seconds, Logan had my jeans and panties down around my ankles. The warm humid air hit my exposed flesh, cooling my fevered skin and making me shiver.

"Oh no, baby." He delivered a firm smack to my ass, causing me to curse and rise up on my tiptoes. "I'm going to give you what you fucking need."

God yes.

He leaned over, folding his hard body over mine and softly growled in my ear.

"You think you want nice."

I winced at the slight stab of pain when he roughly shoved a finger into my pussy. My body wasn't prepared for the intrusion. That didn't matter to Logan, he forced in another finger.

"But you really want to be used, don't you?"

I thought I wanted to be loved and cared for. Be someone's something special. Not a toy to be used. One pump of Logan's fingers told me otherwise.

Not only did my inner walls clench around him, but I could hear how wet I was. The sucking sounds that rang through the air as he finger fucked me were like a slap to the face. Each one, mocking me.

Squelch.

You like this.

Squish.

You want him.

Squelch.

You like being used by him.

I whimpered and shook my head.

"What's wrong, sweetheart," Logan growled. The vibration of his deep voice poured through my body, tingling across my skin and sending a shiver up my spine. "This what you wanted, isn't it?"

This shouldn't be turning me on, but it was. Every rough thrust of his fingers made me wetter. The evidence was trickling down my thighs. Logan was right. I needed this. Needed to feel that heady concoction of pain and pleasure that only he could give me.

I mewled and pushed back. My orgasm was right there, just out of my reach. A couple more thrusts and I'd be flung over the ledge.

And then, just as quickly as they came, his fingers were gone. Leaving me empty and wanting.

"Logan," I whined, lifting my head to look back at him, "Please–"

"Shut the fuck up!" he snarled, pushing my face back down into the hood. "You don't tell me when to fuck you." The sound of a zipper, followed by very masculine grunts. "I tell you."

Was he...

I tried to lift my head, but he had my hair fisted so tightly that every breath I took caused my scalp to scream. Laying there listening to him jerk off was doing strange things to my body.

Some sick part of me wanted to see it. To see *him*. My skin prickled with every grunt, while fat drops of wetness slid down my legs.

I felt Logan shudder as he roared out a "mother fuck." And hot, thick fluid hit my skin.

Feeling his cum glide down my ass and across my pussy was almost enough to send me over the edge.

Almost.

Logan's deep, heavy, panting breath rang in my ear, as his hand slid through the mess he'd made.

"You feel that, baby?"

God yes. And it felt amazing.

I whimpered and nodded, hoping he'd give me what I needed.

"That's all the cum you're gonna get tonight."

And then he was gone.

Chapter 15
Logan

I'm not sure what was happening. Lana showed up, Riley introduced her to Shelby, and then I think they were taken over by pod people. That, or I drank way too much.

"…oh my god, did you see…"

"…the red dress…"

"…he is so funny…"

"…and that ring…"

What language were they speaking? Because it sure as hell wasn't English. I should've fucked her. Why the fuck didn't I fuck her? She offered herself up on a silver fucking plater. I had her right where I wanted her, and instead of fucking her body, I fucked her mind.

Did I regret it? Fuck no. Cherry Pie needed to learn who was in charge. How was I supposed to know that I'd end up watching… well, I don't know what the fuck I was watching.

"…the grey dog…"

Laugh.

"…so many gloves…"

I glanced from one to the other and then down at the red Solo cup in my hand. Should've fucked her into a coma again.

Even Naomi was sucked into this black hole of confusion. Her eyes fluttered back and forth, trying to track the words flying through the air. Riley seemed pretty calm. Maybe this was normal for her?

I leaned over and whispered, "Do you understand this shit?"

"Well," she let out a huff of air and tipped her head, "Shell said something about a cat, I think?"

The little chick with glasses beside Riley shook her head. "I'm pretty sure it was a dog."

I recognized her from the tattoo parlor. Only chick I'd ever seen mouth Preston off. She was kind of cute. If her trampy twin was an indication of what was under those potato sacs she called clothes, then she was definitely fuckable.

Not my type, though lately I seemed to have a very particular type.

"No, it was definitely a bird." Parker's brows furrowed. "Or maybe a rat?"

"Ah," I breathed out a sigh. "So no one knows what's going on."

"Nope." Riley shook her head. "Not a clue."

Well, that was a relief. At least now I knew I wasn't going crazy.

"Don't you agree?"

It took me a second to realize Lana was talking to me.

"Um, sure?" I nodded, hoping she was talking about some kinky shit?

Shelby's mouth fell open. "I can't believe you're agreeing with her?"

I looked from the insult on Shelby's face, to the smile on Lana's, and shook my head.

That's it. I'm out.

No need to say anything. Within seconds, they were back at it again. Whatever *it* was. Honestly, I was a little scared.

Micha nodded at me when I walked over to the keg and refilled my cup.

"There's something wrong with your girl."

I leaned next to him and smirked. "At least I know she can hold her breath."

"Feel free to gag her," Micha grumbled.

My best friend did not like being ignored. Especially by Riley.

"Aww," I popped my bottom lip out, "Is someone lonely?"

"I should drag her ass in the car."

"Not happening." There was only one girl getting fucked in Betty, and it sure as fuck wasn't my sister. "Do that shit in your Jeep."

"I would," his eyes rolled to me, "If someone let me drive my damn self."

I nodded at the eyesore of a Volkswagen bug parked beside my Mustang. "You lost the right to drive when you let your girlfriend buy that piece of shit."

"Are you bitching about my car again?" Riley said, snatching a bottle of water off the table behind us. "It's not that bad."

Micha and I both cocked a brow. The fact that the rust bucket made it anywhere at all was nothing short of a miracle.

"Not that bad?"

"That's right," she huffed, crossing her arms.

My sister was a stubborn little thing. It took weeks to convince her to throw out her old ratty shoes. Duct tape did not make them 'perfectly fine.'

I wouldn't be surprised if she hadn't touched any of the new clothes in her closet. Ma did drag her to the salon every week though. I guess that could be counted as progress.

"Hey Silas!" I called to the angry fucker standing by her car. "Do me a favor and smack that rust bucket."

His lip curled at the faded yellow bug. "You want it to fall apart?"

"Just do it."

He shrugged, and slammed his palm down on the roof. A loud groan rang out and then the hood popped open.

"So you know," I said, throwing my thumb over my shoulder, "Cars shouldn't do that."

"So it has some glitches."

Glitches, really?

I didn't say another word, just walked over to her car and kicked the tire, turning the headlights on. "Would you call that a glitch?"

She rolled her eyes and rejoined the foreign alien language Shelby was still engaged in. I shook my head and leaned back on the yellow bug, not at all surprised when the horn blared.

Eventually my sister's car would be fine. Riley hadn't noticed the parts I'd upgraded. Doubted she ever would.

"Hey," Preston tipped his chin as he sauntered up and leaned next to me.

The only time I'd seen Preston come to high school parties was when he was in high school. And that was only because Ava dragged him along. Or someone there pissed him off. Which usually provided an entertaining night for me.

"Since when do you come to shit like this?"

His grey eyes landed on the small chick with glasses. "I have my reasons."

Ah, so that was the mystery girl.

For the first time since I met the girl, I really looked at her. A little plain for my tastes, and not the type I would've pegged Preston to be interested in. Then again, for all I knew, he just wanted to break the girl. Should've felt sorry for the frumpy little thing, but she brought this shit on herself.

"The sister looks like more fun."

"Pfft," he snorted, "Too much fun."

He had a point. The girl had her breasts pushed up against one guy, with her arm around another. Besides, why take a trip down the ride everyone's driven, when you could pluck the fruit yourself? Shelby laughed at something frumpy chick said and turned my way, cinnamon eyes sparkling with innocence.

Yeah, plucking the fruit was much more fun.

My gaze dropped to the red Solo cup sloshing in her hand. How many had she had? I told her not to fucking drink, and there she was, swaying on her fucking feet.

I wasn't the only one that noticed, either. Two motherfuckers in the corner were whispering and pointing at her. Fucking football players.

"Huh?" Preston slapped my arm and nodded at the crowd. "Check it out."

I looked over to see a scowl on Parker's face. Golden boy didn't seem to be having much fun. It didn't take me long to realize what had his panties in a bunch. He was staring directly at Lana.

More specifically, Brandon, who was definitely checking her out. Parker didn't like Brandon on a good day, but right now he looked ready to kill. Fucker wasn't mad though. He was jealous.

Interesting.

"Parker has a thing for Lana?"

Preston rolled his eyes, "He's been talking about her since we were kids."

"No shit." I cocked my head at Parker. "Why the fuck hasn't he gone for her?"

"Have you met our mother?"

Their mother was one of the co-founders of the National Freedom Movement. A group that fought for the empowerment of the rights and freedoms of true Americans. As long as they were the proper representation of their ideal race.

In other words, a bunch of racist and homophobic pricks. Headed up by the biggest cunt I'd ever met. Lillianna Whitley. Preston and Parker's mother.

A mother who would not be happy to find out her youngest son was not only bisexual, but also interested in someone who she'd refer to as 'the local colored girl.' If she was my mother, I'd have pushed her in front of a bus a long time ago.

"Does mommy know little bro likes to suck dick?"

"What do you think?"

That was a no.

Not surprising, considering Parker was the golden boy of the family. He was too concerned with what his parents thought. Fucker even went to a couple rallies with his mom. He hadn't gone to one in a while though. I scanned Lana's mocha complexion. Now I knew why.

"You tell him to go for her?"

"Course I did," Preston snorted. "Even offered to hold her down for him."

"Pfft. Pussy." Who gave a fuck what Mommy thought?

"That's what I said."

"We could lock them in a room together." I happened to know that Lana had a thing for the dingbat. Eavesdropping on my sister had it's advantages.

Preston cocked his head and lit a cigarette. "You got a room in mind?"

There were plenty of places to lock someone up in my house. Some, thanks to my old man, I had intimate knowledge of.

"There's that room in the basement?"

"With the Saint Andrews' cross?"

"That's the one."

Preston and I may have had some fun with a couple girls down there. None recently. He didn't like it when I broke his toys.

"Still got the restraints."

I nodded and sparked up my own smoke. "Just reinforced the welds."

"Alright, you take golden boy. Prick doesn't trust me. I got the girl."

Parker didn't trust his brother because he knew the asshole.

"Deal," I said, watching Shelby's hips sway as she sauntered over. Mischief curled her lips and glinted in her eyes.

What are you up to, Cherry Pie?

"Just so you know," she sang, "I didn't need you to finish me off."

The corner of my mouth lifted. "Is that right?"

"That's right." She was obviously drunk, slurring her words and swinging her hand around before she dropped her finger on my chest. "All I needed was this finger."

Fuck, that was hot.

"This finger?" I said, grabbing her wrist and sucking her finger into my mouth, groaning when her sweet essence hit my tongue.

She even tasted like fucking cherries.

Shelby's pouty pink lips parted, releasing an exasperated gasp. "Logan..."

She argued, but didn't fight. Just stood there staring as I wrapped my tongue around her finger, sucking off every last drop. Next time, I'd get it right from the source.

"She's drunk," Preston muttered.

I rolled my eyes his way and popped her finger out of my mouth. "Your point?"

"I am not drunk." Shelby glanced down at her cup with her brows furrowed. "Where did my drink go?"

Preston gave me an 'I told you so look'.

Alright, she was trashed. While I didn't like it, I couldn't help but notice that she came to me. Not one of the other fuckers eyeing her. Me.

My moment of self satisfaction was tamped down when a Sedan pulled up and four guys piled out. Shelby's attention was drawn off me to the biggest asshole strutting up to the keg.

I pulled her in to me and softly growled in her ear, "Are you seriously eye fucking another guy in front of me?"

"Exactly why I won't let mine drink," Preston muttered. His eyes landed on frumpy girl, who turned stark white and quickly averted her eyes.

I might need to take some tips from Preston.

I wasn't the only one sizing up the newcomers. Micha stood against one of the stone walls, watching them. As soon as our eyes met, he tipped his chin, drawing my attention to the blue ribbons proudly displayed on their chests.

Well, that explained why they were walking around with their shoulders back and heads high. Like they were something fucking special.

Preston slapped my arm. "You see that."

"Yeah, I see it." I nodded at Silas and down to the blonde in my arms, who I think might've passed out. "Didn't know your mom had a rally tonight."

Preston shrugged. He didn't talk much to his parents when he was a kid. Now their relationship was virtually non-existent.

Silas came over and shook his head. "Is she passed out?"

"I think so," I said, handing her over and shifting my eyes to the group of guys. One of whom was headed straight for Lana. "There's trouble on the horizon. Might want to round up the rest of the girls."

These guys were going to push buttons. None of us responded well to that, and we would never put our girls in danger. Naomi included.

Silas carried Shelby away as Preston and I watched one of the jerks throw his arm around Lana's shoulders.

"Hey there, pretty lady."

I shook my head. Funny how all these assholes went right for the forbidden fruit.

Lana frowned at the ribbon on his chest. "Not interested."

"Don't be like that, baby. I know how your kind likes it."

This guy was asking for it.

Lana's brow rose. "My kind?"

"Jungle bunnies."

"Yeah," she grumbled, hazel eyes blazing up at him. Little Lana had some spunk. "Once again, asshole, not interested."

This guy didn't like her attitude. I could hear his teeth grinding from here.

That's right Lana, don't take his shit.

"A black bitch like you should be honored to be with someone like me."

Gotta say, I was kind of curious how Lana would handle this. Except she didn't get a chance. Riley came flying out of nowhere and nut-punched the bastard.

"She said not interested, asshole!"

His face turned purple and he keeled over, making me snicker. I knew from personal experience how hard my little sister could hit.

My amusement died the second his friends walked up behind him. Which was when Parker sauntered over, placing his hand on the girl's shoulders.

"I think you guys should leave."

"And who's going to make us?" the one with black hair sneered.

"Me, prick," Riley said, holding up her fists.

The one with blue eyes huffed out a snicker. "Go figure the cholo would team up with the fag."

Micha beat me there.

"Leave," his voice boomed over the crowd, "Now!"

While the rest of us surrounded them, Silas rounded up the girls. Naomi bitched, Lana argued, and Riley fought. He ended up having to toss her over his shoulder. The only one that didn't complain was Shelby. She just stared, shell-shocked, and let Silas steer her away.

That's my Cherry Pie.

"Last chance," Micha growled, drawing my attention back to the matter at hand.

Parker cracked his knuckles. "I'd listen to him."

"We don't take orders from fags."

I didn't know whose mouth that spewed from, I was too busy eyeing up the big guy who had yet to say anything. He was ready to go, shoulders rolled back and forearms flexing. That fucker was mine.

"You might want to watch what you say to this one," I said, keeping my eyes locked on my target while I tipped my head at Parker.

"Why? You going to shut me up?"

"No," I smirked at Preston who was leaning against a wall behind them, smoking, "I'll leave that privilege to his brother."

They all slowly turned around and one muttered out a curse before Preston flicked his smoke at one and lunged.

It was on after that.

I WIPED the blood off my hands and followed Parker in the door. "Fuckers didn't put up much of a fight."

It was kind of disappointing how quickly that big bastard went down. Didn't stop me from beating on him. Shelby wouldn't find him so pretty now.

"Where the fuck did your brother go?" Micha asked Parker.

Micha and I shared a look. Unsurprisingly, Preston went after the prick that called his brother a fag. The last time we saw them, Preston was dragging him off. Meaning he'd probably never be seen again, and if he was, no one would recognize him.

When we rounded the corner, we all stopped. Riley and Naomi were waiting for us with their arms crossed and feet tapping. The fact that they weren't snarling rude comments at each other was disturbing enough, but when they both turned to Micha, I damn near burst out laughing.

"What the hell, Micha!" Riley shrieked.

"You think you can just have Silas take us away?" Naomi agreed.

Parker slapped him on the back. "Good luck with that," and walked out of the room.

Considering he hadn't shut up about the guy that hit on Lana, my guess was that was who he was going to find.

Speaking of which...

"Where's Shelby?"

I didn't notice Silas standing in the corner until I heard his voice.

"I dropped her drunk ass in the other room on the couch."

Riley swung her finger up in my direction. "You stay away from her."

"Blow me," I said, and spun around to find my girl.

I found her right where the angry bastard said she'd be. Sprawled out on Ma's favorite couch, snoring away. My dick didn't care about the trickle of drool running out of the corner of her mouth, or the fucked up way her leg was thrown over the back of the couch. Right now she was at her most vulnerable, and it was so easy to corrupt vulnerable.

The only thing that held me back was the quiet way she whimpered. That, and for some fucked up reason, I wanted her fully aware when I took her. I didn't just want to tear through her innocence, I wanted to see the look in her eyes when I imbedded myself in her soul.

I sighed and bent over to scoop her up in my arms. This giving a fuck shit sucked ass.

"Logan?" she mumbled out a whimper and wrapped her arms around me.

I kissed the top of her head, inhaling the light vanilla scent of her hair. "Yeah baby, it's me."

My chest tightened at the sight of this beautiful angel in my arms, and that's when I knew I was fucked.

The next morning it was a fucking chore to get out of bed. Half the night I was up holding Cherry Pie's hair while she yakked what I was sure was the last three months of food from her stomach.

I'd be having a chat with her about that later. She'd be lucky if I didn't slap the shit out of her. Trust me, I was fucking tempted, but the smell of Rosy's omelets lured me away. I didn't even take the time to brush my hair or throw on a shirt.

I yawned and headed down the stairs. The green garland with little red bows decorating the railing told me Ma had started decorating for Christmas. Since Riley was here, she was really excited for it this year. It was hard not to dampen her spirits.

I didn't have the same happy fun family memories other people did. Christmas with my old man was just another day of blood and pain. Some years there was less blood, but there was always pain. Mostly for Ma. I didn't understand why she felt the need to bake cookies and hang ornaments.

Rosy gave me a strange look when I walked into the kitchen. "Good morning, Mr. Logan."

Rosy wasn't used to seeing me like this. Usually when I came down, I was dressed and ready to go. Today, I didn't even bother to get dressed. I was still in my sweats.

I stretched and scratched the back of my head. "Morning, Rosy. Something smells good."

"I hope you're hungry." She smiled and slid a plate piled with food on the island.

My mouth watered as I flopped down on one of the stools. "You read my fucking mind."

That earned me a dirty look. Rosy was the closest thing I had to a grandma. She helped Ma raise me. Tucking me in at night, and scolding me when I got out of hand. Not that it did her any good. She still tried though. More than I could say for some.

"There's plenty for your friends. Make sure they eat."

I smiled and loaded my fork with a pile of steaming eggs. "Who could turn down your cooking?"

"I could."

My hand paused, holding the food inches away from my mouth.

No fucking way.

"Am I in the wrong house? I could've sworn Logan Hudson lived here." I turned to see a petite blonde in three inch heels standing in the doorway. "But he's far too full of himself to ever look that messy."

A slow smirk spread across my face. "You like messy."

"Maybe my tastes have evolved," Ava said, placing a hand on her cocked hip. "I am a college girl now."

I scoffed out a snicker. If Ava Whitley evolved into anything, it would be world domination.

She stood there for a second, trying to look serious, but she couldn't stop her perfectly painted lips from twisting. "Well, are you going to just sit there, or come and hug me?"

"Okay," I said, slipping off the stool to wrap my arms around her tiny body. "But if your brother hits me again..."

She tipped her chin up. "Preston hit you?"

"No," I snorted and headed back to my food. "Preston doesn't give a shit who you fuck."

Parker on the other hand... Let's just say the 'I fucked your sister' comment worked quite well on him. In my defense, Ava came to me. Every guy in town was too afraid of Preston to take a swing at his twin, and she was tired of the forced celibacy role.

She knew I wouldn't give a fuck what either of her brothers thought. On a side note, the 'I fucked your mom' shit worked on Silas as well.

Rosy's brown eyes locked on Ava as she sauntered around the island. Watching every move she made.

Most people who knew Ava did the same. She was just as unstable as me, if not more so. Ava, however, just smiled brightly and plucked a piece of bacon off one of the plates.

"Your pretty eyes don't fool me." Rosy swung a wooden spoon through the air, like she was banishing a demon. Not too far off, considering who she was talking to. "I see the evil in you."

"Admit it," Ava batted her eyelashes innocently, "You missed me."

Rosy marched out of the room, shaking her head, while muttering Spanish under her breath.

"Where's the love, Rosy?" Ava called out after her.

I snickered and dug into my food. If she thought Rosy's reaction was bad, wait until Micha got up. Out of all of us, Micha liked her the least.

Almost as if on cue, a loud voice boomed behind me. "Oh for fuck sakes. Who let you in here?"

"I missed you too, Mikey."

Micha pointed at her. "Don't start with that shit."

Ava gave him the nickname in the second grade. He hated it. Can't say I blamed him. Every time she said it, I was reminded of that cereal commercial. 'Mikey likes it'.

Micha sighed and sat down on the stool next to me. "You could've warned me."

"Where'd the fun be in that?" I said through a mouthful of eggs.

"As you can see," Ava waved her hand at me, "He's too busy stuffing his face to do anything else."

"What else is new," Micha grumbled.

Not my fault if they couldn't enjoy good food. Shelby should be down here enjoying this shit. I doubted there was anything left in her stomach after last night. I didn't want to wake her up though. She had a rough night and needed her sleep.

My brows furrowed at my thoughts. Why the fuck did I care? Shelby was in *my* bed. A place no other girl had been before. She should be servicing me.

Why the fuck did I put her in my bed? And more importantly, why did I like knowing she was up there right now?

I dropped the fork on my now empty plate and looked at Micha and Ava, who were both staring at me with weird looks. Did I miss something?

"What?"

Ava dropped her eyes to my plate. "Did you even taste it?"

"When's that last time you ate?" I rolled my gaze over her tiny form, "And bird food doesn't count."

Micha snorted. "She's a carnivore if I ever saw one."

"Leave Ava alone." Ma walked into the room and dropped a box on the floor. More Christmas ornaments I assumed from the jingling. "She's a sweet girl."

"Thank you, Mrs. Hudson," Ava sang sweetly.

Micha and I both rolled our eyes.

"Logan, honey, I don't want to alarm you," Ma leaned in and added in a hushed voice, "But Riley's friend is asleep in your room."

"I know. I put her there."

I realized my mistake the second I saw Micha's smile.

"Wait…" Ava's grey eyes lit up. "*You* took a girl to your room?"

"She's mine."

This must be what Riley meant by word vomit. I could practically see the grandbabies sparkling in Ma's eyes. Funny thing was, it didn't bother me.

"By mine, you mean…"

Micha answered Ma for me. "Same way Riley's mine."

That's when the smile fell off Ma's face.

"You got a contract for her?" I hated that sad look in her eyes. "Logan, you promised."

"I promised I wouldn't use her family against her." I got up and walked around the island to drop my plate in the sink. "I didn't."

"But you still got a contract."

"Yes, Ma," I sighed. "I don't make the rules. If you have a problem with it, take it up with Lou."

I'd never been more happy to see my stepsister than I was at that moment. Riley walked in the kitchen, sporting a Minnie Mouse t-shirt, pink shorts, and a scowl. She did not appear happy to see a crowd of people in the kitchen.

Not that I was surprised. My sister wasn't a morning person, and judging by the way her black hair was sticking up, she'd just rolled out of bed.

Her lip curled when her blue eyes landed on Ava. "I hope Bitchy Barbie recruited a new minion, because I swear to God, Logan, if this is another member of the skank squad, I'll gouge your eyes out with a fork."

Ava threw her head back and laughed. "I like this one."

"Don't worry," I said when Riley turned her glare on me, "I haven't fucked this one in years."

Riley muttered out an incoherent response and headed straight for the coffee pot.

I'm not sure what was more amusing. The dirty looks Riley was giving me, or how Micha was eyeing Ava. He wanted to tell her to stay away from his girl, but saying anything would be like dangling meat in front of a feral dog.

Ava was already getting ready to pounce and my sister tended to do the opposite of what she was told.

Before Ava could make her move, we were interrupted by a ruckus out in the hall.

"Go fuck yourself, Parker!" Lana's shrill voice cut through the air. "You think you can pay me off."

"Calm down, *Koshecha*."

Ava and I shared a glance and then darted across the room to see what was going on. Neither of us was shy about spying. Had to get our amusement somewhere.

Lana stormed towards the door with Parker hot on her heels. Deep lines of anger were etched in her forehead and I could see her teeth clenching from here.

This should be good.

"Don't tell me to calm down," she snarled, while snatching her sweater off the hanger.

Parker rolled his eyes. "I don't know what you're so broken up about."

For some reason, that really seemed to piss Lana off. She spun around and slapped him across the face, causing both Ava and I to silently grimace.

Damn, she got him good. His face twisted to the side. He had just enough time for shock to register in his eyes at seeing his sister, before Lana stuffed a wad of bills in his mouth.

"Choke on it," she spat, and marched out the door, slamming it behind her.

He spit out the money stuffed in his mouth and tipped his head. "Ava?"

"Little brother," Ava tsked and leaned against the doorframe. "What did you do?"

Before I opened my eyes, I knew two things. One, I wasn't in my room. This bed was way too comfortable to be mine. And two, I drank way too much last night. My head pounded so hard it hurt to open my eyes. And then came the problem of trying to focus.

My eyes were not cooperating. Lucky for me my feet worked just fine, though. I don't what was a bigger relief, making it to the bathroom before my bladder exploded, or recognizing said bathroom.

Thank God, I was just in Rye's room.

Feeling a little better about my choices last night, I walked over to the sink to wash my hands. It wasn't until I started brushing my teeth—my mouth tasted like ass—that I noticed all the stuff on the counter. Various bottles of hair gel, cologne and other men's products.

With the toothbrush in my mouth and mint exploding on my tongue, I glanced over at the other side. A brush, a bottle of leave-in conditioner, and a sink. Nothing else. I didn't come from Riley's room. I came from Logan's!

Crap!

I slowly glanced down to see the shirt Logan was wearing last night covering me down to my bare legs.

Double crap!

What the hell did I do last night? I remembered the Causegrove, Logan saying something to me, and that was it.

Wait... there was something warm and wet on my finger. His mouth!

Everything came flooding back at once. My fight with Riley, Jumping Jim's car, and me passing out on Logan. Suddenly my pounding head wasn't the problem. My mind started spinning, unsure what to focus on. The older brother I didn't know I had, or what may have happened with Logan last night.

Did I sleep with him? I didn't feel any different, and I still had my panties on. Logan didn't strike me as the type to re-dress a girl. He wouldn't pass up uninhibited access. Then again, if he got what he wanted, why would he need more? Everyone knew Logan Hudson didn't do return visits. At least that's what he told Riley. I needed to get out of here.

But then again...

I looked over at the open door I came through. Riley and I had always been curious what his room looked like. We'd tried to sneak a peek a couple of times, but he never let us get more than a glimpse.

Riley thought he had some secret sex dungeon in there, with hand-cuffs and whips and stuff. Honestly, I wouldn't be surprised if he did. I couldn't pass up this opportunity. I mean, he did put me in there, so...

The room I saw was not the room I expected. Well, except for the massive circular bed that took up the middle of the room. It looked like something out of a harem, with piles of pillows and black silk sheets.

The soft burgundy duvet matched the rest of the room. Everything was the same deep color with black embellishments. Including the rug on the floor at the foot of the bed.

The dresser, wardrobe and headboard were all made from a dark mahogany wood, and had intricate carvings of the moon's different phases. To the left was a shelf with model cars. Some looked like they were put together by a child, while others were carefully detailed. Right down to tiny scratches on the chrome bumpers.

Next to that was a crescent shaped bar with three stools, and across the room from that was a large poster of a Porsche 916 that took up half the wall, and an open closet door, with rows and rows of clothes. The room was beautiful and huge. Fitting, I guess. How else would Logan's big head fit through the door?

My eyes landed on a single pink rose laying on the dresser. There was a glass of water, two pills and a note next to it.

Cherry Pie,
These will help your head.

Ps, we will be talking about your drinking.

I ROLLED MY EYES. Leave it to Logan to turn something sweet ominous. Didn't stop me from smiling when I touched the rose's soft petals though.

You're falling for his shit.

Shaking away the voice, I eyed the pills. Should I trust them? I was in Riley's house, and her dad was the sheriff. Logan might have an ego, but he wasn't stupid.

I sighed and quickly swallowed the pills before I changed my mind. At this point, I didn't really care where relief came from. Every breath I took made my head throb.

After that, I crawled back in the bed, figuring it would be okay to give the pills time to kick in. I was wrong. Logan was everywhere, warming my body and filling my lungs. He lingered on the tip of my tongue, like some bad aftertaste. Okay, it wasn't bad. More like delicious, but still...

That's when I should've left. Instead, I cuddled into the warm sheets and buried my nose in the pillows. Content to get lost in Logan's cool, masculine scent.

The boy was infuriating as heck, but goddamn did he smell good. And he had style. The shirt I was wearing was so soft, it made sleeping in a bra comfortable. I could wear his clothes all day. Who cared if they were two sizes too big?

Snap out of it, Shelby!

I shot up with my brows furrowed. What the hell was wrong with me? Logan changed my clothes and put me in his bed. I should be slapping him, not snuggling up in his friggin' pillow. My nose tingled as I stared at said pillow.

But he smells so good.

"No," I growled, slapping the temptation away and getting off the bed.

I definitely had to get out of here. Problem was, I couldn't find my clothes. I did find something else though. Sitting on the top shelf of his wardrobe was a small silver bullet–let's not talk about the other stuff I saw in there.

I eyed the tiny dent on the bottom of the bullet next to the switch. One night when I was playing with mine, Mom came into my room. I tossed it before she could see, which is how it got the dent.

That son of a...

I snatched the bullet up and stormed out of the room.

Riley met me at the bottom of the stairs. "Hey Shell," her brows furrowed as her eyes roamed over my unwanted attire, "Everything okay?"

Seeing her face brought a twinge of guilt to my heart. I'd said some pretty horrible things to her last night, but I could deal with that right after I shoved my foot up Logan's ass.

"Where's Logan?"

"He's in the kitchen. Why?"

"Because I'm gonna kill him," I muttered, continuing my angry march.

When I rounded the corner and saw him sitting there, my fist tightened around the bullet. The sparkle in his bright eyes as he talked with Parker, Micha and some small blonde girl, pissed me off even more. This bastard invaded my life, and here he was laughing with his friends. Fuck him.

I stormed over there and slammed the bullet down on the counter, not caring about the loud echo that silenced their chatter.

"Did you take this from my room?"

Asshole sat back and smirked. "Hey Cherry Pie, sleep well?"

"I think you're cool and all Shelby," Parker said, "But most people keep the things they do in the bedroom private."

"Oh, grow up," I growled, turning my glare on him, "Everybody fucks themselves."

Logan tipped his head at Parker. "She's got you there."

"Yeah," the blonde agreed, "I fucked myself last night."

"Jesus Christ, Ava!" Parker called out, "No one wants to hear that shit."

"No, little brother, *you* don't want to hear that shit."

Parker sighed and pinched the bridge of his nose, while Micha grumbled, "That's an image I didn't need."

"I don't know," Logan sat back and swung his gaze Micha's way, "She's pretty good with her hands."

"Hey!" Parker barked out. "That's my sister!"

His reaction just made Logan smile. "Yeah, but she's not mine."

Oh my god!

"Hey, I asked you a question," I yelled, slamming my palm down on the counter next to the bullet. "Did you take this from my room?"

Logan looked at my toy and then back up at me. "Yes."

Smug bastard didn't even deny it.

"So you admit it?"

He shrugged and took a sip of what I assumed was coffee.

"This is mine!"

"No, Cherry Pie," his green eyes locked on mine, "Anything that touches your pussy is mine."

My mouth fell open. *He did not just say that.*

"You know what?"

"What?" He challenged back.

I didn't say anything, because what could I say? How did one respond to having their personal enjoyment toy stolen? It wasn't exactly something you called the cops about. I could imagine the report. One item taken. Small silver bullet used for masturbation purposes.

I'm sure Ashen Springs police department would make it a high priority. I couldn't even use it as proof Logan broke into my house. Riley's dad knew my mom, and that was a conversation I did not want to have. Didn't mean I had to sit here and take Logan's shit.

"Where are my clothes?" I demanded.

Logan sat back and slowly raked his gaze over me. I hated how my body shivered in response. Bastard didn't have to touch me to caress my curves. He could fuck me with his eyes alone.

"I like your current outfit."

Screw him. I didn't need my clothes to leave.

"You know what, keep them." I leaned in, going nose to nose with him, "You can jerk off to them tonight."

Parked coughed back a laugh and Micha shook his head, while Ava pointed at me and said, "I like this one, too."

Good for her, I thought as I spun around, but Logan grabbed my wrist before I could take a step.

He pulled me in and growled in my ear, "You're not going anywhere in my shirt."

"You want your shirt? Fine." I ripped my arm out of his grasp, pulled the soft fabric over my head, and tossed it at him. "Take it."

"Fuck me," Parker hissed.

Micha sucked in a breath, "Goddamn."

"I'd fuck her," Ava added.

Logan shot them all a dirty look, which made me smile as I turned and walked away. Riley would've died of embarrassment walking around in her bra and panties. I didn't care. It was no different than a bikini, and I knew I looked good. I just didn't let it go to my head like some green eyed assholes.

"Where the fuck do you think you're going Cherry Pie?"

"Home."

"Not like that, you're not."

Was it wrong that the harsh tone in his deep voice made my blood sing?

"Watch me." *Prick.*

Micha snickered. "Looks like Mouse isn't the only stubborn one."

"She's not going anywhere," Logan confidently stated.

Fuck him. Fuck Micha. Fuck them all. I was going to walk out that door with my head held high and they could all kiss my lily white ass. The jangle of keys stopped me dead in my tracks.

"Might need these, sweetheart."

Son of a bitch.

I spun around to see a familiar pink pom pom key chain dangling from Logan's finger. Whatever remained of my headache was burned away by the rage rolling through my system. Suzie Q was my baby. I rebuilt her myself. No one drove her, especially not him!

"Don't worry, I didn't drive her back," Logan's lips tipped up. Bastard knew I wouldn't want him anywhere near her, "Micha did."

Well, that was better. Micha was at least responsible. Still…

I thrust my arm out, holding my palm up and marched forward. "Give me those."

"You want them?" Logan smirked as he hooked his thumb in the waistband of his grey sweats and held them open. "Go get them," he challenged, and dropped my keys down his pants.

For the second time that morning, my jaw dropped.

"And that's our cue to leave." Micha stood up and walked out.

Ava's eyes gleamed as she rested her elbows on the counter. "I can't not look."

Parker decided to follow Micha and opt out of our showdown, dragging Ava behind him, despite her verbal objections.

I stood there in a state of shock as everybody left. I knew Logan had a big ego, but I didn't think he'd be so brazen. Honestly, I wasn't sure how to proceed. If I went in after them, I'd be playing right into his game. I watched him lean back, resting his elbows on the island behind him, and inwardly smiled.

Maybe he'd be playing into my game?

I sauntered over to him, swaying my hips a little. Logan's green gaze watched my every move. Rolling over my breasts, around my hips, down my legs, and back up again.

I'd be lying if I said I wasn't eye-fucking him too. His sculpted torso got more defined with each step I took. The tattoos somehow emphasized every hard muscle. I suddenly got the appeal of grey sweats.

Then again, what wouldn't look good on this man? He could probably rock the shit out of hot pink track pants. Hell, I'd still want to lick him if he was in a skirt.

Focus, Shelby!

"You think I won't go after them?" I tore my eyes off his abs to meet his intense gaze.

He arched a daring brow. "Go ahead."

I leaned in close enough to feel his breath warm my mouth, and flattened my palms on the counter behind him.

"I'll do it."

"No one's stopping you, sweetheart."

He was calling my bluff. He knew it and I knew it. Other girls might've backed down. Give him what he wanted and let him win.

Well, I wasn't the meek timid thing he thought I was. Sexuality didn't scare me. I wasn't embarrassed of my body, and I sure as hell wasn't going to shy away now. So what if I touched him? It was just a dick, right?

Wrong.

It wasn't just a dick.

It was Logan Hudson's dick, and he was ready for me.

I slipped my hand under his waistband, gasping when my fingers grazed the smooth hot head of his very erect cock. That's when Logan pounced, seizing a handful of my hair as he crashed his lips down on mine.

I fought, struggling to pull away, but one growl and a tug on my hair had my lips parting enough for him to thrust his tongue in my mouth. Logan Hudson didn't just kiss me, he claimed me. Pulling me deeper into that dark pit of sin with every drop of his sweet, smoky taste.

I could feel my mind slipping away as my body melted, and knew my soul wouldn't be far behind. So I did the only thing my befuddled mind could think of. I wrapped my fingers around his thick shaft and squeezed.

"Fuck," Logan groaned, dragging my bottom lip through his teeth, "That's it baby, jerk me."

He yanked my head to the side and slid his hot tongue up my neck. I shouldn't like the rough way Logan used me, but I did. The tiny pricks of pain tingling across my scalp shot straight to my core.

My hand continued to move along his hard shaft, reveling in the silky feel of his skin. That's when I knew I was done. I wanted Logan Hudson. I couldn't deny it anymore. And neither could my mouth.

"Logan, I need…"

"Tell me what you need, baby," he purred in my ear.

My mind was gone. I didn't notice he'd stood up until my back hit the island, let alone figure out how to voice what my body was asking for.

"Tell me," he demanded, pressing in on me.

One word left my lips. "You."

A primal growl rang through the air and the next thing I knew, my feet were lifted off the ground as I was slammed down on the island. My hand immediately missed the feel of him. I sat up and whimpered my objection, but Logan had other things in mind.

He gave me a devilish grin and pushed me back down. "It's my turn, Cherry Pie."

That was the only warning I got before he pulled my legs apart and dove between my thighs, wrapping his mouth around my clit and sucking me through my panties. Pleasure shot through me, making my eyes roll to the back of my head. If I thought his fingers felt good, they were nothing compared to his mouth.

"So fucking sweet," he growled, sliding his tongue across me while nipping at that throbbing bundle of nerves.

I openly moaned, and somewhere in the back of my head a little voice warned me that someone might hear. But the wrongness of what we were doing, and the possibility of being caught, only made me wetter.

I wanted it. Wanted to give in to that dark part of my soul. So, I did. I burrowed my fingers in Logan's hair and stopped fighting it. For once, I let go and let myself just feel.

It was wrong.

Dirty.

And freeing.

The only regret I had was the scrap of fabric between his mouth and my flesh. But Logan had that covered. With one loud growl, he tore my panties away and really ate me. He dove down and feasted on my flesh like a starved man. Thrusting his tongue in my opening and fucking me with his mouth, while sucking on my clit.

No book or porn had prepared me for the intensity of the ecstasy rolling through me, and it quickly became too much. I whimpered and tried to move away, which only spurred Logan on.

He dug his fingers into my hips and pulled me back. I'm not sure if it was his demanding touch, or the shivers of pain that threw me over the edge. But all I could do when waves of bliss seized my body, making my back bow, was pray my heart wouldn't give out.

And Logan didn't stop there, he continued to lap up my juices faster than I could produce them. Each swipe of his tongue tensing my muscles and reminding me of the orgasm that nearly took my life. At least that's what it felt like.

Afterwards I lay there limp, praying that he wasn't going to force another one out of me.

"After the shit you pulled, I should eat you all day." He kissed my inner thigh and I whimpered. I couldn't take any more. "Are you done fighting me?"

Was I done fighting him? Yes. Really, what was my other choice? Death by orgasms?

I frowned and nodded.

"Say it," he demanded. "Say you're mine or I'll fuck you with my mouth again."

He didn't need to tell me twice.

"I'm yours."

"Look at me when you say it."

When I finally pushed my tired body up and met his intense stare, I saw it. The seriousness shining in his eyes caused my breath to hitch. This wasn't a game to him. When he said he wanted to keep me, he meant it. Logan Hudson, the demon of sin and lust, wasn't going to stop until he had my soul.

I was so fucked.

About fucking time she admitted it. It took a bit to get Shelby to say it while looking at me, but two more orgasms and she was screaming it to the heavens. Just to make sure she got the point, I gave her another, and then left her there a sopping mess.

Let's see her question me again.

Gotta say, the last thing I expected her to do was rip my shirt off and prance around in her underwear. Parker and Micha both got a punch for that. I would've given Ava one too, but she probably would've stabbed me for it. Then I would've had to stab her, and Parker would've got involved. That was a mess I didn't have time for.

I leaned against my Mustang and lit a smoke. Ma would like this place. It was littered with fucking flowers. She spent half the damn day out in her garden. I kept telling her we had people for that, but she insisted on doing it herself.

She'd also like the fountain they had out front. Fuck, I liked this fountain better. It was that simple three tiered shit. No happy cherub trying to convince everyone that the people inside weren't completely fucked up. Pretty sure the big sign saying, *'Cedarbrea addiction clinic'* would give that lie away.

Let's get this show on the road.

I flicked my butt and sauntered through the sliding glass doors. Micha would cringe at the ding they made announcing my arrival. Fucking parents, they fucked us up more than anyone else. Sometimes I wondered what Micha would be like if his mom didn't drive into that lake, or if Riley's never took that first drink.

They weren't the only ones shaped by the mistakes of their parents. Parker's mother was a racist cunt that used her youngest son as her shining beacon of white male success.

Silas's whole family had sticks shoved so far up their asses, they tasted wood when they coughed. And then there was my old man... The only one of us unaffected by our parents' crap was Preston, and that was only because he didn't give a shit.

Fuck sakes-, Mase was in rehab because he'd rather fill his veins with poison than deal with the reality of his genetics. Last time I was here, Mase chewed me out for not telling him he was my brother. Then I chewed him out for even acknowledging that shit.

The Kessler name gave him a hall pass. Lou might be an uptight prick, but he was a good dad. He loved his boys. No amount of drugs or alcohol could make me forget how my old man loved me.

"I hope you're here to visit someone."

I smirked down at the receptionist openly eye-fucking me. She was decent. Big tits, small waist, and with lips like those, I bet she sucked a mean dick. Any other day I might've taken her up on the offer, but there was only one pussy on my mind. The one I could still taste on my lips.

"Mason Kessler."

She ducked down, trying to hide the pink tint that flashed across her cheeks. "Mason's a fine young man."

I just bet you thought he was a fine young man. How many times did you swallow his cock, sweetheart?

"And you are?"

"Logan Hudson," I said, leaning my elbow on the counter just enough to sneak a peek at her cleavage. *Not bad, Mase. Does daddy know what you're up to at the Cedarbrea Addiction Clinic?* "I'm on the list."

"Oh, you're his brother." She lifted her head and gave me a quick scan. "I should've known. You don't see eyes that green often."

Sorry sweetheart, your fantasies of brotherly love will have to wait.

"He was moved down to the main floor. Room 1013."

That must mean Mase was being a good boy. Good. Maybe now we could talk about real shit, like pussy, and how to fuck with Silas.

"Thanks." I tapped the counter and sauntered down the hall.

This place wasn't exactly the plaza. The stark white walls were so sterile I could smell it in the air. The security was top notch though. It was locked down tighter than a nun's cunt.

Every door I went through, I had to get buzzed in, and the guard on either side asked for my ID. All this shit and I still had to argue with Lou to get put on the visitors' list. He was worried Mase would slip something by me because I was too impulsive and didn't pay attention.

Problem was, I paid too much attention. Situational awareness was a by-product of my childhood. Not paying attention could mean a lot of blood and even more pain.

Down one hallway I saw two people getting high on cleaning products, a girl trying to jimmy her window open, and an orderly getting his dick sucked behind a housekeeping cart.

This place wasn't keeping Mase clean–there were more drugs here than on the street–Preston and I were. We threatened every one of these fuckers and their families. The orderly was the only one that called my bluff. Preston paid his girlfriend a visit. She wouldn't be sucking anybody's dick anytime soon.

"Your recovery is coming along Mason, but it would help if you took part in group."

"I show up, don't I?"

"Showing up is only half of it. You need to open up. Share with the others."

"Why the fuck would I want to open up to a bunch of crackheads?"

I leaned against the doorframe to Mase's room and watched the doctor push his glasses up his nose.

"We've talked about using that kind of language." He sighed and wrote something down on his notepad. "Not everyone in group has the same issues."

"Sure we do, Doc." Mase was sitting on the bed with his arms crossed and a smile tugging on his lips. "That's why we're all here in the lockdown hotel."

"Well, Mr. Kessler, if you ever want to get out of the lockdown hotel, I suggest you start committing to your recovery."

Mase rolled his eyes. "It was a phone, Doc, not a fucking needle."

So that was how Mase was fucking with everyone. My personal favorites were the male strip 'o' gram he sent to Lou's office, and the barber shop quartet that followed Silas around school.

"You know the rules." The doctor stood up and finally noticed me standing in the doorway. "Oh," he paused long enough to eye me, "And who is this?"

"My dealer." Mase smiled and nodded at me. "You bring the good stuff?"

"Always."

The doctor sighed and crossed his arms. "Your visitors should be helping you on the road to recovery, not downplaying it."

"Don't worry, Doc," I smirked and shot the obviously unimpressed doctor a wink. "I'll keep him on the straight and narrow."

I already had the cheerleading squad set up to give Mase a proper welcome home party. Minus Naomi, of course. Mason couldn't stand her.

"I'm not sure you should be having visitors right now."

Sorry Doc, that's not going to fly.

"I think you should be more worried about the girl in 1039 that's getting ready to dive out the window. Wouldn't look too good on you, Dr. Spielman," I sauntered up to him and flicked the silver name tag pinned to his white lab coat, "If someone jumped ship on your watch."

A second later, a bunch of guys in orderly scrubs rushed down the hall as alarms rang out. I smirked down at the anger curling Dr. Spielman's lip. Fucker didn't say anything else, just glanced back at Mase before running out of the room.

"You bring it?" Mase said once we were alone.

I tossed him the phone in my pocket and took the chair the doctor formerly occupied.

"How the fuck do you get this shit in here?"

I looked at the painting hung above his bed. A black dragon. The same black dragon I saw Riley painting. Mase still wouldn't talk to her. Riley should take it as a compliment, because if Mase didn't care about her, he wouldn't give a shit.

Rape play was one of his favorite games. Something my old man probably knew. What he did to Riley wasn't what ate Mase up, it was how much he liked it. The painting was progress, I guess. He had it out in the open, instead of tucked away like her letters.

"Told security I needed to keep it on me in case my wife went into labor."

"You, with a wife?" Mase arched his brow at me. "And they believed that shit?"

I grinned back at him. "I can be very charming."

Besides, lately I'd kind of grown to like the idea of having a wife. Tying Cherry Pie to me forever and watching her belly swell with my baby. I jerked off to that image three times in the shower this morning.

Fortunately for me, I wouldn't have to fuck my hand anymore. I decided this morning when I watched Shelby prance out that door, all defiant with her chin up in the air, that that would be the last time she walked out of my house a virgin. Tonight, her pussy was mine.

I looked at Mase, eyes locked on the phone as his thumb scrolled the screen.

"How'd they find the last one?"

"Fucking bitch Brandi ratted me out," he muttered. "She can fuck the staff all day long, but I make one pass at her and she loses her shit."

"Ah, so you have to have something to get a taste of her pussy?" I knew girls like that. They were the ones I had a little extra fun with. Didn't want shit from me after that.

Mase shrugged. "Guess so."

He was all wound up. I could see it in the way his muscles tensed and brows furrowed. Normally he'd find some poor fucker to beat the shit out of, but he didn't have that option here. Not if he wanted to get out anytime soon. There were other ways he could let off steam.

"Huh?" I leaned forward, resting my elbows on my knees. "What do you say we test that theory out?"

For the first time since he was put in this shithole, a genuine smile spread across Mase's face.

SOMETIMES, it was too easy. One smile and a few words had this bitch following me like a fucking puppy. Brandi was a little too skinny, and way too fucking stupid–she was following me–but cute. I could see why Mase was lusting after her.

He always did have a thing for redheads. And this one, with her petite frame and sad eyes, reminded me of one particular redhead. Her hair was obviously dyed, and her eyes were blue, but she was pretty damn close to Harper. Even had the freckles across her nose. Which meant good times for me. Not so much for her.

"This way, sweetheart," I said, rounding the corner.

This part of the clinic was long forgotten. Dust hung in the air and half the rooms had the windows boarded up. I led her down a dimly lit hallway to a door marked Storeroom B. The only thing stored in there were a couple of old mattresses stacked against the far wall. Empty, solitary, with nowhere for her to run. The perfect place.

"After you." I pushed open the door, waving Brandi inside.

The girl wasn't as stupid as I thought. She took one look into the dark room and turned her suspicious eyes my way. Never underestimate an addict. They dealt with sketchy fuckers every day. But none of them had my charm.

"Come on sweetheart, I don't have all day." I gave her one of my winning smirks, making sure to flash just the right amount of teeth. "You want your world rocked, or not?"

Her eyes rolled over the ink on my arms and down to the bulge in my jeans. Was I hard? Fuck yeah, I was hard. I was about to get one hell of a show. Didn't mean I'd touch her. That privilege was reserved for the blonde goddess back in Ashen Springs. Tonight I was going to get myself a slice of cherry pie.

Brandi glanced in the room and back at me, licking her lips. "How did you find this place?"

"I have my ways." Mainly an orderly named Alex that didn't want his boss to find out he was supplying the clients, in exchange for sexual favors.

Guess she decided my pretty ass was worth it, because her shoulders visibly relaxed and she sauntered inside. One way or another, she was going in that room. This way was just more fun.

"You coming?" she called over her shoulder.

I smirked and followed.

Welcome to my parlor, said the spider to the fly.

Once we were both inside, I shut the door and leaned back against it. Mase took that as his cue to spark up a smoke in the far corner of the room. Prick got ten points for adding to the eerie factor. This room was so fucking dark, I could barely see my own hand in front of my face.

Hence why we brought candles with us. But Mase didn't light them right away. No. The fucker waited long enough to suck in a deep drag of his smoke so the ember cast a red glow across his face.

"Welcome to my playroom, Brandi," he added, while blowing a stream of smoke into the darkness.

I was so fucking proud, a tear almost rolled down my cheek.

Brandi's back went ramrod straight as her unsure gaze shifted back to me. "What's going on?"

That was when Mase decided to light the candles, allowing me to see that spark of fear in her blue eyes. They reminded me of something else. The big wide cinnamon eyes of a tempting blonde angel I had cornered in a corn maze.

That was the best Halloween of my life. The fear coming off Shelby while I whispered all the dirty things I was going to do to her was fucking delicious. One of these days I was going to fuck her in that angel costume.

Mase pushed off the wall and stalked slowly closer. After seeing him so broken, this was fucking beautiful. Like watching a cat stalk its prey. My old man didn't destroy him. Mase was still in there. Maybe not the same version of him, but he was there.

"She's not very fucking smart, is she?" Mase said to me.

I shook my head. "She followed me down here, didn't she?"

"I only came because you said we were–"

I tsked, cutting her off.

"I said you were going to get your world rocked." Smirking at the shock on her face, I pulled out a cigarette and placed it between my lips. "Not that I'd be the one doing the rocking."

"If you do anything," Little Miss Brandi huffed up, sticking her chest out and lifting her chin, "I'll tell."

Mason's face twisted in a scowl. If she wasn't fucked before, she was now. Like his brother, Mase didn't handle betrayal well.

"He won't have to do anything," I stated confidently. "You'll do it all on your own."

She openly scoffed her disagreement. "I don't know what makes you think I'd do that."

"These," I said, shaking a bottle of Oxy.

Both of them stopped and eyed the pills. Unlike Brandi, who was practically salivating–Alex informed me her drug of choice was prescription meds–Mase was eyeing me out of curiosity. He really needed to stop underestimating me.

Like the obedient addict she was, Brandi looked right at me and said, "What do you want me to do?"

I tipped my chin at Mase, expecting to see a smile of satisfaction. Instead, he stared down at her with his brows furrowed. As if he was unsure what to do next. No, not unsure.

I cocked my head at the shame in his glare. It was guilt. Maybe he didn't play with the pretty receptionist? Had he fucked anyone? Well, fuck that. I was putting a stop to this shit right fucking now.

"Suck his cock." When she took a step towards him, I shook my head. "Uh huh. Betraying bitches don't deserve to walk."

There was no hesitation. Brandi dropped down and crawled over to Mase. When her hands shot up to his belt, he moved to step back. One look at my arched brow stopped him.

"Isn't that right, Mase?"

"Yeah." He looked up at me like a scared little boy afraid he'd get caught with his hand in the cookie jar, and I was gonna make sure he ate every last fucking crumb.

A few seconds later Brandi had his jeans open and was slurping his cock in her hot mouth. Though Mase was hard and ready to go, he fought it.

I could see the frustration behind his closed eyes. Heard the guilt in his groan. This bitch had one purpose. Help him get past this shit. If she couldn't do that, she was fucking useless.

"Do better," I growled, spurring Brandi to shove him down her throat.

It didn't work. Mase was two seconds away from pushing her off. I was losing him. Time for another tactic.

"She's smiling more, you know." That worked. Mase's eyes popped open and locked on mine. "Might even be a little happy."

I smiled when his jaw ticked. That's it. Come out and play.

"You're in here, and she's out there. Laughing and having a good time with her new friends." That was a lie. Harper was just as timid and scared as ever. I made sure of that. But Mase didn't need to know that. "Even went on a date the other day."

It was on after that. Mase held Brandi's face down on the dirty floor while he took his frustration out on her.

I sat in Suzie Q, listening to the purr of her engine while staring at the dips of roller coaster road. Releasing the e-brake, I popped the clutch and soared down the first hill. This was exactly what I needed.

That sinking feeling dropping my stomach, along with the adrenaline rush from speed, helped me sort out my muddled thoughts. And right now, my thoughts were more than muddled.

My dad's infidelity, Rye hiding things from me, and the brother I never knew about. All this crap floating around in my brain, and yet it was one thing. A single solitary thought that brought me here today. Logan friggin Hudson. The one person in my life that didn't treat me like a fragile princess that couldn't handle things.

Suzie Q roared up the last hill and I slammed on the brakes. Kicking up dirt as the back end swiped along the gravel road.

"God damnit!" I growled, slamming my palms down on the steering wheel.

Making me say that I was his wasn't a power trip for Logan. It was his way of shoving the truth down my throat. And now, I was choking on it. Because as much as I hated to admit it, he was right.

I did want him. But it was more than that. I liked the deep timber of his voice, and dreamt about that stupid charming smile. Somehow the bastard had ingrained himself in my soul.

How the hell did this happen?

I brushed my hands over my face, sweeping away the thought. I didn't have time to deal with that now. I had to be at Pop Pop's for work in ten minutes. Thankfully, the shop was just around the bend and through the scrapyard, so I was there in under five.

When I pulled up, Pop Pop had his head under the rusted out hood of a 1956 Cadillac. I called it the cursed car. He'd been trying to get that thing running for years. Kind of like Rye's car, that Cadillac belonged in the junkyard out back. Stubborn old man.

"Hey, Pop Pop," I said, climbing out of Suzie Q, "Still fighting with that thing?"

He stood up and wiped his greasy hands on his overalls. "I'm not ready to give up on her yet."

Staring into his light eyes, I couldn't help but wonder if my brother had the same color. Mom and Mags did. They got the blue eyes from Pop Pop. Which posed a bigger question. Did he know? I mean, he had to. She was seventeen, and still living at home when she had him.

"Why didn't you tell me I had a brother?"

He sighed and answered like a true southern gentleman. "That's none of my business."

"A grandson is none of your business," I challenged, "What about a brother? I suppose that should be none of my business either."

"Don't sass me, child," he snapped at me before returning to the Cadillac. "Don't you have work to do?"

I muttered under my breath and marched into the shop. Why did I expect anything else? My mom's side of the family was built on secrets. At this point, I wouldn't be surprised to find some forgotten relative chained in the attic. Well, my brother wouldn't stay forgotten.

If it took the rest of my life, I'd find him. All I needed was a place to start.

Once I got to work, there wasn't much time to dwell on anything. I had three oil changes, a tire rotation, and a transmission replacement to keep me busy. Before I knew it, I was closing up the shop and getting ready to go home. Which was the last place I wanted to be.

It was my mom's day off and I wasn't ready to face her. Mostly because I knew she'd just give me the run around. The last thing Mags needed to hear was more arguing. She got enough of that with our parents.

Unfortunately for me, everyone was busy today. Rye had an art class to teach at the YMCA tonight, and Marnie and Trina were at Saturday Mass with their parents. I was half tempted to text Logan. Even had my phone out, ready to tap the screen, when it went off.

Noah? Why was he calling me?

"Hello?"

"Hey sweetness, sorry to bug you, but I'm kind of in a bind. I'm at Evan's and my car won't start."

"Evan's?" I didn't really want to go out there. Beside the fact that he was a piece of shit, he lived twenty minutes outside of town. "I don't know."

"Come on, you'd be really helping me out," Noah sang in a sweet tone.

I hummed in contemplation. Did I really have anything else to do? And I was looking for something to delay my inevitable homecoming. But still... Evan's house? I didn't know about that.

"You do kind of owe me."

Damnit. He was right. I did lead him on and then break our date at the last minute. Fixing his car was the least I could do.

"Alright," I sighed. "I'll be there in thirty."

Noah and Evan were waiting for me when I pulled up. A lot of my school's parties were held at Evan's place, so I'd been here a couple of times. This was the first time I was able to really look at it though.

If it wasn't for the scumbag that lived here, I might've admired the ambiance of the massive log cabin tucked in the middle of a patch of trees on the south side of the bluffs. Not many people lived up here. You had to have a lot of money and be okay with the geysers roaring in the background.

Evan March was one of the few rich kids at Ashen Springs High. Rumor was he couldn't beat out Parker for Ashworth's football team, and that was how he wound up in public school.

Ashen Springs was a football town after all, and considering Evan wasn't in middle or elementary school with any of us, it was a pretty believable rumor.

"Hey sweetness," Noah smiled and jumped off the deck when I stepped out into the cool night air. "Thanks for coming. You're really saving my ass here."

Evan leaned back against one of the bannisters and rolled his glare over me. "Does your boyfriend know you wear that shit when you're working?"

"I wear what I want," I snarled back. "And I don't have a boyfriend."

"That's not what I heard."

"Right, cause I'm sure your sources are reliable." *Pffft. Creep.*

"I don't need any sources. Not when Logan Hudson shows up at school to mark his territory."

I rolled my eyes. "Drama queen much."

"Honey," Evan pushed off the bannister and rested his elbows on the railing to smirk down at me, "He may as well have pissed all over you."

"Shut it!" Noah growled and twisted his neck to glare back at Evan. "She's here to help. Quit being a prick."

"Whatever," Evan grumbled under his breath.

His hatred for the Knights was no secret. I'd lost count of how many times I'd heard him talking smack about Micha. Maybe that was why he targeted Rye. What better way to out-alpha the king than by taking his queen? Not a very smart choice on his part.

Everybody knew how tightly knit the Knights were. If you screwed with one, you screwed with them all. That kind of loyalty was hard to find. Which is why I knew this thing with Logan was a losing battle. I wasn't just fighting him. I was fighting them all.

I shot Evan one last menacing glare before smiling at Noah. "So, what seems to be the problem?"

"I don't know." He shook his head and sauntered over to his truck, "It just wouldn't start..."

I watched his hands wave through the air as he explained what was going on. Things would be so much easier if I could've just fallen for him. Noah wasn't a bad guy. If I'd broken a date with any other guy, he'd treat me like crap.

Not Noah. He'd said he appreciated my honesty and hoped we could still be friends. Which I thought was one of those lines people tossed out to make themselves feel better. But here he was, smiling at me like nothing had changed. How understanding was that?

Noah Torres wasn't just sweet and thoughtful. He was literally the perfect guy. Everything I wanted. Or at least what I thought I wanted, until Logan Hudson came along and messed everything up.

"Think you can get it going?"

"Shouldn't be a problem." If I could keep Riley's car running, I could fix anything. I looked over at Evan. "You got any tools around here?"

He tipped his chin to the left. "In the garage."

Thankfully, Noah took Evan inside before things got uncomfortable. Well, more uncomfortable than they already were. Which they definitely would've been if I'd had to work on Noah's truck in a skirt in front of Evan.

The guy made my skin crawl before he attacked Riley. He had this creepy pervert vibe. Didn't seem to bother some of the girls in school. Though I had a feeling his family's financial situation had a lot to do with that.

It took some time, but I eventually found the problem. The starter had come disconnected. Not a super common problem, but not unusual either. My guess was, since Evan lived off a gravel road, a rock had jumped up in the engine and rattled around.

It wasn't too bad. A ten minute fix that didn't require any parts. After which, I went inside to tell Noah the good news. I found them playing video games in the living room.

"All fixed," I sang.

"That's great." Noah beamed up at me. "What was wrong with it?"

"The starter came a little loose. No big deal. But you should take it easy going down gravel roads," I pointed out.

He touched his fingers to his forehead and gave me a small salute. "Aye, aye captain."

With a giggle, I shook my head. "Well, I should get going."

"Really? You can't stay for a drink?"

The frown on Noah's face tugged at my heart, but I drank way too much last night and just the thought of alcohol turned my stomach.

"Not really in the mood for a drink."

"A soda then." Noah held his hand out palm up, inviting me to take his offer. "Come on, when's the next time I'm going to see you."

He had a point. We weren't in the same school anymore, and he did say he wanted to be friends.

"Okay," I sighed. "Just one though."

"Great." Noah jumped up all excitedly and headed for the kitchen. It was kind of cute. "Have a seat."

I looked over at Evan, who had his feet kicked up on a stool while battling some giant robot thing on the T.V. Since he was in a chair by the window, I chose the farthest spot from that.

I pulled my sweater tighter around my chest and flopped down on the far end of the couch. I had to admit, Evan's place was just as nice on the inside as it was on the outside, and this couch was comfy as heck.

There were family portraits hung on the wall, with little Evan and his parents. He was kind of a cute kid. Wonder what happened.

"Where are your parents?"

"Europe," Evan said, without so much as looking at me.

"They just left you here alone?" That explained a lot. If his parents weren't around, who was going to stop him from being a dick.

"Fuck," he growled, tossing the controller on a nearby table.

Guess the robot won. Also guess he wasn't going to answer me. Whatever. Small talk with Evan March wasn't high on my priority list.

"Here you go, sweetness," Noah said, handing me a glass with a little pink umbrella and small lemon wedge.

"Wow. You really went all out on the soda."

"Nothing but the best for you." He smiled and dropped down on the other end of the couch.

The longer I sat there talking to Noah, the more relaxed I became. He told me about the football team's latest victory and a date he had with Sarah Miller. I was happy that he found someone, plus it was nice to be able to confide in someone.

Logan wasn't a topic I was super interested in talking to Rye about. Besides, Noah could give me an outside opinion. I didn't tell him everything, of course. Anything sexual I kept to myself. He didn't need to know that stuff.

By the time I was ready to go, I felt a lot better. Like a huge weight had been lifted off my shoulders.

"I should go," I said, rising off the couch. When I went to take a step, my knees gave out and I stumbled.

"Whoa," I felt Noah's hands slide under my arms, helping me steady myself. "Are you okay?"

"I must've gotten up too fast."

I blinked away the fog starting to haze my vision. *Did I eat today?*

"Yeah. I'm fine." If I splashed some water on my face, I'd be fine. "Is there a bathroom around here I can use?"

"Down the hall. Last door on the left."

Noah tipped his head. His eyes were sparkling brightly. Like really bright. They looked so unreal.

"You want me to help you?"

"No," I shook my head and made my way down the hall.

Which was really long. And the walls were super smooth. I couldn't stop myself from sliding my hand across them.

So soft.

The bathroom sink was soft too. Silky even.

I watched water run over my fingers, amazed at how the heat tingled up my arm, warming my skin. It made my hand look distorted. Like a cartoon. Maybe I was a cartoon. I was smooth like a cartoon. Logan was smooth too.

All smooth and warm and hard.

God, I wanted to touch him. Run my hand over the hard ridges of his abs.

Would he let me lick them?

Wait...

My brows furrowed down at my wet hand. That wasn't right. Since when did I want to lick Logan?

I bet he'd taste good.

He probably would. He sure felt good. When he ran his hand down my body, my skin lit up. I got all hot and wet. My pussy clenched. I could almost feel him.

Hang on... I did feel him?

But it wasn't his hand touching me. It was mine.

That's not right?

I looked at myself in the mirror. I had really nice boobs. They felt good too. Everything felt good. Except my teeth. I couldn't feel those at all. Oh no! What if there was something wrong with me?

Why couldn't I feel my teeth!

I opened my mouth and tapped my finger off my bottom tooth. *Crap.* I couldn't feel that either.

Rye will know what to do.

That was a good idea. I should call Riley. She always knew what to do.

Chapter 20
Logan

"How's Mase?" Micha plucked a muffin off the plate on the island. "He still riding the guilt train?"

"Well, I got to watch him fuck some snitching bitch today, so…" I tossed the last piece of my third muffin in my mouth and grinned.

He sat down next to me and grumbled, "About fucking time."

We'd all been worried about Mase. The fact that he found his dick again was reassuring.

"What about your girl? She still pissed?"

Micha gave me a sideways glance. "What the fuck do you think?"

To say my sister wasn't taking the news about Shelby and I well would be an understatement. Too bad for her. Despite what Riley thought, Shelby was a big girl. She could make her own decisions.

Not that I'd give her much of a choice. Cherry Pie was mine and that was that. She'd just have to get used to it. Both of them would.

"Where is your girl?"

"She's at home." Shelby'd gotten off work an hour ago. I figured I'd give her some time with her mom before heading over there. They had some shit to talk about. "You talk to your old man?"

Micha shook his head. "I'm saving that for after the council meeting."

Keeping his long lost brother to himself gave Micha leverage in case things didn't go his way. He had nothing to worry about though. I had his back, and Chase had Riley's. But that little tidbit of information I'd leave for a surprise.

I couldn't wait to see the look on the Creswells' faces when that scruffy motherfucker walked in and took his seat. Uptight fuckers.

My thoughts were interrupted when my phone went off, ringing Warrant's 'Cherry Pie'. Maybe Shelby didn't need as much time as I thought.

"Hey baby," I sang into my phone, "Miss me already?"

"Riley told me to call you."

A slow smile spread across my face. "Did she?"

Looks like little sis is coming around after all.

"Can you feel your teeth?" She whispered as if it was some secret. "Because I can't feel my teeth."

My brows rose. That was not the response I was expecting.

"Uh, no, come to think of it, I can't feel my teeth. I don't think anyone can."

"You have really nice teeth."

Well, that was a weird fucking compliment.

"Thank you. You have nice teeth too."

Was she drinking again? If she'd decided to get drunk after last night's shit show, I was gonna whip her ass. I don't give a shit what happened with her mom. My brow rose as I thought back to one particular fantasy.

Maybe I'd whip her anyway.

"I have nice boobs also."

"Yes you do," I agreed.

Shelby let out a long breathy sigh. "I like touching them."

Was this my little virgin's version of phone sex? I'd play along. Why not. This shit was cute as fuck.

"I like touching them too," I said, cocking a brow at Micha who was answering his own call.

"Baby, calm the fuck down," he yelled into his phone.

My face dropped at Shelby's next words.

"I want to lick you."

Okay, something was definitely wrong.

Micha slapped his hand down on the counter, grabbing my attention. My pulse picked up the second I met his stare.

"Noah drugged Shelby."

"What!?" I knew I should've killed that prick.

"She wouldn't tell Riley where she is." Micha pointed at me. "Find the fuck out."

"Why is everyone yelling?" Shelby whined. "Are you mad? I don't like it when you're mad."

Yes, I was fucking mad. I was goddamn livid. Noah Torres was a dead man. Anyone he knew, looked at, or talked to was a dead man. Tonight blood would run down the streets.

"No one's yelling baby," I said, trying to keep her calm. "Where are you?"

"In the bathroom. Do you have ears?"

"Yes baby, I have ears. Whose bathroom are you in? Are you at Noah's house?"

"No, silly," Shelby giggled. "Why would I be at Noah's house? Noah's not home. This sink is really smooth."

"Shelby, focus!" I clapped at the phone, ready to reach through and strangle the answer out of her. "Tell me where you are."

"There was an umbrella in my soda."

I'll just bet there fucking was.

"That's great, baby. But you need to tell me where you are."

"I feel really good." She released a long breathy moan. "These towels are soft. Evan has a lot of towels in here."

"Evan? Evan March."

Micha looked over at me with death in his eyes. Evan lucked out last time, only because of Riley, but she wouldn't be there to save him this time. Evan March's clock had just rung out.

Ding Dong motherfucker.

A new voice came over the other line. "Hey sweetness, you okay in there?"

My hands instantly balled.

Noah Torres.

"Why don't you come out? Evan and I are making a movie."

"I'll like movies," Shelby sang happily. "Can I be in it?"

"No baby, you don't want to be in his fucking movie!"

I tried to get her attention, but she wasn't listening to me anymore. Not even my old man could make me feel as helpless as I did now. When I heard the door open and Torres's voice ring across the line my heart damn near broke.

"Of course you can in our movie. You're our star."

"You mother–" the line went dead before I could finish the threat.

"Fuck!" I yelled, throwing my phone at the wall.

Noah Torres was fucking done. I was going to paint the walls in his fucking blood, and then I was going to go after everyone he cared about. The whole fucking Torres family was going down.

I looked over at Micha and said, "Call Preston," before marching out of the room.

"Where the fuck are you going?" he called out after me.

"To get my gun."

"Jesus fucking Christ," Micha growled as I screeched to a stop. "Who's gonna save your girl if we're fucking dead?"

I rounded the corner and screeched to a stop behind Preston's BMW. Fucker just lit a smoke and tipped his head down at the front bumper inches from his knees.

"Cutting it close, don't you think?" he said when I jumped out of the car.

I cocked my 9mm, popping one in the chamber and glanced over at him. "You're fine, aren't you?"

What the fuck was he worried about? Betty was a finely tuned instrument and I knew how to drive. I could stop on a motherfucking dime. Micha didn't agree. He lurched out of the car, hunched over and held up his hand.

"Give me a second to swallow my stomach."

"Didn't have to come." Preston flicked his butt into the bushes by the house. "Kid Rocket and I could've handled this shit."

He had a point. Preston and I were more than capable of taking care of this.

Micha snorted in disagreement. "Riley would cut my nuts off if I let anything happen to her friend."

He had a point too.

Preston nodded at me. "So what's the game plan?"

"Go in, get my girl, and kill the motherfuckers that thought they could touch her."

"Hold up," Micha said. "No one's killing anyone."

Preston and I both cocked a brow at Micha. Who the fuck was he kidding? This wasn't an Order job. There were no rules here. And even if there was, I wouldn't give a shit.

"I'm fucking serious. I don't want any messes."

Micha was paying too much attention to his old man. He might be our King, but he didn't get a say in this shit. Preston got it.

"Don't worry." Preston popped a magazine in his Beretta and pulled the slide back. "There won't be a mess."

"Fuck sakes," was the only response Micha grumbled as we made our way up the steps and through the front door.

We could hear them further in the house. Stupid fucks didn't know we were here.

"Fuck," Torres grunted, "Hold her still."

"You sure this shit is worth it?"

Micha and I looked at each other. We'd assumed March was the ringleader of their little gang, but ringleaders didn't question shit.

"Quit fucking worrying. We'll be long gone before anyone knows what happened," Noah growled. "The Piper has our back."

My hand tightened on my 9mm. I should've known my old man had something to do with this shit.

"Logan," Micha whispered in a harsh tone, "They might know something."

Who fucking cared? Anyone associated with my old man should be put down. Letting them breathe was doing this world a disservice.

"Logan," Micha growled a little louder.

Even Preston had that condescending look. There was a bigger threat out there. Mainly, Micha's illegitimate older brother.

Who the fuck knew what my old man did to him. Or turned him into. Fucker was either dead, or working against us. Either way, we needed to find out. And we literally had nothing to go on. Didn't even know his name.

"Fuck, fine," I grumbled, tucking my gun in the back of my jeans. "But if they touched her, they're fucking toast."

When did I become such a pussy?

We made our way through the kitchen and into the living room. I heard her before I saw her.

"No," Shelby murmured, "I want Logan."

My heart lurched at the sight of my beautiful angel struggling on the couch as Evan held her arms and Noah fought her kicking legs. She'd never have been in this situation if it wasn't for me.

Did I care? Yeah, I fucking did. It fucking killed me that I put her in danger. Not enough for me to let her go, but enough that I got Micha's obsession about knowing Riley's every move.

"Get away, " Shelby growled, landing a hard kick in Noah's shin.

The pained look on the prick's face made me want to kiss her. My little Cherry Pie had some power in those legs. I felt that power when I held her down, but she didn't use all her strength on me. Noah got it full force.

She really does like me.

"Jesus Christ, slap her or something," Noah snarled at Evan.

The last thing I saw before red bled into my sight was Evan's hand swinging back...

. . .

BLOOD...

So much blood.

"Logan..."

It was everywhere. On the bed and bleeding down the walls in fat drops.

"Snap the fuck out of it..."

My fists pounded down, spraying more blood. Across my face, over the floor and seeping into my clothes.

"Fuck sakes, Preston stop her..."

I laughed as the warm drops hit my skin.

"No, I want Logan."

That voice...

I BLINKED my eyes down at the mess that was Evan March's face. There wasn't much left of it, and what there was, was covered in the gurgled blood he was choking on. Noah was sitting on the ground staring wide eyed at the mess. Prick was scared. Good, he fucking should be. Thought he could touch my Shelby.

Shelby!

Where the fuck was she?

I jumped up to my feet and spun around to see Micha holding her back. My sweet girl swung her fists, beating his chest while yelling, "Let me go."

Micha just tightened his hold, keeping her from me.

"Let her go."

He cocked his head. "I don't think that's—"

I plucked my gun out and held it up, aimed right at him. "I said, let her go."

He released her and held up his hands.

Shelby immediately rushed forward, slamming into me and wrapping her arms around my waist. Only then did the fire pumping through my veins calm to a mild burn.

"I missed you," she mumbled into my chest.

I tucked my gun away and kissed the top of her head. "I missed you too, baby."

Micha visibly relaxed and grumbled out a string of curses. I probably shouldn't have pulled a gun on him, but he shouldn't have kept her from me. She was mine. He'd do the same if it was Riley.

"I told you she'd be fine," Preston said, and tipped his chin at Noah. "What do we do with this one?"

Micha and Preston started arguing about Noah's fate, but I didn't give a shit about that. I was too occupied with the gorgeous blonde running her hands under my shirt and up my back. Who knew nails could feel so fucking good?

"You smell good," Shelby purred and nuzzled into my neck, running her tongue across my skin. "I want to lick you all over."

"Baby, I know you're high right now…" I yanked on her hair, tipping her head back, and swept my thumb across her cheek.

Whatever I was going to say was lost the instant I saw Evan's blood painting her perfect skin. I'd never wanted anyone so bad in my life.

"Take her home, the doctor will meet you there," Micha said, tipping his chin at Noah. "We'll find out what this one gave her."

I glared at the prick that drugged my girl. My job here wasn't finished. Was about to tell Micha as much, until Shelby reached down and grabbed my dick through my jeans.

Fuuuck.

"You're wearing too many clothes."

I'd never agreed with a statement more in my life. Unfortunately, she was high as fuck, and as much as my dick didn't care, I did.

When I fucked her the first time, it sure as hell wouldn't be in front of the prick that drugged her, and she'd be completely aware. So, as much as it pained me to do, I pulled her hand off my dick and steered her out the door.

She pouted when I buckled the seatbelt across her. "I want to touch you."

How fucking high was she?

I sauntered around the car, shaking my head. What the fuck was wrong with me? I had the girl of my dreams begging for it, and I did nothing. *I should get a fucking medal for this shit.*

Chapter 21

Logan

Where was Ma? I could hear her crying. I just couldn't see her. I couldn't see anything. I could feel the blood dripping down my face. Heard each drop softly land on the hard ground.

I could even hear the breeze whistling through the trees outside. That's how I knew we were at the cabin. It was past the geysers, up so high on the bluffs that even the softest breeze turned into an echoing cyclone.

"I told you not to interfere."

I could feel the anger in my old man's voice. He was close. Close enough that I could smell the whiskey on his breath.

Why couldn't I see him?

"Don't," Ma cried from somewhere in the distance. "He's just a boy."

A loud smack rang through the air.

"You're making him weak. The boy would be better off without you."

My heart picked up. It wasn't a threat. I knew that, and so did Ma.

"Leave him alone!"

She should've kept quiet. Why didn't she keep quiet?

Her scream pushed me to force my swollen eyes open. Only one listened, but it was enough for me to see my old man hovering over Ma with a bloody knife in his hand.

"Don't!" I cried out, scared for the one good thing in my life.

Hand still in Ma's hair, my old man turned around. "Look at you calling out for your mother. It's pathetic. Give me one good reason I shouldn't carve this weakness out of your life?"

I looked over at the woman strapped down to the bed. My nanny. She'd tried to get Ma and me out. Took us here to wait for her husband, who was someone she said could help.

His body was somewhere at the bottom of the cliff. My old man had some fun with her first. He said he wanted to show me what a real man did. I was amazed she was still breathing. Bruises and blood marked her body, and still, she hung on.

Maybe she enjoyed the agony?

Pushing myself off the floor, I moved my aching body closer. Nancy was okay. I had nothing against her, but I knew what my dad wanted.

Blood and misery.

That was what he always wanted.

I didn't think twice. Just picked up a knife and plunged it into her neck. Nothing. That's what I felt, standing there and watching her choke for life as her blood soaked the bed. Ma cried behind us and my dad beamed with pride, but I felt nothing.

Not happy, not sad, I was simply there. Listening to the wind whistle as the spark bled out of her eyes. I cocked my head at her cold dead stare.

Ma cried and called out to me, hoping to find her sweet boy.

She wouldn't find him here.

There was no sweetness. No innocent child to save.

After all, I was my father's son, and the boogeyman didn't have a soul...

"Logan, stop."

I wasn't in the cabin. I was in my room, on my bed, with Shelby squirming under me. The way she moved, wriggling her butt while weakly slapping at the arm wrapped around her neck... I liked that. Liked seeing her helpless and afraid. My dick liked it too.

I loosened my grip on her neck enough for her to suck in gasping breaths, and rolled my eyes down to her heaving chest. Her pert little nipples pressed against the fabric of my shirt with each deep breath.

"How are you feeling?" It'd been a while since Silas's old man gave her the shot to flush the drugs out of her system. She should be sober now.

"How do you think I'm feeling?" she squeaked. "You just tried to choke me."

Yes I did, and I wanted to do it again. I could feel her pulse throbbing under my fingers. Each beat timed with the need coursing through my cock. My hand slid around her hip and up, to palm the warm flesh of her breast.

I liked the way she shuddered beneath me when I pinched her nipple. What I didn't like was the fabric between us.

Why the fuck did I put her in my shirt after Silas's old man gave her the shot? Right now, I didn't give a fuck if she was high or not. I needed to be inside her tight little pussy. Still...

"Are you," I twirled her nipple between my thumb and forefinger, watching her pouty pink lips part to release a strangled moan, "Still high?"

Her cinnamon eyes glowed in the moonlight as they locked onto mine. "Why?"

That single word was all I needed to hear. I pushed my knee between her thighs, fisted the collar of her shirt, and tore the fabric apart. This time when her breath hitched, it wasn't because I was choking it out of her.

It was because my mouth latched on to one of those perfect rosebud nipples. One taste and I was fucking done. Growling, I dove in, feasting on her perfect salty skin while my dick throbbed with every tiny whimper I dragged out of her.

"Logan, we can't." Her hands clung onto my shoulder, little fingers digging into my flesh. "Stop."

Her mouth was saying no, but her body pulled me in closer.
"Not this time, baby."
There'd be no stopping me this time.
She was mine now.

Chapter 22

Shelby

I don't know what happened. Logan's voice tugged at my subconscious. It came from far away at first, pulling me out of my drug induced sleep. When I opened my eyes and found myself in Logan's room, on his bed, I was confused. I remembered bits and pieces.

Helping Noah fix his truck, suddenly feeling really weird, and then someone holding me down. I was scared. Fought back, kicking and swinging my arms at the hands on me. Then they were gone, and all I could see was a pair of beautiful green eyes. Logan's eyes.

When I woke up, I looked for the safety of those eyes. But they were tightly closed as Logan thrashed about. I couldn't understand what he was saying, I didn't need to, to know he was having one hell of a nightmare. So, I did what anyone would've done. I called his name and reached out to touch him.

Big mistake.

He attacked. Glaring down as he choked the life out of me. My only thought, as blackness seeped into my vision, was how cruel fate was. It was that lost look in his eyes that got to me. I could feel his pain and sadness. Taste his desperation.

This man staring down at me, broken and vulnerable, that was the real Logan Hudson, and he was more beautiful than I thought. How ironic was that? The very moment Logan took my soul, was the same moment he'd take my life.

And then, just as suddenly as it started, it switched. The pain and anger on his face was replaced with hunger and lust. My shirt was ripped away and his mouth was on me. I couldn't think. I could barely breathe.

My mind was a myriad of emotions. I needed a moment to collect myself, but all I could focus on was his hot tongue swirling around my nipple. The sensation tingling across my flesh like a thousand tiny shivers.

"Logan, we can't." Even though I said the words, I couldn't stop myself from clinging onto his shoulders and arching deeper into his touch. "Stop."

He pulled my nipple through his teeth and growled, "Not this time, baby," as he moved over to my neglected breast.

The fire in my body was heightened by his hot mouth nipping my sensitive flesh, and scraping his teeth along my stiffened peak, sending a tiny zing of pain straight to my clit.

I knew I shouldn't like this. I shouldn't want more. But pain took on a whole new meaning when it came to Logan Hudson. It became this twisted, erotic thing, controlling the motions of my body. Drawing out quiet mewls from my parted lips as I threaded my fingers through his hair.

My mind was swirling. One voice told me to push him away, while another told me to give in and pull him closer. When my panties were torn away and he flicked my throbbing clit, I felt a little more of my resistance slip away.

"Logan," I whimpered, "I can't."

"You can, baby," he purred, and pinched my clit, while kissing his way up to my neck. "Just let go."

Liquid lava poured through my veins, igniting my nerves and

making me moan when he began to circle my opening. I shook my head, trying to deny my inner walls tightly clenching, silently begging for more. But Logan knew. He sensed what my body wanted, and happily obliged.

Shoving two fingers roughly inside my wanton opening. That was when the second voice bitch slapped the other, shutting off the logic part of my brain. My body took over, gyrating my hips as pleasure slipped through my lips in soft moans.

"That's it, sweetheart," he purred in my ear while spearing his fingers in the back of my head to grab a fistful of hair. "Now grab my cock. I want you to jerk me while I finger fuck you."

I whimpered out an objection, which was met with a rough yank on my burning scalp.

"Do it now!"

God help me, I did it. Slid my hand over his washboard abs and into the waistband of his sweatpants. His cock was thick and hard and ready. I'd never wanted anything more in my life.

I gently stroked his shaft, watching his beautiful face twist in the same agonizing pleasure he was drawing out of me. It was empowering and terrifying at the same time. This man was well experienced and I was just... a girl.

"Am I doing it right?"

I don't know why, but my question seemed to please him. A smirk spread across his lips as his green eyes met mine. He pulled away and withdrew his fingers from my pussy, leaving me feeling empty and confused.

I didn't say anything as he stood up and shed his clothes. I was too mesmerized by the way he fisted his cock, slowly stroking the long shaft.

"Spread your legs."

That's when panic started to set in. "Logan..."

"Now, Cherry Pie."

I don't why, maybe it was the sternness in his tone, or the wicked gleam in his eyes, but my legs slowly fell apart. He was on the bed, hovering over me, before I had time to think about it.

When I felt the thick head of his cock slide through my folds, my body started to tremble. He was going to hurt me. His size alone guaranteed that. Yet, for some reason, I felt safe with him. Logan didn't give me time to think about it.

With one hard thrust, he forced his length inside me. Stealing my breath as he tore through my virginal wall. My muscles tightened, fighting against the uncompromising hardness as I clung to him and buried my face in his neck. Seeking refuge from the pain he was inflicting on me.

"Fuuuck," he groaned and snapped his hips, sheathing his entire length in my walls.

Logan Hudson didn't take it easy on my virgin body. He didn't whisper sweet things in my ear, or give me time to adjust. He fucked me. Thrusting so deeply inside me, that my very soul wept. Tears spilled down my face as I shook my head, silently begging for mercy. But that just spurred him on.

He threw my leg over his hip and licked the tears off my cheek. "So fucking sweet."

I swear I felt his cock grow bigger right before my vision blurred. My body seized and I screamed out his name as the most agonizing orgasm rocketed through me.

"Jesus fucking Christ," Logan growled, and pulled out long enough to flip me over.

This new position drove him deeper, letting him touch places I didn't know existed. Still, I fought to hold on to my sanity. Struggled against the unbelievable pleasure forced on me.

Every time I thought my mind was winning, he slapped my ass, or sank his teeth into my flesh. Giving me just enough pain to throw me back over the edge. But it wasn't until he pushed his thumb in my ass, that I truly let go.

"One day, I'm going to fuck you in both holes," he growled, shoving his thumb deep in my back door. "Ingrain myself so deeply in your soul that every time your thighs rub together, you'll feel me."

"Oh god," I moaned. "Hurt me."

I needed it. I needed the pain as much as I needed my next breath.

He speared his fingers in my hair and yanked me up against him. I moaned at the burn spreading across my scalp and tipped my hips back to meet his thrusts. Logan groaned loudly and dragged his tongue up the side of my neck. I shrieked and jumped back when his hand landed on my pussy. Striking my clit in a hard smack. It hurt, but in the best way.

"You like that, baby?" he growled in my ear while delivering another tiny slap. "You like a little pain with your pleasure?"

For the first time since I met Logan, I looked deep into his eyes and told him the truth. "Only with you."

He lost it after that. Pushed me up against his headboard and fucked me like a deranged animal. And I loved every second of it. I hung onto the hard leather board and swung my hips back, fucking him as hard as he was fucking me.

"God fucking damnit." His palm pressed down on the back of my head, squishing my face into the headboard. "You feel that?" he growled, pulling my hand down the front of my body to the place we were joined.

I could feel his shaft sliding into my opening. Each rough thrust causing more wetness to soak my fingers.

"That's my cock claiming your virgin pussy, and it's the only cock you'll ever have."

With one last thrust, Logan released a long masculine grunt and buried himself deep inside me. I could feel each and every warm shot of come move up his shaft, twitching his dick inside me. That's what sent me over the edge into oblivion. Only this time, I didn't fight it. I spread my arms and dove head first into the cloud of bliss. Logan was right, I was his. And he was mine.

I TRACED my finger along Logan's hourglass tattoo, stopping to follow an angular scar. He'd fucked me twice more, and now we were just laying there in each other's arms. "Can I ask you a question?"

"Depends if you want to know the answer."

"Was Riley really in a car accident?"

His chest rose with a long sigh. "No."

I rested my chin on his chest and looked up at him. God, he was beautiful with his arm behind his head. Focus Shelby!

"What happened to her?"

"Sorry baby," he said, tucking a lock of hair behind my ear. "That's not my story to tell."

Figures.

"Of course it's not," I muttered, flopping my head back down. "It's not like anyone tells me anything anyway. Why would I be able to handle it?"

"Hey," Logan tipped my chin up, forcing me to look at him again. "I never doubted your ability to handle shit. If you want to know something, ask. Just make sure you want to hear the truth before you do."

My eyes narrowed. "You're going to tell me the truth?"

"Why not?" He shrugged.

I practically snorted. Sure. Logan Hudson was going to tell me the truth, because he'd been so forthcoming so far.

"I'm serious, Cherry Pie."

Alright, fine. I'll play along.

"Okay," I sighed and pushed myself up to sit. "How did you find out about my brother?"

"Overheard your mom and Lou talking about it."

That I did snort at. "Right, cause my mom is open about her life with strangers around."

"She didn't see me." Logan looked my way with a smirk on his face, "Or the cameras I have in your house."

My mouth fell open. "You have cameras in my house?"

"Had to jerk off to something until I got you in my bed."

Oh my god! I didn't know if I should be outraged, or flattered.

Outraged, definitely.

"Logan!" I shrieked, "You can't put cameras in people's houses."

"Actually, I can."

I didn't know what to say. Not only was he admitting to basically stalking me, but he was acting like it was a normal thing to do.

"So, what? You think because you're the sheriff's stepson, you're untouchable?"

"Fuck no," Logan choked out a laugh. "That prick hates my fucking guts. He'd love to lock my ass up."

"Well, maybe I'll tell him."

"Go ahead, he's probably right downstairs."

My brows furrowed as I cocked my head at him. "Aren't you afraid of going to jail?"

"I won't go to jail, Cherry Pie."

It was the seriousness in his tone that got to me. I sat there staring at him, wondering if he really was crazy. That's when I saw it. A raven tattooed on his inner right wrist.

Unlike the rest of them, the raven stood out on it's own. No other tattoos blended into it, or even touched it. Like that one small bird was somehow sacred. I hadn't noticed it before, because he usually had a watch on.

I glanced over at Logan's Richard Millie watch resting on the dresser. Come to think of it, they all wore one. On the same wrist. I didn't think I'd seen any of them without it.

Was Marnie right this whole time? No, that was ridiculous. There wasn't some secret society ruling the town. My eyes once again landed on the raven.

Or was there?

"There you go, sweetheart." Logan smirked at the expression on my face. "Now you're getting it."

I had to get out of here. I couldn't breathe.

My morning was off to a good start. Drained my balls in the greatest pussy ever created, and now I was enjoying some of Rosy's cinnamon buns.

All in all not bad, except for the part when Shelby tried to run. But it'd been awhile since I tackled a girl and tied her to my bed, so I couldn't really complain about that either. She should cool off after spending some time alone with a gag in her mouth.

"Gonna share those cinnamon buns, pretty boy?"

And there goes my morning.

I glared at Junior strutting into the kitchen like he owned the place. *Little shit.*

"Don't you have somewhere else to be." *Like at the bottom of a deep dark well.*

"Well, I'd go home," he growled, snatching one of the cinnamon buns off the plate, "But that's apparently not an option."

"Quit mouthing off," Micha snarled as he joined us in the kitchen.

Junior stuffed half the bun in his mouth and grinned up at him. "Welcome to parenthood, asshole."

Tension filled the air as Micha and the little shit stared each other down. It was scary how similar they were. I was honestly curious to see who would win.

Gotta say, I was a bit disappointed when Junior grumbled under his breath and marched out to the patio doors. I'd kind of hoped I'd get to see the little shit get slapped.

"Where the fuck do you think you're going?" Micha called after him.

"To drown myself," Junior barked back and slammed the patio doors.

"I guess things are going good then," I said after Junior left.

Micha sighed and gave me a sideways glance. I laughed at his frustration. My best friend was a sucker for punishment. Not only did he pick a chick that would have no problem ripping his nuts off, but he chose a kid that would help her do it.

I couldn't even feel sorry for him. Riley, I got. Your dick wanted who it wanted. I knew that better than anyone. But Junior wasn't his responsibility. He chose that shit.

"You know, one of these days, you'll have a kid."

A week ago the idea of having my own spawn would've freaked me the fuck out. So much so that I had seriously contemplated getting snipped. Now, I wasn't entirely opposed to the idea. I thought about the image of Shelby's belly swelling with my seed. Might've even jerked off to said image a few times.

"Yeah, *my* kid," I said, "Not some little shit I found on the street."

"Speaking of little shits," we both turned to see Silas standing in the doorway, "This one wouldn't leave me alone until I brought him to see you assholes."

A head darted out from behind the grumpy bastard and rushed right for me.

"Finn!" I cried out, throwing my arms open to catch him.

He crashed into me, almost knocking me off the stool. From the time he was born, Finn was my shining beacon of innocence. Always happy, and pumped to take on the world. My little spark of light in a blacked out nightmare. Except the little bastard wasn't so little anymore.

"What the fuck are they feeding you at that genius school?"

His light eyes rolled up. "We eat a balanced diet, complete with the four food groups. It's very important for the human body…"

My brow rose as he continued to spout off the nutritional facts for someone his height and weight. Minus the scowl, Finn was the spitting image of his cousin, they both had the same black hair and light eyes, but the second he opened his mouth…

"Where the fuck is my hug?" Micha growled, stealing him from me while Finn was explaining complex carbohydrates.

My gaze shifted from the little man wrapped around Micha, over to Silas. What else did the little prick inherit from his cousin?

"Did you ask for an extra dose of piss in your cornflakes this morning, or is something on your mind?"

Silas narrowed his glare and pointed at me. "You know exactly what the fuck is on my mind."

I did. Helped Mase pick out Silas's new bedroom furniture myself. It was amazingly hard to find a pink carriage bed big enough for that bastard.

"What's wrong Princess, didn't you sleep well?"

"My room is pink." Silas huffed and crossed his arms. "And there's a Tinkerbell costume in my closet."

Not as hard to find as one might think.

"Mase wanted to make sure you had the complete package."

"I'll make sure he gets the complete package when I see him tomorrow."

"Hey," I sang, swinging my hand through the air, "What you and Mase do with your package is your business."

Silas's scowl deepened, making me chuckle. Like Mase, I got a kick out of bugging the grumpy fucker.

"Speaking of packages," I said, reaching over to ruffle Finn's hair, "You learn to use your dick yet?"

"Of course," Finn's brows knit as if I'd just asked the strangest question in the world. "The penis has many functions. Urination for one."

I arched a brow at Silas. "What the fuck are you teaching your cousin?"

"Nothing," Silas grumbled. "And neither are you."

"Someone's got to teach him how to use that monster cock."

"Not fucking you. You use that shit way too much."

"You should make an appointment with my uncle," Finn said. "Frequent urination can be an indicator of an underlying medical problem."

I sighed and scrubbed a hand down my face. "Do you see this shit? What the fuck, Silas?"

"You are not corrupting my cousin."

"He thinks the only use for his dick is to take a piss."

"Of course it has more functions." Finn tipped his head and continued speaking. "Sexual encounters…"

It was physically painful. I was in real pain here. Which Micha must've sensed, because he ushered Finn outside.

"Alright Finn, go play with Junior before you give Logan a heart attack."

That was a gangbuster idea. Send the nerd to play with the crackhead's kid. Junior was going to punch him in the face two seconds into his quantum theory lecture. Ah well, might toughen the kid up. Besides, any idea I had of going to Finn's rescue fled the second Riley walked in the room.

"Where's Shelby?"

"She's fine."

"I didn't ask how she was," she snarled at me, "I asked where she was."

"She tried to run, so I tied her to my bed."

"What the hell, Logan!" Riley shrieked while throwing her hands up, "Go untie her now!"

I sat back and eyed her for a second. Riley was Shelby's best friend, it was only natural that she'd be concerned about her, but I didn't like being questioned on what *I* did with *my* girl. "No."

Micha nudged me while Riley continued to rant. "You guys were going at it pretty hard this morning. Why'd she try to run?"

"She figured shit out," I said, looking over at him.

That's when Riley's face went white. "What do you mean, she figured shit out?"

She knew exactly what I meant.

"I mean, she figured shit out." I braced my elbows on the counter and leaned in closer, "Did you really think you could keep her in the dark?"

"Logan, Shelby's too sweet. She doesn't belong in this world."

Shelby was stronger than she thought. She was drugged by a couple pricks, found out she had a brother, dealt with all her father's shit, and she hadn't broken yet.

When she saw my scars did she give me a sympathetic look, or try and kiss my wounds away? No, she got pissed. There was a fire in her begging to come out, but I had a feeling Riley knew that.

"What are you afraid of Riley? That she can't handle it?" I rolled my gaze up to the fear shining in her eyes, "Or you can't?"

Not even Micha, Riley's knight in shining armor, came to the rescue. My best friend was the first to shove the truth down someone's throat. If she was going to survive in our world, she better learn to suck it up and deal with it. Life wasn't full of sunshine and lollipops. Reality was a bitch that slapped you in the face when you least expected it.

Riley's throat bobbed with a heavy swallow. "You need to give her time to process."

"I don't need to do shit."

"If you care about her at all, you'll give her time," Riley said as I strutted out of the room. "You can't force someone to love you, Logan."

"Worked for Micha," I snarled over my shoulder, and left.

What the fuck did Riley know? You can't force someone to love you. Pfft. Who said I wanted love, anyway? She was mine, and that was all that mattered. A warm pussy for me to come home to every night.

Well, I liked the way she smelled, like fresh jasmine on a spring morning. And how her smile lit up the room. In the right light, the golden flecks in her eyes sparkled and the sweet tone of her laugh rang through the air, making everything seem brighter. Hell, just watching her walk in a room made me want to smile.

I stopped in the hall and stared at my closed bedroom door. Did I love this girl?

Fuck, I think I did.

No. Riley just got in my head, that was all. But when I opened my door and Shelby's angry glare rolled my way, I felt my heart swell.

Fuck.

Maybe time wasn't a bad idea? I needed to get this shit under wraps before I was pussy whipped like Micha. Problem was, the last thing I wanted to do was let her go. The mere thought of it made me ball my hands into tight fists. Luckily, my phone dinged, giving me the excuse I needed.

Lou: If you want to see your father, meet at HQ at noon.

After Logan untied me, he didn't try to stop me from leaving. He simply said he'd find me tonight, and let me go. And go I did. I ran down the stairs and out the door, ignoring Riley's voice calling after me.

I saw her come out of the house as I sped down the driveway and still didn't stop. I didn't know where I was going, just that I needed to go.

The irony of the situation was that I was running from the one person that told me the truth. For all his faults, Logan never once lied to me. He didn't deny the supposed secret society, even when I freaked out.

What really scared me was the image of Logan covered in blood that I couldn't shake from my mind. I lay trapped on that bed, wondering what happened to Noah and Evan. When I could finally speak, I was too terrified to ask. Because if even half the rumors were true, I wouldn't like the answer.

The Order of Ravens and Wolves was real, and I didn't know who to trust. It certainly wasn't Riley. She was hiding something from me, just like my mom, and my dad, and who knows who else. Which is how I found myself parked in front of a little white church, staring up at the large cross on the roof.

I wasn't a religious person. My family didn't go to church on Sunday or pray before dinner, but right now, I could use a little faith.

I walked inside and dropped down in the closest pew. It was quiet, only a few people remained from Sunday service. None of whom paid me much attention. Except for one. Marnie was putting away hymn books when I walked in.

She looked as confused as I felt. I didn't see Trina anywhere; she usually left the second their father was done preaching. Marnie stayed behind. She said she liked the peace, which I got now. It was calm in here.

"Hey," Marnie said, slipping in to sit next to me. "Are you okay?"

I didn't know if anything would ever be okay again.

"Did something happen with Logan or Riley?"

I huffed out a snort. Did something happen with Logan or Riley. *Everything happened.*

If anyone would understand, it'd be Marnie. She researched the Order, and it wasn't like I could talk to Rye. But I really wanted to talk to her. I missed my friend. My heart hurt when I thought about how things used to be. Rye was gone, my dad was with someone else, and my mom hid a kid. I had no one except Marnie.

"You were right you know, about the Order." I turned my teary eyes her way. "I don't know what to do?"

Marnie's lips tipped down in a frown. "There's nothing you can do."

Like I said, no one.

I sniffed and stared at the cross on the altar. "I could run?"

"You wouldn't make it far."

Marnie and I turned our heads to see Preston standing beside us, his cold dead stare focused on me. "You and I need to talk."

He was the last person I wanted to talk to.

"You shouldn't be here," Marnie whispered.

His eyes snapped up to her, and for just a second I thought I saw a spark of life in their cold dead depths.

"We've had this discussion, Little Bird." He leaned over me, brushing his jean jacket off my shoulder, and added in a soft growl that scared even me, "You don't get to tell me what to do."

The Marnie I knew would've thrown his words back in his face. This Marnie didn't do that. She squeaked a quiet apology and hung her head.

"Leave her alone," I snarled and pushed him back.

I was so tired of all this bully bullshit. That's when I learned Logan might be scary, but Preston was terrifying.

"Here's what's going to happen." He braced his palms on the pews and leaned in, "You're going to walk out that door with me and not say a goddamn word."

"And if I don't?"

"You see that sweet little old lady?"

I assumed he was referring to Mrs. Jenkins, who was on her knees deep in prayer.

"Yes."

He didn't say anything, just held open his coat enough for me to see the butt of a gun.

I swallowed a lump of fear and whispered, "You wouldn't."

"He would," Marnie answered.

With my heart pounding loudly, I hesitantly rose off the pew. Preston smiled and waved his hand at the door. I didn't want to go. It was the look on Marnie's face that convinced me.

Pushing the door open, I took one last look at my friend and tried to reassure her with a smile. It didn't work. For either of us. All I could think as Preston marched me over to his car, was how normal life was before Logan. My biggest worry a week ago was Christmas for my little sister. Now, I felt like I was walking to my execution.

Once we were seated in his BMW and the doors were closed, Preston turned to look at me.

"There are very few people I actually care about in this world. My parents don't even make the cut." He pulled out a cigarette and placed it between his lips, before holding out the pack to offer me one.

"No thanks," I said, shaking my head.

He shrugged and tucked the pack back in his pocket before continuing. "Logan does. I'm sure you know he didn't have the most ideal childhood."

My chest tightened thinking about all the scars marking his perfect body. I nodded.

"He's not the most stable person, but last night I saw something I never thought I would. He was frenzied, going off on that prick that drugged you, and *you* pulled him out of it. You didn't have to hit him, or pin him to the ground, you just had to say his name. One word from you and he snapped back."

How was I supposed to take that?

"Are you trying to tell me Logan's crazy?"

"He's most definitely crazy." Preston exhaled a stream of smoke and rolled his eyes my way, "But you make him sane."

Was it wrong that my heart melted a little? That five words from Death Himself made me fall deeper for a man I should be running from?

"I only have one question. Do you love him?"

"Mom!" I called out and closed the door. "I'm home!"

I wasn't excited to see my mom, and even less so when she walked around the corner with Riley.

I sighed and hung up my coat. "What do you want?"

"Shelby Harlow Grace, is that any way to talk to your friend?"

I glared at my mom. She would never talk to someone like that. God forbid she show an ounce of attitude. Perfect Cheyenne Grace and her happy little life.

"Would you prefer we talk about the kid you're pretending doesn't exist?"

"I understand you're upset, Shelby."

That was an understatement.

"I was young and alone. What was I supposed to do with a baby? I was still a child myself. The responsible thing was to give him to parents capable of raising a child. As much as it hurt, I had to think about him."

I didn't think about that. Mom loved Mags and me, she'd never given me any reason to think otherwise. It was probably incredibly hard for her to give up her baby.

"I'm sorry, Mom," I cried, and threw my arms around her.

"It's alright, sweetie. I understand." She kissed the top of my head and smiled down at me. "You should talk to Riley. She was worried about you."

Mom walked away, leaving us alone. We stood there in awkward silence for a few seconds before breaking down and embracing in a violent hug.

"I'm sorry," Rye cried.

"No, I'm sorry," I cried back.

We let our tears wash away our anger and guilt before sitting down to talk. That's when I found out about the horrible things that happened to her. The stuff Logan's dad made Mason do, and how Micha saved them.

She told me a bit about The Order, but didn't know much about it herself. She didn't want to. After what she'd been through, I couldn't blame her. When I asked her where Logan's dad was, all she'd say was that he couldn't hurt anyone anymore.

That wasn't true though. He hurt Logan every day. I saw it in his eyes when he looked in the mirror. He was haunted by his past. It tormented him.

'You make him sane.'

But maybe I could save him.

My hands tightened on the steering wheel as I pulled to a stop at Manning Keep. Lou's town-car was already there, along with Martin Creswell's Lincoln.

Both were standing by the open entrance, waiting for me, along with Marco and four security guards. I swung open my door and stepped out with a smirk on my face. Guess they didn't trust me alone with my old man.

"Little overkill, don't you think, Lou?"

"I prefer to call it cautious."

I looked over at Marco, who cleared his throat and shifted on his feet. He was a big fucker, but he wasn't dumb. He'd seen me in a rage.

Sucking in a long drag of smoke, I said, "I hope it's a big room." I flicked my butt and slowly exhaled, "Otherwise someone's going to take it up the ass."

"You'll be going in alone."

My brow rose at Lou's statement. He had to know I'd kill the fucker the first chance I got. It didn't matter how many men he had ready, they weren't fast enough.

I glanced over at Martin, eyeing his doctor bag. "What's the catch?"

"You have the right to talk to your father." Lou straightened himself and smoothed his suit jacket.

Since when?

My gaze narrowed in on him. "He wouldn't talk to you, would he?"

"No," Lou sighed. "He said he'd only talk to you."

The Kings must've learned the hard way that you can't torture someone who has nothing to lose. My old man already lost the only thing important to him. Power. He could give a fuck less about anything else.

Lou waved his hand at the stairs leading into the ground. "Shall we?"

"After you," I said, and followed him down the stone steps.

We went through the Ravens door and took a left down a hallway I'd never been down before. Not that I paid attention to shit here. The only time I came to Manning Keep was when I had to. At the end of the hall, Lou punched in a code and creaked open a metal door.

My heart pumped adrenaline through my veins. I knew my old man was in there. I could sense him.

"So you know," Lou turned and looked at me, "If you kill him, you fail."

I scoffed out a laugh. Seriously? This was what they decided to use for my *Dominare la paura?*

"You think I give a shit if I fail your fucking test?"

Martin grumbled, "I told you."

No one accused the doctor of being stupid.

"I have faith in the boy."

"You shouldn't," I said, and sauntered through the door.

My first thought was, *what the fuck was this?* This shit wasn't some deep dark hole, it was closer to a luxury room at the Plaza. Complete with plush furnishings, and a goddamn bar.

"Hello, boy. How's your mother?"

My eyes locked on my old man. Smug fucker stood there with a smile on his face, sipping fucking brandy.

"Come in, have a seat." He waved at a wingback chair. "You want a drink?"

"Only if I get to drink it out of your skull."

My old man tsked. "You should play nice. That is, if you want your little girlfriend to find her brother."

He was bluffing. No way my old man would take Lou's kid and let him live. "He's dead."

"Is he? Come on boy, you know me better than that." He tipped a brow in my direction. "Would I waste perfectly good leverage?"

No he fucking wouldn't. Did I care? No. *But she would.*

Fuck sakes. For some goddamn reason, I cared about that shit. Thinking of Shelby crying over her lost brother broke my heart.

"God damnit!" I snarled and flopped down in the chair.

Fucking Shelby jacking up everything.

I could've come in here and gotten some satisfaction, and maybe a little blood. But no. I had to play along. And why? Because of some chick.

Not 'some' chick. My chick.

My old man snickered and walked over to the bar to pour a drink. "She's a fine piece of ass, son. You fucked her yet?"

None of your fucking business.

"Of course you have," he said, holding out a glass for me. "You are my son, after all."

"I'm nothing like you," I hissed and snatched the cup out of his hand.

"Yes you are." He sat down in a chair opposite me and stared me straight in the eyes. "You're exactly like me."

I wanted to rip that fucking smile off his face. Instead, I downed the contents of the glass, letting the alcohol burn it's way down my throat.

"See that look right there?" He lifted his glass and pointed at me. "That's all me, boy."

"Shut the fuck up."

I was nothing like my old man. Everything he touched turned to shit.

"Let me ask you a question." He sat back and crossed his ankles. "You hit her yet?"

My eyes locked on his as I forced a swallow down my throat. I did, but only because she hit me. She needed to learn.

"She deserved it."

"Did she?" He tipped his head, "Or do you just like seeing her suffer?"

That was different. She liked it too. At least, I think she did. She asked me to hurt her. What if she only did it because she knew I wanted to?

"It's okay boy, I like it too." He held his glass up and stared longingly at the amber liquid inside. "There's nothing quite as exquisite as your woman's tears."

"She laughs with me," I said, attempting to refute his argument. "I make her smile."

"I'm sure you do. Your mother smiled all the time, too."

Ma's smiles were fake. Shelby's were real. *But are they?*

"You're more like me than you thought, boy."

I jumped out of the chair and threw my glass at the wall. Fuck him. He was just messing with my head. "You don't scare me anymore, old man."

"Yeah, well come on then, boy. Show me what you got."

"ANOTHER," I said, slamming the glass down on the bar.

Lou had his goons pull me off my old man before I could do any real damage. I had the fucker, too. He was down on the ground, facing the full fury of my fists, and the fuckers pulled me off.

Son of a bitch laughed at me when I was dragged from the room. I got a couple good shots in though. I should be happy about that. I wasn't.

The bartender slid another shot of scotch my way. "Here you go."

I nodded at him, tipped the glass to my lips, and downed the alcohol.

My old man said I was like him. That Shelby would end up just like Ma. Scared and alone. Maybe he was right. His blood did pump through my veins like a fucking plague. Everything I touched turned to shit. Why the fuck should she be any different? I was a fucking idiot to think I could have something good in my life.

"Hey there handsome. You look a little down."

I tipped my chin at the brunette and raked my eyes down her frame. If her shirt got any tighter, her nipples would be on display. They kind of were already.

She leaned in, giving me a good view of her ample cleavage. "You know, I have a knack for cheering people up."

"Oh yeah?" I leaned back to sneak a peek of her ass. Not bad. "Well, what do you say we get out here then, sweetheart?"

Two minutes later, we were behind the bar in the back of her shitty car.

$\mathcal{I}$ pulled out of a rather good dream by a strange noise. I stared up at my darkened roof as I blinked away the remnants of a wedding dress I'd never be able to afford. Logan looked good in a tux. With his hair all styled, and a smile on his face. I wouldn't argue if I got to see him like that one day.

I still couldn't believe what Rye went through at the hands of Logan's dad. If he could do that to her and Mason in a couple of hours, what did he do to Logan over years? It broke my heart just thinking about it. I pushed myself up and grabbed my phone.

> Me: I'm sorry I ran out on you. Can you come by? I'd like to see you.

I hit send, even though Logan was probably asleep.

Ding.

What the heck?

My heart flipped when I looked up and saw the red ember of a

261

cigarette glowing in the dark. My brows furrowed at the figure sitting on the end of my bed.

"Logan?"

I thought I smelled smoke, but I'd assumed my mind was still in my dream. For half a second, I thought I might still be asleep. I'd never seen him like this.

His shoulders were hunched over, and even in the dark, I could see the deep lines etched in his brow. I gently reached out and placed my hand on his back, as he sucked in a drag from his cigarette.

"I had to see you."

His statement sounded more like an apology.

"It's okay." I shuffled a little closer and tipped my head, coaxing him to look at me. "Are you okay?"

"Am I okay?" The muscles on his back flexed under my palm as he scoffed out a snicker. "No, I'm not okay. Nothing's okay," he added in a mutter before sucking on his cigarette.

Logan still wouldn't look at me. He continued to sit there and stare at something in the dark. The pain coming off him physically tugged at my heart.

I wanted to comfort him. Wrap my arms around him and tell him everything would be okay. So that's what I did. I pressed myself up against his back and held him tightly.

"I fucked up." His fingers grazed over the back of my hands. "I fucked up bad."

"I'm sure it's not as bad–"

Seven words. That's all it took for Logan Hudson to destroy me.

"I met a chick in a bar."

My arms dropped away from him as my heart physically shattered.

The only thing that stopped me from moving away were his red rimmed eyes. When he lifted his head and I saw the dry streaks on his face, I froze. He'd been crying.

"I didn't fuck her," he explained, "But I came damn close."

"How close?" I don't know why I said that. I didn't want to hear the gritty details.

"I had the condom ready, and my dick out."

That was pretty close.

"So, you touched her?"

He let out a strangled sigh. "Yes."

"Did she touch you?"

He didn't have to say anything, I could see the answer on his face.

I sat there quietly chewing on my lip while struggling to blink back the tears filling my eyes.

This was stupid. He'd been with countless girls, why would one be enough for him now? Let alone one so inexperienced. Then I got angry. I didn't want this. He made me fall for him. Why? Just so he could rip my heart out?

"Sounds like you had everything in order."

"It wasn't like that." He grabbed my arm, stopping me when I tried to back away. "I didn't want her baby."

"Don't call me that!" I growled, tearing my arm out of his grip.

He reached out for me again, but I kicked his hand away and slapped him. Everything got quiet. So quiet that I heard the sizzle of his cigarette when he dropped it in my cup of water.

Then he lunged. Grabbing my ankles and pulling me down on the bed so he could crawl over me.

"I couldn't do it," he said while I swung my fists, taking my anger out on his solid chest. "I had her right there, and I couldn't do it."

"You expect me to have sympathy for you because your bar whore couldn't cut it?"

I couldn't get away, his weight had me pinned, but I could still hurt him. Make him feel an ounce of the agonizing pain I was feeling. I swung my hand and slapped him hard across the face.

"Fuck you, Logan."

Was this all some twisted way to hurt me? It worked. For half a second, I'd let myself think that Logan Hudson did care about me. I was a fool. The dam holding my tears back broke.

"You win," I huffed out a sigh and rolled my head on the bed. It hurt too much to look at him. "I hope you're happy."

"Fuck." He dropped his head and nuzzled in my neck. "I was scared I'd break you, and I broke you anyway."

What?

"Everything I touch turns to shit. I should've stayed away from you. But I can't. I fucking love you. I can't let you go."

My heart fluttered as I twisted my neck to look at him. "You love me?"

When he lifted his head and I saw those beautiful green eyes glimmering with unshed tears, my breath hitched. I could feel the desperation in them. Logan wasn't just guilty, he was terrified.

"I don't just love you baby, I need you." He cupped my face and swept the tears off my cheeks with his thumbs. "Your beautiful smile is the first thing I think about in the morning and the last thing I see when I go to sleep. I let my old man get to me and I shouldn't have."

He *saw his father today?*

"I'm so fucking sorry. You have no idea how fucking sorry I am. I swear to god I'll never look at another woman again. Just tell me I didn't lose you."

My heart swelled as I stared up into his pleading gaze. Was it too late? Did he lose me?

"I saw Preston today. He asked me if I loved you."

A spark of hope flashed across his face. "What did you say?"

"That I didn't know. But I lied."

No, he didn't lose me. He couldn't, because Logan Hudson didn't just own my heart. He owned my soul.

"I do love you."

His lips slammed down on mine, taking me in a possessive kiss that I felt in the depths of my soul. It was desperate, tinged with the mingled taste of our tears, and absolutely perfect.

We became a frenzy of teeth, tongues and hands. A tangled mess of passion. I threaded my fingers through his hair and wrapped my leg around his waist, groaning when I felt his hardness press against me.

Logan growled against my mouth and tore away my shorts and panties, while I unbuckled his belt and pushed his jeans over his hips with my feet.

I didn't care what happened. I need him, needed to feel him inside me. When he lined his cock up and pushed into my opening, we both groaned.

Our bodies moved up the bed as he fucked me hard and rough. Every time I came close to that blissful edge, Logan would bite me or pinch me, giving me just enough pain to toss me over.

I cried in my pillow, my hand and blanket. Anything I could to muffle the sounds I was making. But when he wrapped my leg around his hip and changed the angle I couldn't hold my moans back.

"Quiet, baby," Logan growled while clamping his hand over my mouth, "You're going to wake up your mom."

I muttered behind his heavy palm, "I don't care."

"You will, when she has to watch me fuck you," Logan chuckled, "Because I'm not stopping."

That just made me moan louder as my pussy clenched tightly around him.

"Oh, you like that?" he hissed in my ear and picked up the force of his thrusts. "My dirty little girl wants everyone to know who owns this pussy."

I screamed behind his hand as waves of orgasmic bliss rocked my body.

"Fuuuck," Logan grunted, flipped us over and pressed my face down into the crook of his neck.

I was nervous at first. The new position gave me control. Or at least I thought it did until Logan grabbed my hips and started rocking me.

It didn't take me long to fall into the rhythm he set and soon I was fucking him. It was empowering watching his face twist in pleasure, knowing I was the cause.

"That's it, baby, fuck me." He palmed my ass, digging his fingers into my flesh and ran his hot tongue down my neck. "Ride my cock."

This time when my orgasm took me, I dug my teeth into his shoulder, using his muscle to muffle my scream. That seemed to set him off. Two hard thrusts later and he was holding me down on his cock as it twitched inside me, bathing my walls with his warm cum.

As I lay there slumped over him, panting my exertion into his neck, a thought occurred to me. "You didn't use a condom."

"I'm clean and you're on birth control."

"Birth control isn't always a hundred percent," I pointed out. "What if I get pregnant?"

"Well, then we'll have a baby." He turned and looked at me, green eyes sparkling with delight, "And it'll be the cutest little shit this world has ever seen."

Chapter 27

Shelby

My first day at Ashworth was better than I expected. Everybody was so nice. Except for Naomi, who I suspected was a bitch to everyone, and the receptionist, Mrs. Grier.

I think Rye was right and she was a demon sent to collect high school kids' souls. That, or an alien. Most of my classes were with Rye, and the few that weren't were with Lana or Harper.

All I wanted to do when I first met Harper was put make-up on her and dress her up. She was so friggin cute, and absolutely terrified. Of everything. I saw her jump at her own shadow. Twice. It was sad.

I kind of wanted to punch Mason, but something told me the youngest Kessler wasn't her only problem. Otherwise, why would she still be scared? Mason wasn't even here.

Her brother Sean was cute, and fun to be around. Until Logan punched him in the face. Which led to my current situation. Sitting in the cafeteria, watching Logan and Sean snarl insults at each other while their friends held them back.

Welcome to Ashworth, Shelby.

"It's usually Mason."

"What?" I said, looking over at Lana, who was eating her lunch like normal.

"It's usually Mason that's fighting with Sean."

"Can you blame him? He's not exactly nice to his sister."

Riley sighed and grumbled, "They're all idiots."

"Agreed," Naomi added.

"Stop agreeing with me," Riley curled her lip and shot Naomi a look, "It's freaking me out."

Naomi returned her glare with a lip curl of her own.

"When you two are done, maybe you can help me figure out how to break this up."

Micha and Silas were holding Logan back, while two of the football players had Sean. I don't know what infuriated me more, that no one in the cafeteria seemed to care, or that Harper was two seconds away from a heart attack.

"Fuck you, Hudson," Sean snarled, "The second you fuck up, I'm gonna be all over that shit."

Sean had no idea how close to home that hit. Logan held me tightly all night, like he was afraid I'd change my mind if he let go. It might be odd, but I trusted him more now than I did before. He'd told me the truth, knowing he might've lost me doing it.

"I'll fucking kill you!" Logan yelled, loud enough to fill the whole room with his voice.

Harper squeaked and ducked under the table.

Alright, that's it.

I got up and sauntered over to Logan.

"Shelby," Micha growled, "Now's not the time. Go sit the fuck down."

There was only one thing that cut through a guy's macho alpha crap.

"But the chair's uncomfortable," I whined with a fake pout. "I was hoping Logan could give me something better to sit on."

A woman.

Logan stopped fighting against Micha and Silas's hold and cocked a brow at me.

"I'm kind of cold too." I swung my hips and twirled my hair, "could you warm me up?"

I could practically hear Riley's eyes roll as she groaned, "Good God."

Whatever my best friend thought, it worked. Logan shook Micha and Silas off him and pulled me into his arms.

"You need me to warm you up, baby?"

"Uh huh." I widened my eyes into a sappy puppy dog stare and wrapped my arms around his neck. "I'm really cold."

He moved in, brushing his lips against mine, and softly said, "Well, we can't have that."

"Pussy," Micha grumbled as he walked by to rejoin Riley at the table, who was making gagging noises.

When Logan shot him a dirty look, I leaned in and whispered, "Don't worry about them. They won't get to do to me what you will tonight."

"Oo, I like the sound of that." He pushed his fingers through my hair, tucking it behind my ear. "Do I get any details?"

"Well, I saw all that stuff in your wardrobe."

I couldn't stop thinking about it. Whips, and sticks, and other things I didn't know what to call. I had to admit, I was curious.

"Let's go now," Logan growled, pressing in on me. "Fuck school."

"Not so fast, big boy," I said and led him back to the table, where he pulled me onto his lap.

Micha looked at us and cocked a brow at Riley, who waved her fork at him. "Don't even think about it."

Despite Riley's objection, he grabbed her and pulled her onto his lap.

"I swear to God, Micha, I'll stab you with this fork."

He nuzzled in her neck and growled, "You like it."

As amusing as the flush on my best friend's face was, I was much more interested in what was happening at the other end of the table.

Parker's death glare was locked on Lana. His jaw ticked every time she lifted her fork to her mouth.

For the first time since I met him, I could see the similarities with his brother. The dark look on his face reminded me so much of Preston, it was scary.

Lana didn't seem to mind. She completely ignored him, and continued to eat her lunch as if he wasn't boring holes in her skull. Which he did not like.

"You sure you should eat that?" Parker tipped his chin at the cupcake on her tray. "Your ass is fat enough."

Without so much as a word, Lana lifted her cup and threw the contents in his face.

Logan burst out laughing while Parker spit out a mouthful of orange juice and glared at Lana.

She returned his look with a sweet smile and went back to her lunch.

Go Lana.

"Damn girl, you've got good aim," Logan sang, "Not even a drop on Silas."

Silas frowned and ran his light eyes over the juice dripping off Parker's face. "You might want to clean that up."

"I'm fine," Parker grumbled, and tore his shirt off, using it to wipe off his face.

Damn. The boy was cut. And I mean cut.

"Do I need to fuck you in front of my friend?"

"Why would you need to do that," I rolled my eyes over my shoulder to Logan, "When you say such sweet things to me?"

He smirked. "Next step, poetry."

Speaking of poetry…

"I think you need to work on your poetic skills," I said, passing him the note I found in my locker this morning.

It was sweet that he tried, but the poem was kind of creepy:

Shelby Grace, Hudson's cherry pie,

She kissed the boy that made her cry,
Now The Piper is ready to play,
Shelby Grace should run away.

The Piper.

"Sorry, but The Piper isn't the kind of cute nickname I'd give you."

All the guys got suddenly really quiet and Riley was staring at me with wide, worried eyes.

"What?"

Did I miss something?

"Baby, where did you get this?"

"It was in my locker." I didn't like the way Logan was staring at the piece of paper in his hand. "Didn't you put it there?"

"No, I didn't put it there."

"He could've mailed them before?" Riley said with a hopeful gleam in her eyes, "Post dated them?"

"How'd he know she'd be here?" Logan pointed out, "Or that I call her Cherry Pie?"

Micha's dark eyes rolled up. "You know what this means…"

"What, what means?" I was so confused.

Instead of answering me, Logan answered Micha. "He has a partner. Probably…"

"My brother."

"What about our brother?"

I swear it was like I suddenly manifested the power of invisibility.

"Better call your old man."

I slammed my hand down on the table. "Will someone tell me what's going on?"

SOMETIMES IT WASN'T bad to be in the dark. I wish I was still there. Cloaked in an illusion where everything was safe. Now I saw danger around every corner. Every new face was the monster in my closet.

My only saving grace was Silas's angry scowl, watching me from the sidelines. I had to send Logan to pick up Mags. I was more afraid for her, and didn't trust anyone else to keep her safe. So he left Silas to watch me. Didn't make me feel any better.

"Come on, Grace, pick it up. I know you can do better than that."

The assistant coach, Luke Lannister seemed nice enough. The other girls on the team seemed to like him. Can't say I blamed them. He was handsome. Dark hair and kind light eyes that reminded me of my mom, but all I could think when I looked at him was, does he want to hurt me?

"Sorry," I said, hunching over to catch my breath. "I don't know what's wrong with me."

Lie. I knew exactly what was wrong.

"Hey, I get it." Luke laid his hand on my back. "It's tough being the new kid in school."

Or having your life threatened.

"You just got to push forward and move on."

Easy for you to say.

"Now, come on." He ushered me back onto the track, "I know you've got the speed to out-run every girl on this team."

I smiled, and took off.

Let's hope I was fast enough to out-run the boogeyman.

I'd never been happier to babysit in my life. The look on Junior's face when I walked in with Shelby's little sister was fucking priceless. He looked like he just got kicked in the nuts.

It was fucking awesome. Even better was the fact that currently had him out back playing tea party with Finn, who was also dumped on me.

Ma was fucking ecstatic to have three little ones in the house. Which gave me time to look into the note Shelby got, and I think I'd found the culprit. The handwriting on her note looked familiar, so I started rifling through my shit. I found a match in my chem lab notes.

More specifically, the ones Sean Callaghan took. Prick probably found one of the notes Riley got and figured he'd fuck with the new girl. I'd have a conversation with him about that tomorrow. In the meantime, I told Silas to let Shelby know every-thing was fine. It was just a stupid prank.

"Oh my god, I love that kid," Ava said, slipping in through the sliding glass doors. "She's got the boys in big flowery hats."

I closed the newspaper I was reading and looked up at her. "Fuck off."

"Seriously, Naomi's out there right now explaining why the colors should match their outfits."

This, I had to see. I got up and walked over to stand next to Ava and look out the glass doors. Sure enough, there they were. Sitting at a table Ma had set up by the pool with big flowery hats on their heads.

Shelby's little sister poured fake tea, while Naomi's hands swung through the air, pointing from one hat to the other. Finn was watching her intently, soaking up every word she said, while Junior was slumped over with arms crossed and a scowl on his face.

"I don't think I've ever seen your mom so happy."

Ma was playing the part of servant, standing off to the side and bowing every time Maggie said something to her. "That's dreams of grandbabies dancing in her eyes."

"You gonna give her any?"

I glanced at Ava and said, "What are you doing here?" before returning to my paper.

"Well, I heard that *you* were babysitting and I just had to come and see for myself."

"Parker has a big fucking mouth."

Bastard was there when Shelby asked me to pick up her sister. Of course he had to tell his sister. *I was so playing the 'I fucked your sister' card tomorrow.*

"Ugh, I don't get kids these days," Naomi sauntered in joining us. "They are impossible to talk to."

"I don't think they're worried about the finer points of fashion," I pointed out.

"Finn listened to me," she sang.

I glanced over at her smug face. "Finn listens to everyone."

Kid was like a sponge.

"Anyway," Ava waved her hand, interrupting us. "I'm more interested in why the great Logan Hudson is babysitting. Never thought I'd see you bow down to a girl."

I'm not bowing down to her.

"Should've seen the way she played him today," Naomi added. "The girl is good."

She didn't play me. Did she? I thought about Shelby's hips swinging and the tempting smirk on her face.

Son of a bitch, she did.

"I'm cool with it." A slow smile spread across my face, "Especially since I get to play with her tonight."

"Ah, so she promised you sexual favors."

Naomi nodded at Ava's statement. "Told you she was good."

"The question is," Ava pointed at me "What is Logan going to do for her?"

"What do you mean?" My brows furrowed. "I'm gonna give her my dick."

What the fuck else did she need?

The girls exchanged a look before Ava sighed and turned back to me. "As fantastic as you think your dick is…"

Hey now.

"What are you going to do for *her*?"

"What? Like eat her out?"

"He's hopeless."

"Utterly," Naomi agreed.

I sat there listening to them argue about how much of a lost cause I was, wondering when my house became the community drop in center. When did my life become so fucked up?

Things used to be so simple and quiet. I bring a chick home, bang her, and then send her on her way. Now I had my own chick and I was sitting between two bickering divas, and my chick wasn't even a diva. What the fuck? How was this shit fun?

My phone dinged, making me smirk.

Chase: We're here.

Now this shit would be fun.

Me: Come on in. we're in the kitchen.

The girls were too busy discussing the crap I needed to do for Shelby to hear the roar of bikes coming up the driveway.

"We can set up a romantic dinner," Ava said.

I nodded in agreement while anxiously staring at the door. "Totally."

"And you have to get her something nice," Naomi added. "Something she likes."

"Nice." I held up my thumbs. "Got it."

"Logan, are you even listening to us?"

Nope. Not one bit.

I smiled when the door opened and Chase and Tanner sauntered inside.

Naomi's face instantly dropped as her eyes rolled over the scruffy biker that tanned her ass. I heard all about her little Daddy incident, and honestly couldn't be more excited to see a reunion.

Tanner whistled as his eyes swung around. "Nice digs. How many rooms you think they got in this place?"

"Too many," Chase muttered, and marched straight for the kitchen, with Tanner swaggering behind.

The first I'd seen a smirk tug on the big bastard's lips was when his eyes landed on Naomi's scowl. Tanner seemed much more interested in Ava. Poor fucker.

"Damn," he sang, flashing her a charming smile, "I'm definitely a fan of the kitchen."

Ava's brow rose. "Is that your attempt at flirting?"

"Depends. Is it working?"

I almost felt sorry for the bastard when Ava got up and sauntered over to him. Almost.

The girl may be tiny as fuck, but she knew how to command a room. Like when she slid her hand up Tanner's chest. I guarantee, at that moment, she was all the fucker saw.

"Are you gonna give it to me good, big boy?" Ava purred with a seductive look on her face.

I knew what that look meant. Unfortunately for Tanner, he didn't.

"Oh yeah baby, I'll give it to you good."

The only warning he got before her fist landed in his gut, was a tiny smirk.

"I'm going to find Logan a suit," she sang, and flipped her hair over her shoulder before strutting out of the room. Leaving Tanner behind in a hunched over heap.

"Fuck," he coughed while glancing back at Ava's retreating form. "I think I'm in love."

"You might want to stay away from that one," I warned him, "She's psycho."

He beamed up at me. "I like psycho."

His funeral.

"Can I help you?" Naomi snarled at Chase, who was standing in the middle of the room with his arms crossed.

"Still mouthy, I see." He slowly raked his gaze over her body and cocked his head. "Does Daddy know you're out this late?"

She glared at him and I couldn't be happier.

Welcome home motherfuckers.

HOW THE FUCK did I end up in this situation? Oh, that's right. The diva's decided I had to take my girl on date. While they set up the backyard like a scene from a chick flick, I was sent out to get Shelby something *nice.*

"Why the fuck do I have to wear this monkey suit?" I tugged at the tie around my neck.

Ava slapped my hand away and straightened my tie. "Because you look handsome."

I rolled my eyes and snorted. *Tell me something I don't know.*

"I always look handsome."

Riley grumbled out a groan. Still wasn't sure how they roped my stepsister into this shit.

"Did you get her something?"

Don't know who said that. Didn't care. Just held up the stuffed unicorn.

Naomi's lip curled. "You got her a unicorn?"

"She likes unicorns."

Riley's brow rose. "How do you figure?"

"She's got three in her room." I know, because I counted that shit. Fucking stuffed animals and flowers everywhere. Shelby was going to love this thing. I'd prefer to burn it, but hey, I wasn't a chick.

"Uh huh." Ava nodded at the unicorn in my hand. "Can I see that?"

I handed it over, only to be smacked in the back of the head with it.

"Ow," I cried out rubbing my head. "What was that for?"

"You're an idiot," Riley answered.

Ava placed her hands on her cocked hips. "He's clearly not equipped to deal with this."

"Agreed," Naomi nodded.

I was really starting to feel ganged up on here.

"Well, I can't stay," Riley said, "I've got a class to teach in fifteen minutes."

"I've got dinner with my parents," Ava said. "I guess that leaves you, Nay."

Naomi rolled her eyes.

I was there with her. This was bullshit.

"And who exactly, is supposed to be my date?"

Chase and Tanner chose that moment to saunter in. I tried to warn them and wave them off, but the stupid fucks didn't listen.

Ava immediately ran up to Chase and slapped her hand on his chest. "This strapping young man right here."

"What?" His brows furrowed as he glanced around the room, confused. "What's going on?"

"Just go with it man," I sighed. "It's not worth fighting."

I got a text telling me to come to Logan's and to wear something nice. I had no idea what was going on, but I never refused a chance to dress up.

So I went all out. Rolled my hair up in a French twist. Put on my best jewellery, and dressed in a red spaghetti strap dress with a plunging neck-line and slit up to my thigh. The shoes were my favorite black strappy sandals, with just enough heel to give me a bit of height while not making me too tall.

When Logan opened the door I was stunned. His blond hair was styled in that perfect 'messy yet not' way, and his green eyes glimmered against the black jacket of his suit. My favorite part of his outfit was the deep crimson dress shirt. It wouldn't suit him if there wasn't some dark flare to the outfit.

If the look on his face was anything to judge by, he seemed to appreciate my outfit too. Particularly the plunging neckline.

"Damn, baby," he growled and pulled me in for a kiss, "I can't wait to rip that dress off you."

"You better not rip it. This dress was expensive."

He kissed a trail up my neck and muttered, "I'll buy you another one."

"Uh um!" That's when I noticed Naomi standing there tapping her foot. "See, this is why you need supervision. You'd have the poor girl naked before the first course."

"And what's wrong with that?" he snarled over his shoulder.

"Focus," Naomi snapped her fingers in front of his face. "Do what you were told and I'll meet you outside." She stopped halfway into the kitchen and glanced back at him. "Don't make me come back in here."

I was definitely curious what was going on now.

Logan grumbled something, rubbed the back of his neck and looped his arm in mine. "Come on."

We walked through the kitchen and out to the backyard, all lit up with fairy lights. Everything was so beautiful I didn't know where to look first. At the string quartet playing on the far left side of the patio, the lilies floating in the pool around a small fountain, the two tables lit by candle-light, or Naomi and Chase…

Wait…

"Chase?"

He looked just as surprised as me.

"Shelby?" He tipped his head and glared at Logan. "You and I are going to have words later."

"Careful now, Jim Bob," Logan smirked down at him, gleaming like a sly cat. "You don't want to ruin her special night."

Chase just scowled at him as Logan led me over to the other table.

He was so cute, trying to act like a gentleman and pull my chair out for me. I almost chuckled when he thrust a bouquet of daisies in my face. Instead, I smiled and held the flowers up to my nose.

"You got me flowers."

"*I* got you a unicorn," he said, sliding into the chair opposite me, "But Ava smacked me in the head with it."

My nose crinkled as I cocked my head at him. Why would he get me a unicorn?

Everything was going great. We talked and shared a meal. Even though Logan fumbled his way through, I couldn't have imagined a better date. It was so cute, seeing him unsure, but trying anyway. He even tried to do the Lady and the Tramp thing, which didn't work as well with lobster as it did with spaghetti. I suspected a kiss was his ulterior motive there.

Chase and Naomi were clearly not having a good time. Though, I wasn't sure Naomi would have a good time anywhere. Not to mention her supposed date looked more ready for a-peanuts-on-the-floor type bar than a five star restaurant. But I didn't care.

This night could be an epic failure and I'd still love every minute of it. Because Logan did this for me. He put on a suit, slow-danced in the moonlight and used the proper fork, for me.

I was entranced, staring at Logan starry-eyed and wondering if I could possibly love him more, when everything took a violent left turn.

"You need a serious attitude adjustment, Princess," Chase growled loudly, "And I'm in the mood to give it."

"If your grubby paws come anywhere near me–"

Chase slammed his hands down on the table, causing the plates to clatter, and leaned in to glare right in Naomi's face. "You'll what?"

Naomi stared at him for a second before huffing out a frustrated grunt and storming into the house.

"That's what I thought," he called out after her, "Go back home to Daddy."

I kept waiting, holding my breath, to hear Naomi's car drive away. Instead she came back out of the kitchen with a glass in her hand and threw it in Chase's face.

"Should we do something?" I whispered to Logan.

"Fuck no," he said, eyes locked on Chase with interest. "Let's see how this shit plays out."

Chase swept the liquid off his face and rolled his eyes up at her. If looks could kill.

"Did you just go in the house to get water to throw in my face?"

Naomi tipped her head and crossed her arms. "I didn't want to waste perfectly good champagne."

None of us expected what happened next. Chase stood up and puffed his chest out.

I thought for sure Naomi was about to get another spanking. I couldn't believe it when Riley told me about that. That's not what Chase did.

He grabbed the back of her head and crashed his mouth down on hers. It only lasted for about three seconds, but it was enough to stun not only me, but Naomi as well.

"If I'd have known that was all it would take to shut you the fuck up," Chase grinned down at Naomi's stunned face, "I'd have kissed you a lot sooner."

And did Naomi slap him? No.

She calmly reached down into her purse and sprayed him in the face with a can of mace. Chase roared and fell back into the pool.

After which Naomi looked at us, said, "You can fuck her now," and sauntered away with her head held high.

When Chase finally popped his head out of the water, he grumbled, "She fucking maced me."

We didn't say anything. Pretty sure he wasn't asking for confirmation anyway, since he promptly climbed out of the pool and marched after her.

AFTER OUR DATE, Logan took me up to his room. I knew what was coming next, and for some reason I was more nervous now than I was the first time. Maybe that was why I was hiding in the bathroom? I told him I needed a minute, but that minute was long gone and I still couldn't calm the butterflies in my stomach.

"Calm down, Shelby," I said to my reflection, "It's not like you haven't done this before."

This was different though. I wanted to please him and the longer I thought about how to do that, the more nervous I got.

How many girls had he been with? Did I compare to them? I know he said he loved me, but what if he got bored? What chance did I have of keeping a man like him satisfied? It was a lot of pressure.

A male grunt interrupted my thoughts.

"Fuck, Mouse, just like that."

Micha and Riley must be home. *Were they…*

"Please, Micha."

Oh my god, they were.

I shouldn't eavesdrop. At least that's what I told myself as I slid over to her side of the bathroom. There was nothing wrong with a little curiosity, right? My pulse picked up as I pressed my ear to the door. I could hear faint sounds on the other side. Soft moans and tiny grunts. All that did was peak my interest. I looked down at the door knob, chewing my lip.

This was a private moment between them. I shouldn't. Then again, what would it hurt if I took a tiny peek? They wouldn't know.

Before I could stop myself, I was creaking the door open. Just a gap at first, then a little more, until I could see Micha's body glistening with sweat. But it was Riley that had my attention. Micha's big hand was pressing her face into the mattress as he pumped furiously into her.

I'd never seen her look so vulnerable and small. I couldn't stop watching her tiny fingers clutch the blanket as she moaned her pleasure in the bed.

My breathing picked up with theirs and I could feel wetness gather on my thighs. This shouldn't be turning me on. I needed to get out of here. Except I couldn't look away. Micha flipped Riley around, stuck his fingers in her mouth, and slowly sunk back into her.

"Whatcha doing, Cherry Pie?"

I quickly clamped my mouth shut, swallowing my startled groan, and moved to close the door. But his hand shot out, stopping me.

"Watch them," he breathed in my ear while slipping my straps over my shoulders. "See how much she trusts him."

He smoothed his warm palm over my breasts and down my stomach, pushing my dress down to pool at my feet. My breath hitched with a small moan as his fingers skirted over the red lace thong I was wearing. The whole time he kept his mouth next to my ear, warming my skin with his breath.

"He can do anything he wants to her." His finger pressed down, toying with my clit. "He can choke her, slap her, bite her." I shivered as his tongue traced the shell of my ear. "And she'll love every second of it."

My head fell back on his shoulder. "We shouldn't," I whispered, despite my hands moving behind me to stroke him through his pants. "It's wrong."

"They like it." My panties were torn away. I had to bite my lip to muffle the moan when he shoved two fingers inside me. "And so do you."

"It's wrong." I shook my head even though it was a lie. Having him touch me while my ears were filled with the sounds of grunting pleasure, I'd never been more turned on in my life. "We shouldn't be watching."

"We're not the only ones watching."

I swear my heart stopped when I looked up and saw Micha's dark eyes locked on us. And he wasn't the only one. Riley was watching us too, and moaning loudly every time Micha pumped inside her.

"Are you gonna fuck her?" Micha growled while wrapping his hand around Riley's neck, "Or just tease us?"

It took me two seconds to get rid of my clothes and another one to bend Shelby over and slam my cock inside her. I groaned at the pleasure of her walls clenching around me. This, right here was everything I needed. The whole world could go to shit and as long as I had her, I wouldn't give a shit.

"Watch your friend get fucked, Mouse."

Oh, Micha wanted a show, did he?

I pushed Shelby into the room and slammed her up against the wall. She opened her mouth to argue, but when I slammed back into her, all that came out was a moan.

"That's right, baby," I said, grabbing a handful of her hair and pulling her head to the side. I wanted to taste the sweat on her skin. "Show them how much your pussy loves my cock."

That was all it took to make her tight cunt squeeze my dick. Fuck, I loved how easily she came. I could fuck her all night and watch those beautiful lips part.

I wanted those lips somewhere else. My dick wept when I pulled out of her wet heat long enough to push her to her knees.

"Open your mouth, baby."

Her glazed eyes rolled up to me as her perfect lips fell apart. I smiled down at my good girl and slipped my cock into her mouth. And fuck me, I was right. The girl was built for sucking cock.

My little Cherry Pie pulled me down her throat like a pro. Tongue swirling around my head, slurping up every drop of precum my dick leaked. Any more of this and I was gonna blow in her mouth.

Can't have that, the fun's just getting started.

I popped my dick out of her mouth and pulled her back on her feet.

"Not so fast, Cherry Pie," I said, walking her back to the bed, "If you want the true voyeuristic experience, you need to get fucked beside your friend."

Riley moaned at that, but I knew she'd like that. Mouthy little vixen had a thing for being watched. Micha hadn't let it happen until now. Fucker was probably scared my dick would end up in her again. He didn't have to worry about that.

There was only one place my dick wanted to be. And I slammed right back home after pushing Shelby on the bed and spreading her legs.

She called out my name while creaming all over me. Yeah, she liked it too. I didn't know how I felt about that. Might've punched Micha in the face, if it wasn't for her hand entwining in Riley's. Micha wasn't who she was interested in. I looked over at Micha, who looked back at me. We both felt the same relief.

"Oh God," Shelby moaned, drawing my attention back to her.

I folded over her, wrapped her leg around my hip, thrust in and held myself deep inside her. "You like that, baby?"

She ground her hips needily against me and feverishly nodded.

"You want more?"

"Yes, please."

Fuck me.

My voice rumbled when I spoke. "Say please again."

"Please."

I rewarded her with a small thrust and said, "Again."

"Please," she whimpered.

This time I rotated my hips. "Who do you love, baby?"

She whimpered out a moan and rocked her hips.

"Come on, baby." It was fucking agony to hold myself still. "I want to hear you say it."

Micha whispered to Riley next to me. I didn't give enough of a fuck to care what the hell he was saying. My sole focus was on the blonde beauty under me and the way my dick looked sliding in her tight little pussy.

"Come on, baby," I coaxed and rotated my hips, making both of us groan.

Her beautiful eyes fluttered open and locked with mine. "I love you, Logan."

That's what I wanted. I leaned down and brushed my lips against hers. "I love you too, baby."

"I love you so much," she cried out, wrapping her legs around my waist.

I lost it after that, fucking her into the wee hours of the morning.

"This is bullshit!" Martin Creswell slammed his hand down on the stone table. "The wolves were wiped out."

"Apparently one family survived," Lou stated calmly.

I couldn't help but smirk. Something told me the fucker knew all along that the Mathers line was out there.

"Even so, how do we know we can trust him?" Martin's brother Sebastian pointed out.

Of course it would be the Creswells' who objected. Stuck up bastards. Honestly, I thought they'd be a little more pissed at my claim to a vote. Surprisingly, they didn't argue it much.

"It doesn't matter," Dean Whitley piped in, "You know the rules. Blood is law."

That meant there wasn't a fucking thing they could do about it. Chase's vote stood. Whether they liked it or not.

"I still don't like it," Martin grumbled.

"Too fucking bad," Micha barked back. "Junior's in. Deal with it."

I looked over at the rest of the Knights, suiting up for the hunt. Even Silas cracked a smile. Martin might be his old man, but that didn't mean he liked the prick.

"Three minutes," Lou announced.

The hunt was one of the Order games I liked. It was an initiation, of sorts. When a Knight reached the age of maturity, which according to Order doctrine was eleven, they were given a twenty minute head start and sent into the woods.

The object was to avoid capture until sunrise. For the rest of us, it was to capture. No cell phones or communication devices of any kind were allowed. Just man versus man. Initiates were told that if they were caught, they failed. That was just an added incentive to try harder. We were all caught. Except Preston.

I was looking forward to this hunt. When it was just Finn, I thought this would be another Mase situation. He didn't even try. Now Junior was in. The kid was a pain in my ass, but he was street smart. Might actually get a challenge for once.

I slipped my mask over my face two seconds before the bell rang.

"Don't fuck with Junior," Micha growled, throwing a finger my way.

"Whatever you say, chief." Fuck that. The little shit was mine.

The doors opened and I was off.

Parker looked at me as I rushed by. "What the fuck is he so excited for?"

"Shut up and do your job, boy," Martin growled. "This year I'm going to beat that prick."

"Bring it, Doc," I smirked and ducked behind a tree.

I was un-fucking-defeated. Like a bloodhound, I sniffed out my prey and waited for the right time to pounce. The doctor was just pissed that I'd caught his son in under an hour. Silas was predictable though. I didn't get so lucky this time. Two hours later and I hadn't come across a thing. Had to actually use my flashlight this time.

I thought for sure I'd have come across Finn by now. Or someone else would've. But the bell hadn't rung, so both boys were still out here. Maybe they decided to work together?

Smart on Finn's part. Not so much for Junior. Finn was intelligent when it came to other shit, but he had no real world knowledge. The kid didn't even know what to do with his dick, for fuck sakes.

"Fucking urination," I muttered, kicking a rock. "What the fuck, Silas?"

I stopped and cocked my head at something glinting in the flashlight beam. When I picked it up I was even more confused. A 9mm shell casing? Still warm.

My brows rose as I looked around the dark trees. There were drag marks in the ground too, right beside a pool of blood. I knew what it looked like when someone dragged a body away.

This wasn't good.

I shielded the beam of my flashlight and crept forward, around the tree the marks led to. All I got was a quick glimpse of a man's body before a foot swung down from above and kicked me in the face.

I flew back on the ground, stunned and spitting out a mouthful of blood. Booted feet dropped down next to me and delivered another swift kick to my gut, causing me to hunch over in a coughing spasm.

"How many times have I told you, boy." The figure leaned down into the light so I could see his face. Though I didn't need to. I recognized the voice. It was the same one that haunted my nightmares. "Always watch your surroundings."

One word flew through my mind as I glared up at my old man.

Fuck.

"I thought you would've gotten better over the years, but you're the same pathetic good for nothing you always were."

"Fuck you," I choked out in a coughing snarl. He didn't see me grab the flashlight. "I took you down once, old man," I swung the flashlight through the air, cracking it off his jaw. "I'll fucking do it again."

The second the prick fell back, I lunged. Diving on top of him in a fury of blows. Each hit I landed fueled my rage.

"That's it, boy," my old man hissed and snatched my arm when I went in for another punch. "Feed that anger."

I swung my free hand back and snarled, "I'll fucking feed it, alright."

My strike never landed. Instead of taking out my old man, he took me out. One throat punch and I was on the ground, struggling for air.

"See, that's the problem with anger." He kicked me once in the ribs and then again in the gut. "It blinds you."

As he crouched over me and tapped my face, all I could do was lay there and struggle to pull air back into my lungs.

"You stay here and collect yourself." He pulled out a gun and grinned down at me, "I have some toys to catch."

The last thing I heard before darkness took me, were his footsteps falling away.

WHEN I CAME TO, the first thing I did was check the body. Sebastian Creswell's dead eyes stared up. One less Creswell in the world wasn't the worst thing. Finn wouldn't be happy. He actually liked his old man. Fuck, Finn…

I scooped my flashlight off the ground and sprinted off in the direction my old man went. I had to find the boys before he did, or just find him. This time though, I'd make sure the motherfucker was dead when his body hit the water.

Fifteen minutes into my search, I spotted the first clue. One of the boys' backpacks with the water and food we gave them, hung on a branch pointing north. I knew it wasn't my old man that put it up there.

He wouldn't waste the time and risk that I'd catch up with him. No, this was Junior. Finn couldn't climb a tree if his life depended on it. I just hoped Junior was smart enough to take Finn with him.

Next was a scrap of fabric, again hung on a branch pointing north. By the third clue, I'd figured out Junior was headed for town and populace. The kid was smart, I'd give him that.

There were more places to hide in town. Not to mention, if he could make it to the police department, he'd be good. No way my old man would take on a building full of cops. He wasn't suicidal.

I hurried my way through the thick foliage, hoping I'd break the treeline before them. The boys knew which direction to go, but I knew these woods. Unfortunately, so did my old man, and he beat me to it. I knew that the second I broke the treeline and saw Finn's shoe laying in the grass next to a cell phone. I failed. He had them.

Whatever my old man had planned for them, Finn wouldn't survive. He might come out of it alive, but the little boy we all loved and protected would be gone.

It'd only take my old man minutes to kill his innocence. I studied the field in front of me, searching for signs of which way he took them. There was nothing. Just when I thought things couldn't get worse, the phone rang.

"You motherfucker, if you touch a hair on their heads…"

My old man tsked into the phone. "I didn't do anything to those beautiful boys. I was busy hunting my own prey. Say hello, Angel."

"Logan?"

My heart stopped. No.

And Shelby wasn't alone. Her father's voice sounded out from the background.

"Just do what he says, sweet pea. Everything will be fine."

This dumb fuck probably thought this was another debt shake down. He had no idea. It wasn't going to be fine. It was so far from fucking fine. Didn't stop me from trying to comfort her, because right now, it was all I could do.

"It's gonna be okay, baby, I'll find you. I swear to fucking God, I'll find you." And I meant every single motherfucking word.

"Aw, isn't that sweet, the boy's trying to console you. He might actually care about you. That's too bad." My old man tsked, mocking my proclamation. "You were just an inconvenience before. Now you're a puppet."

I heard the resounding sound of a slap, followed by Shelby's angry voice.

"Screw you, you creep."

My heart lifted as I listened to their struggle and silently prayed she'd get away. It was a prayer that wasn't answered. The echoing vibrations of a gunshot filled my ear and just like that, my whole world fell apart.

I couldn't breathe, couldn't move. Images of my beautiful girl flew through my mind. The smile on her lips. Those bright shining eyes, and her sweet melodic voice. Things I'd never experience again.

And then the greatest fucking thing I'd ever heard rang through the other end. My girl wasn't gone. She was full of piss and vinegar, and snarling back in the face of darkness himself.

"You hit like a girl."

My knees gave out. I collapsed on the ground and let out the longest breath of my life. *She's alive. Thank fucking God.*

"This one's got fire." My old man chuckled. "I like it."

I bet he did. Sick fuck. "If you touch her, I'll never stop. I'll hunt you down to the ends of the earth, until the last thing you see is me smiling over your corpse, holding your fucking heart in my hand."

"I look forward to it, son. In the meantime, I have some pretty new toys to play with."

"This doesn't end well for you. You took Finn and Junior. Every single member of The Order is gonna be hunting your ass." Not only that, he killed Finn's dad. A King. He wasn't coming out of this in one piece. He'd be lucky if he came out of this alive. "Not a lot of places a man alone can hide."

"Am I?" My old man said, "Yes, I have the boys, and now your girl, but ask yourself this, son. How can a man be in two places at once? I couldn't have gotten all three on my own."

Son of a bitch. I wasn't hunting him in the woods. It was his accomplice. A decoy, so he could go after his true target. My girl.

"I'm never alone, son. Never."

"What do you want?"

"For you to feel my pain. While I'm playing with your pretty little girlfriend, I want you to think what it felt like, being dumped in that cold water and left for dead." His voice deepened with every word. "By my own fucking son. I told you to make sure the job was done, boy. Now you're going to learn what happens when it's not."

The clicking of a gun cocking twitched my ears, followed by Shelby's desperate scream.

"Say goodbye to Daddy, Angel."

He fired, and then the line went dead.

Chapter 32

Shelby

The whistling rang through the air, reminding me I was still in hell. I don't know how long I'd been here. Hours? Days? Maybe years? It felt like I'd been locked in this cabin, cold and afraid, for an eternity.

My body ached. It wanted to give up, but my mind wouldn't let it. It held on to the image of a charming smile and twinkling green eyes. The same color as the devil. They weren't the devil's eyes though. They were someone else's, someone who'd made me a promise.

"I'll find you. I swear to fucking god I'll find you."

Logan.

I shot up and cried out as pain seared up my spine.

"Ah good, you're awake." Ryker swung the door to the cage shut, locking Finn and Junior inside. "I feared I lost you in that last round."

I could still hear the whip slicing through the air and cracking down on my flesh. Logan may have come from this man, but he was nothing like him. The devil wasn't capable of love or kindness.

He was the warden of agony. The keeper of misery and suffering. There was no light in his dark soul. Nothing hidden inside to save, only survive. And I would survive. If not for Logan, then for the boys.

Bile rose in my throat as I watched his fingers zip up his jeans and buckle his belt. The boys had it worse than I did. The things he made me watch him do made me physically sick. I'd throw up again, if there was anything left in my stomach.

"Don't worry, Angel," Ryker smirked and shot me a wink, "Our time is coming."

"Sorry," I growled, looking past him to the boys. Finn stopped crying a long time ago. Now he just lay in the corner of the cage, staring vacantly into space, while Junior sat in front of him like a tiny little watchdog. "I don't think I'm your type."

"Careful, Angel, you remember what happened last time you pissed me off. I don't think poor Finn can take much more. Junior though," he glanced over his shoulder and chuckled at Junior's scowl. "That boy's a trooper. Someone trained him well."

That was as sad as it was true. Finn was broken, I was beaten, but Junior… Junior was unphased. So much so that anytime Ryker came for Finn or I, Junior would do something to anger him and take the punishment for us. That eleven-year-old boy was more brave than anyone I knew, and I didn't know how much more his little body could take.

"Congratulations prick, you can overpower a kid." Junior rolled his dark eyes up to Ryker and slowly clapped his hands. "You must be so proud."

I think it pissed Ryker off that he hadn't broken Junior yet. I know it pissed him off that he hadn't broken me.

"You seem rather protective of our sweet little Shelby. Perhaps I'll play with her?"

"You'd have to be able to get hard for someone over the age of puberty in order to do that."

"I had a wife, boy," Ryker's nostrils flared. "You think I didn't fuck her?"

Junior cocked a brow. "I think you thought about your son when you did it."

"I'm not a pedophile!" Ryker roared.

"Exactly what every pedophile says, and trust me, I've met a lot." Junior's lip curled as his dark gaze slowly took in Ryker's form. "You're not even the worst."

I could see the rage bubbling up inside him. The devil was getting ready to blow. I couldn't watch him hurt those boys again.

"Show him," I called out, leaning back against the headboard of the bed my foot was chained to. "Show him he's wrong."

Ryker's brows furrowed as he tipped his head and studied me. "What's your game?"

"No game."

I fisted the blanket, pushing down my nausea, and slowly parted my thighs, inviting him in. I still had panties on, and the tattered remnants of my shirt. The rest had torn during my whipping, but I'd never felt more naked than I did in that moment.

I tried not to think about it when Ryker slowly stalked towards me, shedding his clothes as he went. Tried not to focus on what was going to happen, and instead stared at the table in the far corner, and the cellphone resting on top.

My stomach rolled as Ryker crawled over me, finger tracing the edge of my panties. "I like these."

The lacy pink panties with little bows on the butt that, I wore for Logan. Maybe instead of turning him on, they'd help me get back to him. I forced myself to look him in the eye and flattened my palm on his chest. Couldn't bring myself to touch him more than that.

"Why don't you take them off?'

He let out a longing sigh and grazed his hand over my flat stomach. "You really are a beautiful girl."

He was hard and ready to go. I didn't have to look to know that. I could feel it, pressing against my thigh like some nauseating leech. My skin crawled and everything in me begged to squirm away, but I stayed put.

"Is it my boy's face you're picturing right now? Do you think he's going to come charging through that door and save you?" He cocked his head and stared down at a bite mark on my shoulder. "Save the day, like a knight in shining armor?"

"Are we going to do this or what?"

I knew he wanted to.

I'd seen the same lust shining in his eyes in another set. But he didn't move. Didn't pull down my panties, or remove the rest of my clothes. He just stayed there. Hovering over me with his hand on my stomach while staring at the mark on my shoulder.

"You can't, can you?"

His green eyes snapped to mine. "I assure you child, I'm quite ready to do this."

That wasn't the problem.

"It's because I'm his." A slow smirk spread across my face. "You can't touch me because I belong to him."

In some sick way, this man actually loved his son.

His gaze narrowed in on me. "Oh, I can touch you."

"Do it then," I lifted my head enough for him to see the challenge in my glare. "Taint the one thing he has in this world."

I snickered when his nostrils flared.

"What pisses you off more? That he hates you, or that he loves me?"

"The boy is mine," Ryker snarled. "He's my flesh and blood. My son! And he always will be."

I let out a little chuckle. "He's not yours. He never was. He's mine. He'd take a bullet for me. What would he do for you?" The amusement fell off my face as I stared him right in the eye and said, "Nothing."

I watched his throat bob with a heavy swallow and smiled.

Gotcha, asshole.

I lifted my lips to his ear and whispered, "Who's the scared little boy now?"

All the crap he did to Logan. The scars, torture and torment. It was all for one thing. To tie his son to him. To ingrain himself so deeply in his child that he'd never be forgotten. All because the boogeyman didn't want to be alone.

"You want to see a scared little boy!" Ryker roared and jumped off me to march over to the table and grab the phone. "Let's see how strong your precious Logan is when I gut his mother," he snarled while throwing his clothes back on and stormed out the door.

"He killed my brother!" Martin bellowed.

"I understand that," Lou said, "But there are more pressing matters. Like the whereabouts of your nephew, my adoptive grandson, and the girl. When we find them, you'll have your revenge."

I'd been sitting here for far too long, listening to them bicker over stupid shit. It'd been two days of dead end leads. Who was going to kill him? How were we going to find them? What was the rescue plan? How fucking stupid was it that we had a rescue plan, but no idea where we were rescuing from.

"I'll be the one to pull the trigger." They all stopped and looked at me.

"Why shouldn't I be the one to do it?" Marin growled.

"Because you're a King." I shifted my gaze his way. "And so is he."

"Sebastian was a King," Dean pointed out.

Martin nodded. "And my brother."

Two seconds grace, that's all I got before they were back at it again. I looked back at my generation, sitting around the table shaking

311

their heads. That was the difference between us and them. The Knights banded together. The Kings fought.

"Fuck this shit," I muttered and walked out of the room. "I'll find him my damn self."

God knows what he was doing to Shelby. Had a good idea what he was doing to Finn and Junior, since the sick fuck liked to send me pictures. Hadn't got one of my girl yet. But why would I?

That would give me hope. My old man couldn't have that. If Finn was here, he could track her phone.

"Fuck!" I screamed, throwing my fist in the wall.

"We'll find them," Micha said, joining me out in the hall. "We won't stop until we do."

I dropped my forehead on the wall and sighed. "I've never felt so helpless."

"You were right," Micha placed his hand on my shoulder. "She's strong. He won't break her."

"He broke Riley."

He huffed out an exhale and shook his head. "No, I broke Riley."

Micha had never forgiven himself for the way he'd treated his girl before my old man took her. He blamed himself for making her vulnerable.

"Shelby knows you love her. That will help her hang on."

Maybe he was right. She fought me, didn't she?

My phone went off in my pocket and I almost didn't want to answer it. Probably another picture, or my old man calling to gloat. It was neither.

"Ma?"

"My sweet boy."

Something was wrong, she didn't sound right.

"Ma, are you okay?"

"I'm fine, honey." I could hear the smile spread across her face. "I'm at peace."

"What do you mean, you're at peace Ma?" I looked over to Micha, who had the same worry in his eyes. "What the fuck is going on."

"Your father called."

No, no, no, no.

"Ma whatever you're thinking about doing…"

"It's okay," she shushed me, "I didn't get my happy ending, but you can."

Fear rushed through my veins as a tear slid down my cheek. "Ma, don't do this."

"I love you, my sweet boy."

And then she was gone.

Tears dripped down my face as I stared down at my phone, trying to will her to call again. Hoping the power of my mind could stop her.

"Logan, what's going on?"

My heart broke as I looked up at my best friend. "Ma's going to sacrifice herself."

I didn't notice Preston standing there until he spoke. "You set up her phone, right?"

"Yeah." Ma could barely work a remote, let alone a smartphone.

"So," Preston arched his brow, "Track it."

IT DIDN'T TAKE me long to figure out where Ma was going. The GPS only pointed to one location. The cabin up on the bluffs. I hadn't been here since that day with my nanny. My old man told me it was the only time he was proud of me.

That this place was special to him. I wanted to burn it to the ground and forget everything that happened inside. This was his lair. The boogeyman's hunting ground. The hell he brought all us kids to play.

I left while Micha was getting everyone ready. Preston saw, but he didn't stop me. He knew I had to handle this shit alone. Ryker Hudson was my demon to defeat. I sucked in a breath and stepped through the gateway to hell.

The first thing I saw were the boys, locked up in the same cage I'd spent many hours in. On the floor in front of them was my old man, grunting as he violently pumped into Ma. She had a peaceful look on her face. Like she'd accepted this was her fate.

And then, finally, my girl tied to the bed, in nothing but a scrap of a shirt and panties. As soon as she saw me, she smiled. That big beautiful smile I dreamed about. I saw the bruises on her skin and knew from the tears in her shirt that she'd been whipped. But had he done more? The thought of him touching her made me sick.

As if she could read my mind, Shelby shook her head and mouthed the words, 'He *didn't*.'

Relief washed over me, until I looked back at my old man. Then rage bubbled through my veins. I pulled out my gun and crept closer.

"Hello, boy," my old man grunted, and stilled with a shiver. "You mother and I were just getting reacquainted."

"Yeah, well you're about to get acquainted with the wrong side of my gun."

"How many times have I told you?" he tsked and rolled off Ma. That's when I saw the 9mm pressed to her head. "Pay attention to your surroundings."

My eyes locked with his. "Think you can pull the trigger before me?"

"You want to risk it?"

I looked at Ma, to the gun, and his finger on the trigger. My old man was a Navy Seal. I honestly didn't know if I could beat him to the punch.

Fuck.

"Drop it."

I did.

"Good boy. Now kick it over here."

Did that too.

My old man grabbed the gun, sat up, resting his back on the cage, and sighed. I cocked my brow at the bags under his eyes. He looked tired.

"Get much sleep up here, old man?"

"I get enough," he said, rolling his eyes up to me. "Your girl here says you'll do anything for her. Is that true?"

No hesitation. "Yes."

"Careful, boy. Anything can mean a lot to a man like me."

"Let me guess, you want me to kill Ma or one of the boys." I shrugged. "Give me a gun."

He huffed out a chuckle and jumped to his feet.

"I may have been born at night, boy, but it wasn't last night."

"Really," Shelby snarled, "I didn't know scum was born. I thought it just kind of oozed into being."

I can't explain how happy I was to see my girl's fire burning bright. My old man, however...

He shook his finger at Shelby and tipped his head. "That one's mouthy. You need to nip that in the bud."

"I like her mouthy."

"I suppose you do."

He lifted the gun and fired, sending a bullet through my calf. Shelby screamed, Ma sprung forward and I fell. Pain crawled up my leg and across my spine, but I didn't show him. I learned that lesson long ago.

"That's all I wanted." My old man swung his hands through the air while Ma cradled me in her lap. "A little reaction."

Ma looked down at me and then screamed at him, "You shot him!"

"Shut the fuck up, Paisley." He held up his arm, pointing the gun at her head, "I'm enjoying the moment."

"Don't give him the satisfaction, Ma." I reached up, placed my hand on her cheek and turned her teary face my way. "Fuck him."

"Fuck me? You have a lot to learn, boy." He grabbed my leg and dragged me across the floor, smacking Ma in the head with the gun when she reached out for me. "Lucky for you, class is back in session."

I don't remember much after that, other than the screams in the air and the fury my old man rained down on me. Feet, fists, knees. Anything he could use to hit me, he did. I accepted it. Took each blow, knowing the second I got my chance, he'd be the one on the ground.

And then it all stopped.

I forced open my swollen eye and rolled my head to the side to see Lou standing in the doorway. A pistol held firmly in his raised hand.

"If it isn't the almighty King of Kings," my old man declared, while delivering another kick to my gut. "Did you come to watch the show, old friend?"

"I came to do something I should've done a long time ago."

"You going to pull that trigger?" My old man scoffed, "Break one of your sacred rules."

"No." Lou flicked the safety off and pulled the slide back. "I'm going to claim my son."

My old man snickered and waved his hand through the air. "You can have Mason. The boy is useless."

A shot echoed through the air.

I watched my old man's face drop and the shock register in his eyes as he glanced down at the growing red spot in his chest. He took one last look at me, and fell.

Lou sauntered over, smoothed his suit jacket, and looked down at my old man's body. "I'm not talking about Mason."

I stared into his dead eyes for a long time, waiting for a spark of life to come back into them. It never did.

He was finally gone.

I was free.

A DULL ACHING pain spread through my body when I woke up. Everything hurt, and I mean everything. Cherry Pie once asked me if I could feel my teeth. Well, I sure as fuck could feel them now. Might not be so bad if there wasn't a heavy weight on my chest.

"Fuck sakes," I grumbled and forced my lids open to look down at the top of a blond head.

Well, that I didn't mind.

I really liked how tightly she was curled up against me. Not that this shitty hospital bed gave her much room. Maybe I should get a smaller bed?

Shelby shifted, digging her shoulder into my ribs.

"Ow, shit," I groaned, wriggling away from the jagged bone of death, "I don't think these beds are made for two."

My beautiful girl shot up, wide eyes sparkling with unshed tears.

"Logan? Oh my god!" She crawled over me and threw her arms around me. "I thought I'd lost you."

"I missed you too, but fuck, baby, take it easy."

If she heard me, she didn't listen, because instead of backing off, she began peppering kisses all over my face. My bones ached, but my dick couldn't be happier. Hot little pussy pressing down on me every time her hips swayed. Didn't stop the wince from escaping my lips.

"I'm sorry," Shelby's face dripped with worry, "Did I hurt you?" Before I could answer, she bent down and gently kissed my ribs. "Is that better?"

"A little lower."

Without a word, she scootched down and pressed her lips to my abdomen.

Fuck.

"Lower."

Her lips moved down another inch.

That's it, baby, almost there.

"Keep going."

I watched her shuffle down the bed, laying kisses as she went, and smirked when my dick twitched under her chin.

"I think it might help more without the gown."

"Logan," her unimpressed eyes rolled up, "This is a hospital."

So?

Playing on her sympathy, I popped my bottom lip out and whined, "Come on, baby, I'm in so much pain. Don't you want to make me feel better?"

Her eyes darted around the empty room. I knew I had her when she looked at me and sighed.

"Alright, fine," she said, lifting my hospital gown, "But just a quick kiss."

Whatever helps you sleep at night, sweetheart.

The second her lips touched my dick all my pain was forgotten.

Guess she forgot about the 'just a quick kiss' too, because the next thing I knew, her mouth was wrapped around me.

"Fuck," I grunted as her hot tongue slithered over my shaft. "Just like that, baby."

My fingers wove in her hair, pushing her down until I could feel her throat constrict around me.

Fuck, that's it.

Shelby didn't struggle. She relaxed into my grip and let me fuck her mouth. It was close to the greatest fucking feeling in the world. But something else was much better. Growling, I pulled her over me by her hair and slipped my hand under her gown, smiling when my fingers met her wet lips.

Good girl.

Her mouth opened, and before she could argue, I fisted my dick and slid inside. Her walls instantly clenched around me. This was what I needed. Shelby Grace taking my cock like a good little slut.

"Logan, " She moaned, "Someone could come in."

Like I give a fuck.

"Let them," I growled, pumping up into her, "Then they'll know who owns this sweet little pussy."

She gyrated her hips, making me groan, and then furrowed her brows.

"But, what if someone hears?"

I wanted the whole damn hospital to hear my girl scream my name. Which is why I flipped us over and fucked her like we both wanted. The bed screeched against the floor with every hard thrust.

Shelby tried to muffle her moans, slapping her hand over her face, but I couldn't have that. I pinned her arms above her head and picked up speed. My spine was tingling and my dick throbbed, screaming for release. But I wanted to hear her scream first.

"Come on, baby," I growled against her mouth, "Give me what I want."

She did. Screaming my name to the heavens as her pussy sucked the come out of me. I collapsed on top of her, completely spent, and kissed her neck.

"I love you, baby. Don't ever forget that." I swept the hair off her face and gazed into those beautiful cinnamon eyes. "No matter where you are, or who you're with, I'll be right there with you. Because you belong to me. You're mine, Cherry Pie. Always have been, and always will be."

A smile spread across my sweet girl's face. "I love you too, Logan."

"Shelby Harlow Grace."

"Oh crap," Shelby muttered and slowly looked to the side. "Hi Mom."

"Hey, Mrs. Grace." I propped myself up and eyed Shelby's mom's nurse's uniform. "No need to check up on me. I feel fucking great."

It took awhile for things to get back to normal. We'd lost so much. My father, and both of Finn's parents. Her body was found in their house afterwards.

Not to mention the emotional scars. But slowly we healed. None of us had any idea where my brother was, or if he was even alive, but I held out hope. Logan promised he'd help me find him.

Mom and Louis—that's what he insisted I call him—were engaged now. Mags, Mom and I lived with him, in his big ass house. The place was seriously huge. Louis wanted to give me my own wing.

My mom put a stop to that real fast. Most nights I spent at Riley's anyway. Well, as many as I could get away with. My mom was less than happy to find out I had a boyfriend, and even less happy when she met him. She and Paisley had become close though, so that kind of helped.

Mags insisted on playing nurse for both Junior and Finn. As far as she was concerned, they were her best friends. Finn liked the attention. He always smiled when my little sister was around, and even though Junior grumbled a lot, I knew he liked the attention too.

He'd do little things for her. Like bring her favorite cupcake, or make sure she got the last cookie. I didn't necessarily agree with his methods–punching a kid in the face for a cookie wasn't the best way to handle things–but, he meant well. Kind of reminded me of Logan.

Over the months, he'd only gotten sweeter and more terrifying. We'd tried out a few of his toys. He steered clear of the whip though. I wasn't ready for that yet, and he didn't want to push me.

That day in the garage I thought going anywhere near Logan Hudson would be the worst mistake of my life. It turned out to be the best thing to happen to me. I couldn't possibly feel anymore loved, and despite his many flaws, he always made me smile.

Riley sighed at me. "I don't know about this."

"You're the one always talking about closure." I nodded at the present on the table. "This is your closure."

"She's right, you know," Lana chimed in.

The three of us had become close friends. Harper too, when she was around. I guess she had strict parents or something, because I never saw her outside of school. All Lana said was that Harper didn't go out much.

"Ugh, fine," Riley grunted, "But if this makes me cry, I'm punching you."

"Deal." I smiled.

Riley's mother may not have been perfect, but she loved her. As long as that present sat in her closet unwrapped, she'd never be able to forgive her or let her go. I anxiously watched her tear the paper off and peeked over her shoulder to see what was inside.

My heart instantly melted and tears sprung in my eyes. At the bottom of the box was her mother's thirty days sober chip, and a note:

I love you baby girl and I'm so sorry I haven't been there for you.
I can't make up the time lost, but I can be there for the future.
This is proof that this time will be different.

"SHE WASN'T DRUNK," Riley cried, "She did love me."

"Of course she loved you." I wrapped my arms around her, tears falling down my face just as fast as they were hers. "Who wouldn't love you?"

"I love you too," Lana blubbered and joined our sobbing heap.

Micha's loud grumble interrupted our moment. "Oh god, what the fuck did we walk into?"

Parker strutted in the room and rolled his eyes. He'd been really grumpy lately. I'm pretty sure it had something to do with the growing animosity between him and Lana.

I was too busy admiring the gorgeous blond god smirking down at us to care.

"They probably saw a puppy on TV or some shit."

"Shut up," I sang, wiping the tears off my face. "We were having a girl moment."

"Oh yeah?" Logan yanked me off the couch and pulled me into his arms, "I'd like to have a girl moment."

Riley groaned. "Do you two ever stop?"

I smiled at her. No, no we didn't. Logan was insatiable, but that was okay, because he made me insatiable too.

"What's that?" I nodded at the bag in his hand bumping against my thigh.

"I got you something."

I swear he got sweeter every day.

"But it's not my birthday for another couple weeks."

I'd been practicing my surprise face for the party he had planned.

He wasn't very good at hiding it. I caught on when I walked in the room and heard him ordering a pink unicorn cake. Not sure why he thought I had a thing for unicorns.

There were more unicorns in my room now than when I was five. I just went with it, because that was Logan. My beautifully broken, sweet and scary Logan. And I wouldn't have him any other way.

He held the pink bag out for me. "It's not for your birthday."

Giddily I grabbed the bag and flopped down on the couch. I loved getting presents. Especially from him. I honestly never knew what to expect.

"You're spoiling her," Micha grumbled.

I answered him by sticking my tongue out.

Logan laughed and sat behind me. "You're just mad your girl won't let you spoil her."

"I don't need any of that fancy stuff," Riley exclaimed, "I do just fine with what I have."

"I took your car to the junkyard."

"WHAT!"

Uh oh. This might be Micha Kessler's last night on earth.

I was just starting to get used to the idea of him being my step-brother. Mason was easier to accept. Especially for Mags. Those two were thick as thieves, and he wasn't coming home for another week.

"Go back and get it!"

"Can't," Micha said, "It's been crushed into a cube."

"That was my car, Micha!"

"No, the one parked outside is your car." He rolled his eyes at the look she gave him. "Don't worry, I bought it used."

I left my friend to argue with her boyfriend and went back to my present.

Um, okay?

Pulling the little blue onesie out of the bag, I eyed Logan and sucked in a breath.

"Baby…"

How the hell was I supposed to handle this?

"I love you." I gave him a smile and reached out to cup his cheek. "And I'd be happy to have your babies one day… But I'm only sixteen."

"It's okay, baby." Logan pulled me in and kissed my forehead. "I'm not mad. You don't have to hide this from me."

I was officially confused.

"Hide what from you?"

His green eyes gazed down at me. "Open up baby, let me in."

"Let me in," I responded, not having a clue what he was talking about.

He huffed out a sigh. "I found the test."

"What test?"

"The positive pregnancy test in the trash."

My brow arched. "I didn't take a test."

"You didn't."

I shook my head.

"So, you're not pregnant?"

"No."

Instant relief washed over his face.

"Thank fucking God. Wait…" Logan stopped and eyed me, "If you didn't take it, who did?"

We both turned and looked at Riley. Even Micha was staring at her.

"Mouse, if you're hiding something from me…"

Riley was not impressed. Her blue eyes rolled up at him and she snarled, "If I was pregnant, you'd wake up with a fork in your nuts."

"Why do you always go to the fork?"

She shrugged. "It's convenient."

"Well, someone took it!" Logan declared, throwing his hands up in the air.

That's when we all noticed Lana trying to sneak out of the room. She stopped and looked back at us with wide hazel eyes.

"Um, I gotta go." She threw her thumb over her shoulder, "Gotta help Gran."

No one said anything while she left. I don't think anyone knew what to say. I sure didn't know what to say. Lana!? I mean she was so sweet and…

Lana!?

Riley tapped my shoulder and pointed at Parker, who was as white as the walls behind him. He stood there, mouth open, with a can of soda held up in his hand.

No.

Friggin.

Way.

"Holy shit," Logan said, coming to the same conclusion as me. "Mommy's not going to be too happy about this."

Parker's brows furrowed and he opened his mouth like he was going to say something, but shut it instead. And then, like the true asshole he was, my boyfriend picked up the bag with the onesie, strutted over to Parker, and hung it off his suspended arm.

"Here you go, man," Logan said, slapping him on the back and clicking a quick selfie. "Good luck."

Spitfire,

How are things going there? Did Silas like his room? He probably didn't tell you about that shit, but don't worry Logan took pictures. Think we could get him drunk enough to wear that Tinkerbelle costume? Relax, I'm not thinking about drinking. You've threatened me enough.

I happen to like my balls by the way. Please stop threatening them

I'm so ready to leave this place. It's fucking depressing. I'll miss the nurse though. Does she have a mouth on her. And don't roll your eyes at me. I know you're doing it. I can feel it from here.

Oh, Hey, what do little girls like? I asked Logan and all he said was fucking unicorns. Literally in those words. Fucking unicorns. Has he been watching unicorn porn or something? I seriously confused.

Anyway, I should go. Nurse Angie just showed up. It's time for my sponge bath if you catch my drift.

Ps. Please take pics of the present I ordered for my brother. Video would be better. Hint, she comes with a lot of leather and a whip. You're welcome.

Your secret wet dream,

Mason

Thank for reading Scartissue.

If you enjoyed this book please consider leaving a review. Reviews are always much appreciated by authors.

If you'd like to be among the first to know about new releases and get an inside look into my world join my Facebook group T.L. Hodel's Murder Of Ravens.

Look for more books in The Order Of Ravens and Wolves.

Next book in the series Happenstance

PARKER

Pain.

The deep-seated agony tearing across someone's nerves could make the strongest fucker bend. It didn't take much. The right poke or prod, hell, even just the threat, had the power to make someone act completely out of character.

What fascinated me was the sound that came with it. Not quite loud enough to give a sense of urgency, but enough to let others know something was wrong. It didn't matter how big someone was, or how much experience they had.

They all made that sound.

A low drowning growl somewhere between a scream and a groan. The same muffled noise the prick I had on the ground was making now. The left side of his face was already starting to swell, and blood trickled from his nose. Pretty sure I broke it. Still, the prick wouldn't give.

He threw his fists up in my ribs and grumbled, "Fuck you."

At this point, I was driven more by adrenaline than anger and answered his strike with one of my own. He wasn't a small guy–I definitely felt his hit–but mine was followed by a loud crunch. The split in my lip reopened as my mouth curled. He was making that sound again, only this time it was louder.

There was no mistaking the agony etched across his face. Broken bone hurt like a bitch. One quick snap sent more pain rushing through a human body than any burn or cut. I'd had my fair share of injuries–part of the job description of being a football player–and still nothing compared to that type of anguish.

The prick on the ground mumbled something incoherent and shifted under me. He was done. About fucking time.

Hurting someone like this probably should bother me. It would bother other people. Micha would say my brother and sister made me numb to it. Preston started torturing people before his preteen years, and Ava... I loved my sister, but she was all kinds of crazy.

The truth was, this shit never really bothered me. Preston stabbed one of our nannies when we were kids, and all I could remember thinking was, 'why is she screaming like that?' Everyone knew my siblings were fucked up, I just hid it better.

My opponent looked up at me and muttered, "Pussy."

I cocked my brow. Guess he had some fight left in him after all. If he wanted to go another round, I was game. I tipped my head down at him, smirked, and dropped my fist into his face. My knuckles grazed his teeth as his head twisted to the side.

That seemed to shut him up. He coughed and spit out a mouthful of blood, but remained silent. I smiled and tapped his cheek.

Good boy.

Happenstance

T.L. Hodel is a Canadian author, poet and artist. Through coming up from a difficult childhood she excelled at writing, having her first poem published in junior high. When not writing she occupies herself with numerous crafts, hobbies and is an avid gamer and horror movie fan. She lives in Calgary with her kids and cat, (who is a complete asshat), and may have a slight weakness for true crime shows.

Connect with T.L. Hodel online:
www.facebook.com/groups/272402970612789/?ref=share
www.instagram.com/tarahodel
www.facebook.com/Author-TL-Hodel-102923044775313/

Also by T.L. Hodel

The Order Of Ravens And Wolves:
Aftereffect
Scartissue
Happenstance
Accident-Prone
Relapse
Panic-Button (coming soon)

Deviant House:
Innocence
Innocence corrupted (coming soon)

The Lost Souls:
Adversaries
Frenemies

Brothers Of Shadow And Death:
Backfire
Backstab (coming soon)

The Seven Sins Series:
Pride

The Buchanan Brothers
Twisted Abel
Twisting Tallon (Coming soon)